Odds and Endings
Fiction Short and Otherwise

by

Joe DeRouen

Small Things Press

Visit Joe's website at www.JoeDeRouen.com

Find Joe on Facebook at www.Facebook.com/jderouenwriter

Connect with Joe on Twitter via @jderouen

First Printing: November 2015

ISBN 978-0-692-32644-2

Cover art by Renée Barratt, thecovercounts.com

Author photo by Sunny Skaggs, SunnySkaggsPhotography.com

Editing by Robin Raven, RobinRaven.com

Proofreading by Lauren Owens Galle

Lyrics from "I Saw a Stranger with Your Hair" courtesy John Gorka, © 1987, Blues Palace Music

Lyrics from "Free My Mind" courtesy Katie Herzig, © 2011, Katie Herzig Music

"Tall Paul" font used in *Good Fortune* courtesy Paul Bobal, © 1997

FIRST EDITION

Printed in the USA

✳ ✳ ✳

Small Things Press | www.JoeDeRouen.com

For my grandmother, Tillie Young. I miss you.

Novels by Joe DeRouen

The Small Things Trilogy:
Small Things
Threads
A Pattern of Shadows✳

Memories of a Ghost
Leap Year✳

Short Story Collections by Joe DeRouen

Odds and Endings: Fiction Short and Otherwise

Anthology Appearances

May the Fourth: A Collection of Stories Across Time and Space
The Cat, the Crow, and the Cauldron: A Halloween Anthology

✳ Not yet published

Acknowledgements

I'd like to thank everyone who contributed to helping make this novel happen, including Andee and Fletcher DeRouen, Bruce Diamond, Rebecca and Jeff Jones, Lisa Smith, Chris Martin, Demelza Carlton, Rose Lintz, Sara Buckley, Dawn Blackerby, Missy Noecker, all the folks associated with NaNoWriMo, Katie Herzig, John Gorka, Brooke Johnson, and Stephen King.

Special thanks also go to Lisa Lauenberg, Tasha DeRouen, my cover artist Renée Barratt, my photographer Sunny Skaggs, my proofreader Lauren Owens Galle, and my editor Robin Raven.

Odds and Endings

Fiction Short and Otherwise

Table of Contents

Preface

I've always enjoying reading and writing short stories, and, on the writing side, it takes a particular mindset to successfully create the perfect short story. I'm not naïve enough to pretend that any of my short stories are perfect, but I hope you enjoy them just the same.

Smoke first appeared in *May the Fourth: A Collection of Stories Across Time and Space*, while *Good Fortune* first appeared in *The Cat, the Crow, and the Cauldron: A Halloween Anthology*, and *Mommy's Favorite* first appeared on Wattpad, racking up nearly 5,000 reads. All of the other stories in Odds and Endings are original to this volume.

Rogers, Arkansas, October 5, 2015

DADDY'S SLEEPING
WITH THE BABYSITTER.

Merryland

Zara Boone was asleep when she got the call. She had been suffering from a nasty cold for the last three days and finally decided to call in sick that Friday morning, to hopefully give her body time to recuperate so she could enjoy the weekend with her husband and daughter.

"I understand," she said, sniffing into the telephone, her nose stopped up and tears starting to blind her deep green eyes. "She just seemed so healthy, so full of life, the last time I saw her."

Zara realized guiltily that had been almost a year ago. She'd been too busy with her family and job in Arkansas to visit the woman who had taken her in when both her parents had died in a car crash, the woman who had nurtured and raised her from just before the age of six.

"I'm sorry for your loss, ma'am," the deep voice that had identified itself as belonging to Hancock County Sheriff Lyle Brady said for the third time in as many minutes.

Lucille Brennan, her 75-year-old grandmother, had apparently died in her sleep. One of her neighbors found her when she missed a breakfast date and immediately called 911, but the paramedics had been unable to revive her. She was pronounced dead at 8:15 this morning.

"Thank you, Sheriff," she heard herself say, almost by rote. "I'll catch a flight out as soon as I can, and hopefully be there tonight or tomorrow morning."

"The body…your grandmother's body, I mean, will be held at Wiseman's Funeral Home on Locust Street in Carthage. If you can tell me where you'll be staying, I can give you directions."

"I grew up in Carthage. I know where it is."

She knew exactly where it was. The Wisemans had handled her parents' funeral when she was just a little girl, and the big funeral home, two stories' worth, was just down the street from where her grandmother lived. At least she wouldn't have far to travel.

"Well, Miss Boone, if you have any questions, please don't hesitate to give me a call." He rattled off a number that Zara dutifully copied down on to the back of an envelope. "And, again, I'm so sorry for your loss."

"Have a nice day," she said, folding the envelope and tucking it into her purse.

She hung up, staring at the telephone. Have a nice day? Had she really just said that? She shook her head. He had called to tell her that her grandmother had died, so why the hell should she care what kind of day he had?

Zara's grandmother had drilled into her the need to be polite even in the face of tragedy, and she supposed such niceties would always stick with her. Like so many of the woman's lessons, and her stories.

Oh, the stories she told! Stories about her life growing up in Ireland, about coming to America with her family when she was just thirteen, tales about her two husbands, but mostly stories about a fantasy land she called Merryland.

She hadn't thought about the stories in years. Merryland, her grandmother had said, wasn't always merry, but even when troubles came to the fantastical place, everything always turned out happy in the end.

The stories began the night of Zachary and Sara Boone's death. Grandma Lucy held her all night, doing her best to comfort her crying, weaving tall tales about majestic knights and great wizards in this wonderful, terrible, beautiful land called Merryland.

Grandma Lucy had promised her that, one day, when she was older and stronger and ready to go on an adventure, she would show her the secret path to Merryland, and they would go together, but of course that day never came. By the time she was twelve or thirteen she had grown tired of the tales, and eventually her grandmother had stopped sharing them.

It had been years since they spoke of Merryland, and she had no idea why she was even thinking about it now. It was part of her past, she supposed, part of the rich tapestry of memories she shared with Grandma Lucy, and would never really go away. She'd give anything to sit on her grandmother's lap one last time and lose herself in those wonderful stories of magic and bravery.

Zara tied her long, brown hair into a pony tail and then, with no small effort, pushed herself up from the couch. Her stomach was grumbling, and she had the start of a headache tickling the edges of her forehead. She desperately needed breakfast, hopefully something that would help clear her sinuses.

She moved from the living room couch where she'd been napping toward the kitchen. This weekend was supposed to be special. Tomorrow was Tildie's fifth birthday, and she and Matt had a fun weekend lined up for her, starting with a Build-a-Bear birthday party for Tildie and two of her friends, and then a trip to the American Girl store, finally ending with a party at home.

She absolutely hated to be apart from her daughter on her birthday, but hated even more the thought of dragging her along to Carthage to prepare for her great-grandmother's funeral. She knew—or at least hoped—that Matt would understand, but five-year-olds weren't nearly as understanding as twenty-nine-year-old medical sales reps.

Speak of the devil, she thought, as her cell phone rang. It was Matt, calling from his office phone. She leaned against the fridge and answered the phone.

"Hey, you," she said, stuffy nose and all.

"Hey babe," Matt said over the phone, "just thought I'd check on you. How're you feeling?"

"Physically, a little better," she lied, "but I just got a call. Grandma Lucy died in her sleep last night."

"Oh no. I'm so sorry. What happened?"

"I don't know. Probably her heart. I just don't know."

Matt and her grandmother had hit it off instantly and had been close ever since Zara married him, seven years ago.

She felt herself breaking down, struggling to stop the tears, but they came anyway. It was hearing his voice, knowing that he shared her grief that did it.

"I'm sorry, Zara. Hey, it's okay. Do you need me to come home?"

"No," she said, sniffling. "I'm fine. I just need to go to Carthage, to deal with all this."

He went silent. "When?"

"Tonight or tomorrow morning," she said, guilt washing over her again. "I'm gonna have to miss her party, Matt. I hate it, but I don't know what else to do. Please don't hate me."

He chuckled. "I could never hate you, Zara. And we'll make Tildie understand. My folks can help. We'll make a big night of it. Unless you want us to come with you?"

Her stomach took a break from grumbling to perform little butterfly flip flops. Matt was wonderful to her and the daughter they had made together, and she loved him more now than she had two minutes ago, if that was even possible.

"I know you'll make it special for her, honey," she said, "and, no, I don't need you to come. At least not until the actual funeral. I can't imagine a worse birthday for a five-year-old girl than watching her Mommy pick out coffins and make funeral arrangements for her great-grandmother."

She held the phone away from her face for a moment, honking her nose into a Kleenex. "...Mom will be happy to help," she heard him say. "We'll handle the birthday gala. You just concentrate on feeling better and taking care of things for Lucy."

"Thank you, my love," Zara said. "I'm gonna check plane tickets and see what I can do. I'll probably have to fly into Quincy, rent a car, and drive to Carthage. Hopefully I can get a late flight so I at least have time to explain all this to her. Poor Tildie."

"Tildie will be fine. We'll make sure of it. She'll miss you like crazy, but I'm pretty sure we'll be able to distract her at least a little with teddy bears and dolls and dresses galore."

She felt herself starting to cry again, but reigned it in. "I love you, Matt. With all my heart."

"I love you too, babe. We'll get through this. And I'll leave work a little early and pick up Tildie from preschool so you can get ready. I'll see you around four."

They hung up then, and Zara finally settled down to breakfast: two slices of bacon, a piece of wheat toast with butter, and two scrambled eggs. *Well, that's one problem solved*, she thought, as her stomach gradually ceased grumbling.

One long bubble bath later, and she almost felt human, or at least as close to human as she was going to get until after the funeral. Zara pulled on a pair of black tights and topped it off with one of Matt's old Batman t-shirts. Nothing she'd wear to the office, but it would work just fine for a last-minute plane flight.

Zara sat down at her laptop and went to the Priceline website. There were no direct flights from Fayetteville to Quincy, but there was a Delta flight that left at six Saturday morning and had an hour layover in St. Louis. She would arrive in Quincy at around eleven in the morning, and from there it was an hour drive to Carthage. Good enough.

Five hundred and twenty-seven dollars, and that was one way. Zara filled out the billing information, wincing as she clicked the button to confirm her purchase. Add to that her return ticket as well as Matt and Tildie's round-trip tickets for the funeral, and there went the funds for their planned Hawaii vacation next year. Easy come, easy go, she supposed.

Saturday

Zara was exhausted. She and Matt had quickly planned a "pre-birthday celebration" for Tildie, which included dinner out at Red Robin and watching her favorite Disney movie, *The Little Mermaid,* over and over until the soon-to-be five-year-old finally passed out in her father's arms.

That had been around eleven last night. She'd promptly gone to bed, ignoring Matt's advances (why he thought she'd want to make love while suffering from the worst cold on earth was beyond her), but then tossed and turned all night. She'd finally fallen asleep around two in the morning, only to be awakened by her alarm at 4:30 so she could get ready for her flight.

And here she was at a quarter 'til noon, in her little red Nissan Altima rental from Hertz, less than fifteen minutes outside of Carthage. She could barely keep her eyes open, and could think of nothing better than passing out on Grandma Lucy's fluffy floral print green couch.

Zara had briefly considered renting a hotel room, but had finally agreed with Matt that she should just stay at her grandmother's house. After all, Zara would soon own the home where she'd grown up.

She knew she was the sole beneficiary of her grandmother's estate, which included the house and everything in it, and probably a couple thousand dollars in the woman's checking account. The house was Zara's now. Still, the thought of sleeping in the house where her grandmother had died just 24 hours earlier felt more than a little bit creepy.

She entered Carthage, a town with a population of less than three thousand people, from the south end. It took her less than two minutes to drive to her childhood home at 1342 Locust Street, a two-story Victorian style house, painted white, surrounded by a waist-level white picket fence.

Zara felt her heart skip a beat. She loved this house, but without her grandmother it felt like it was just a shell, missing its soul. A huge wave of sadness settled down over her.

She shook her head. A house was just a house, of course. A place to live, to eat and sleep, and maybe raise a family. She was half-delirious from her cold and lack of sleep, and the best thing she could do would be to head into the house and zonk out on the couch for a few hours.

"Zara, dear, is that you?" came a creaky voice behind her. She dropped her luggage as she spun around.

"My heavens, child, I didn't mean to startle you," said Mrs. Olinger, her grandmother's best friend and fellow widow. "It's so good to see you, Zara."

The old woman pulled Zara into a hug so tight it brought tears to her eyes.

"Be careful, Mrs. Olinger," Zara said, returning the hug with one arm while covering her mouth with the other, "I have an awful cold. You don't want to catch it."

"Nonsense, child," she said, "I'm strong as a horse. Now, why don't we get you and your luggage into the house and out of the cold, and then I'll make you a nice cup of tea guaranteed to stop any germ in its tracks."

Zara smiled, sighing inside her head. Tea was the last thing on her mind. What she really needed was sleep. Mrs. Olinger, however, was the neighbor who had found her grandmother dead in her bed, and it had to have shaken her up. She probably needed to talk about it almost as much as Zara needed sleep. And so she acquiesced, picking up her luggage from the ground, leading the way up the concrete steps and in-to Lucy Brennan's house.

She had to admit, the peppermint tea did seem to be helping her cold. This old woman, just two years her grandmother's senior, proved to know the house better than she did. She made a beeline for the kitchen and, five minutes later, emerged carrying an antique blue porce-lain tea service laden with fresh gingersnaps.

"She made these the night before she passed," said Mrs. Olinger, pouring herself another cup of tea, "for our card club. That's how I knew something was wrong, you know. Card club was at her house this month, and I was coming over to help her get ready. And when she didn't answer the door, I just…I just knew."

"That must have been awful for you," Zara said, between bites of ginger snap, "to find her like that."

"She looked like an angel, and she had a smile on her face," Oling-er said. "I hope it's some small comfort to you that I don't think she suffered."

"It is," she said, laying a hand on the woman's wrist, not knowing if it was or wasn't. If you go peacefully, how can you know you're really dead?

Stop it, Zara, she mentally chided herself, pushing the morbid thought from her head. Zara didn't believe in an afterlife or a God. Her grandmother was gone. Of course she didn't know she was dead, be-cause she no longer existed.

Mrs. Olinger was looking at her with her head half-cocked. "Are you all right, Zara? I hope it wasn't something I said. I'm just an old lady, and sometimes I prattle on and on just to hear myself talk."

Zara shook herself. "Oh, no, please don't think that. I'm just exhausted. Between this hellish cold and not getting any sleep last night, I'm about to pass out."

"Then that's my cue," smiled Mrs. Olinger, getting up from the couch she shared with Zara. "Let me put this stuff away, wash a few dishes, and I'll get out of your hair."

"I didn't mean it like that," Zara said, though of course she had. "Please, stay as long as you'd like." *Don't listen to me,* she thought silently, *please go and let me pass out three seconds later.*

"Nonsense. You need your rest so you can deal…with what needs to be dealt with."

She started to collect the tea service, but stopped when Zara asked her to leave it.

"The tea was wonderful," Zara said, "and I think it is helping. Please leave it, I might drink some more. And those ginger snaps are heavenly."

She nodded once, then leaned over to kiss Zara on the forehead. "If you need me, just come over or call. My phone number is in your grandmother's book, right beside the telephone in the kitchen. Rest, and we'll talk later."

And with that, the old woman was gone. Zara had meant it about the tea, but decided to close her eyes for a moment before refilling her cup. That was the last thing she remembered before waking up three hours later to someone calling her name.

Grandma? Zara's heart was pounding, and for a moment she didn't know where she was. She sat up on the couch, looking around the living room, and it all came back to her. Had she been dreaming?

Of course she'd been dreaming. She tried in vain to snatch at the rapidly dissolving threads of the dream. Something about Merryland, she thought, and a quest to rescue someone, but then it was all gone.

She yawned, stood up, stretched. Even though she had only slept a few hours, she felt worlds better, and her runny nose had slowed to a small drizzle. The peppermint tea had really helped, apparently. She'd have to remember that the next time Tildie or Matt had a cold.

Zara took a quick inventory of the room, something she really hadn't had the chance to do when Mrs. Olinger had followed her into the house. Nothing much had changed from when she'd been a child, let alone from last year's visit. The hardwood maple floor had been waxed recently, and everything was neat and dust-free.

The Sears portrait of her and her parents, whom she barely remembered, still hung above the mantle, surrounded by various and sundry knickknacks, including the blue and gold ceramic bowl she'd made for her grandmother in junior high.

The Samsung flat-screen, high-definition television she and Matt had given Grandma Lucy two Christmases ago (delivered from Amazon, she thought guiltily, rather than presented in person) stood on a sturdy oak cabinet that had been around since she'd been a little girl, and the huge grandfather clock that had originally belonged to her great-grandparents dominated almost a third of the east wall of the living room.

A plaintive meow startled her. She whirled to see Oscar, her grandmother's old, gray tomcat, staring up at her. How could she have forgotten about Oscar? The poor thing probably hadn't been fed in at least 24 hours.

She walked through the living room, past the dining room and into the kitchen, with Oscar racing back and forth between her legs. Thank goodness, Grandma Lucy had finally purchased an automatic feeder. There was plenty of dry food—Iams, if she remembered correctly—in the feeder, but the water bowl was almost empty. She snatched up the blue ceramic bowl, took it to the sink, and refilled it with cold tap water.

Oscar finally abandoned her legs in favor of lapping up water, then wandered over to the feeder to eat. Oscar was, what? Probably at least fourteen years old. Zara was twenty-eight, and they'd gotten Oscar after their previous cat, a beautiful, long-haired Persian named Emmy (short for Esmerelda) had passed.

She'd been a sophomore in high school when they'd rescued the short-haired tom from the shelter, a scruffy little kitten who she'd fallen in love with instantly. She couldn't believe she'd forgotten about poor old Oscar, the cat who'd mended her heart after Emmy had left them. Something else to feel guilty about, she supposed.

Speaking of feeling guilty, what was she going to do with Oscar? Taking a cat on the plane home seemed like a nightmare, Matt's allergies notwithstanding. Perhaps one of her friends still living in Carthage would take him in? She pushed the thought from her head, determined to deal with it later.

She turned from watching the cat eat, her eyes taking in the room. The kitchen hadn't changed much, either. The house, built in 1899 by her grandfather's grandparents, had been designed well, but apparently people back then hadn't thought they needed much kitchen space. The room was cramped, and had always made Zara feel a little claustrophobic. Her grandmother had often talked of expanding the kitchen, adding on more room, but never did.

Zara looked at the Minnie Mouse watch she'd worn since fifth grade: it was almost four in the afternoon. She'd made an appointment with the funeral home for 4:30, but now regretted it. The thought of seeing her grandmother dead was almost more than she could bear. Still, it had to be done. She had no doubt that Mrs. Olinger would come with her if asked, but the poor old woman had already been through enough. This was something she'd have to handle on her own.

As a child, she'd always been creeped out by the thought of the funeral home just a block away from her house. As an adult, however, having to deal with funeral arrangements for her grandmother, she was glad that it was so close. She'd have just enough time for a quick shower and a change of clothes before the five minute walk that would take her to see her grandmother's body.

She climbed the stairs to the second floor, dragging her suitcase behind her. She followed the hallway to her old room, glancing at the photos that adorned the walls. Black and white shots of her grandmother with her great-grandparents, her own high school graduation photos from ten years earlier, and a candid shot of her mother feeding her father cake on their wedding day were among the mix of memories that decorated the hallway.

She paused for a moment outside her grandmother's room, but couldn't make herself turn the door handle. Soon, she knew, she'd have to visit the room where her grandmother had taken her last breath. But not yet, maybe not even today.

She walked into her room, swinging the luggage onto her old twin-sized bed. The room looked just like it had last year, which wasn't much different than it had looked the day she moved out. Her Bon Jovi poster still hung on the wall, and the set of shelves she and her grandmother had carefully built when she was twelve occupied most of the north wall. They were filled with the stuff of her childhood: teddy bears, books, and school trophies.

Zara pulled down one of the trophies, noting that it wasn't even dusty. At seventy-five years of age, Lucy Brennan had made sure her granddaughter's bedroom was clean and waiting for her. She felt another pang of guilt, but pushed it down.

She stared at the trophy. First place in a swim meet, her junior year. Similar trophies were interspersed throughout the rest of the shelves, a few more for swimming, and the rest for speech and other academic achievements. Although she'd lost her parents in that terrible accident so long ago, she'd never felt like an orphan. Her grandmother had been there for every trophy presented, every milestone achieved.

Oscar pushed through her legs, startling her. She reached down to pet the big gray tom behind the ears, eliciting a loud purring from deep in his belly. Oscar licked her fingers and then jumped onto the bed to settle down for a nap. She replaced the trophy, selected a red skirt, a dark blue blouse, a pair of matching black bra and panties, and other needed accessories from her luggage, and then trudged out of her room and down the hallway for a quick shower.

The shower had always taken too long to warm up, and today was no exception. She used the time to brush her teeth and select a towel from the cabinet before finally stepping into the now-scalding stream. The water felt good against her back and legs, rejuvenating her. She closed her eyes, enjoying the feeling. She slowly worked the Head and Shoulders shampoo into her long, brown hair, feeling better than she had in days.

"Zara," she heard a voice whisper off in the distance, echoing through the house.

Her eyes sprung open, instantly stinging as the shampoo found them. She cried out in pain, thrust out her hands, and pulled the shower curtain open. She squinted against the light but no one was there. Hurriedly washing the shampoo from her hair, she wrapped herself in a white cotton towel and stepped out of the shower.

Oscar was there, starting up at her from the green rug in front of the bathtub. He meowed at her, licked her wet calf, and hopped up on the toilet.

Zara sighed. It was Oscar. It had to be Oscar. The cat meowed, and she'd thought she heard her name. She wasn't used to having a cat in the house because Matt was allergic, and so her mind had translated the cat's mewling into something more familiar.

"Don't scare me like that," she whispered, ruffling the fur between Oscar's ears.

Besides, if it hadn't been Oscar, who else could it have been? Mrs. Olinger would have knocked, and no one besides her, the Sheriff, and Mark Wiseman, the funeral home director, knew Zara was here. The last two didn't even knew she was staying at her grandmother's house and would have no reason for sneaking around in here anyway.

She rolled her eyes at her own silliness. Of course it was Oscar. Zara quickly toweled off and got dressed. It was 4:25, no time to dry her hair. She pulled on a pair of black stockings, followed by the brown leather boots she'd purchased at Kohl's a few weeks ago, and headed down the stairs, out the door, and toward Wiseman's Funeral Home.

She was just about to enter the funeral Home when her phone rang. It was Matt's cell. Crap. She'd promised to call him when she got to Carthage, but had completely forgotten. She tapped answer.

"Before you say anything," she started, "I'm sorry. Edna Olinger, Grandma Lucy's next door neighbor, caught me as I was pulling into the driveway and talked my ear off." A little white lie. "By the time she left, I was so exhausted that I fell asleep, and just woke up a little bit ago."

"Hi Mommy," said Tildie's voice, over the phone, "I love you and I miss you!"

She had just explained why she hadn't called her husband to a four-year old. Scratch that, a five-year old, as of today.

"Happy birthday, sweetie," said Zara. "Mommy misses you so much!"

"I know, Mommy," the little girl said. "Daddy's about to pick up Gretchen and Mikayla and then we're going to Build-a-Bear. He said you should at least wish me happy birthday before we go!"

"Tildie," she heard Matt's voice nearby, "you weren't supposed to say that part."

So he was mad at her. She could hardly blame him. She couldn't believe she'd forgotten to call.

"I'm sowwy, Daddy," Tildie said, mispronouncing her R's as usual.

"Don't worry about it, honey," Zara said. "I don't blame Daddy for being upset with me. I should have called."

"But you couldn't, because that person bit off your ear. Are you okay, Mommy?"

She had to stifle a laugh. "No, honey, she just talked my ear off. That means she talked a lot. My ear's okay."

"Tildie, say goodbye," she heard Matt say. "I need to talk to your Mommy for a minute, and then we'll go."

"Goodbye, Mommy!" the girl yelled into the phone.

"Goodbye, Tildie!" Zara yelled back, "I want you to have the best birthday ever. I love you, and I'll see you soon."

"She knows you love her," said Matt, "and I'm sorry I said that. But what happened? Why didn't you call?"

She repeated the explanation she'd given Tildie earlier, once again laying the blame on poor Mrs. Olinger.

"It's okay, babe, I totally understand," he said when she was finished. "I was just worried. But why didn't you answer your phone? I must have called ten times."

"I guess I slept through it," she admitted. "I zonked out pretty hard there for a while."

"Fair enough. So, when's the funeral?"

Shit. It was 4:40, and she was ten minutes late for the appointment with Mark Wiseman.

"I don't know yet, but I'll find out," she said into the phone. "I'm sorry, I really need to go. I'm late for a meeting with the funeral director."

"Okay. Well, call me when you know, and then I'll book a flight for Tildie and me. Just call when you can. I'll have my cell on."

"I will," she said, running up the wooden steps to the funeral home. "I love you, baby. I've gotta go. Bye!"

She turned the door handle, relieved to find that it wasn't locked. Letting herself into the funeral home, she was assaulted by the smell of roses and gardenias. She wrinkled her nose, smiling as she spotted Mark Wiseman.

"Hi, Mark." She waved across the entryway, smiling.

She and Mark were the same age, and had even dated briefly in high school before he came out of the closet. Now that marriage equality was the law of the land, he had wed a wonderful man named Christopher that he'd met in college. She'd spoken to them both at length last year, when she'd returned home for her tenth high school reunion. Mark had taken over the family business after his father passed away from lung cancer in 2012.

"Hi, yourself," said Mark, wearing a gray sweater vest. His blue eyes sparkled, and she noticed his blonde hair was starting to thin a little. "I was so sorry to hear about Lucy."

She was genuinely happy to see him, even if it was under less-than-ideal circumstances. She gave him a long hug, and felt tears starting to brim in her eyes. She released her hold on the man she'd sat next to in Freshman English and took a step back.

"You look great," Zara said, feeling nervous despite herself to be in the funeral home. Apparently, some childhood fears never go away.

"As do you," he returned the compliment, "just like always. Matt is a lucky man. Now come with me into the parlor, said the spider to the fly. We'll sit and talk for a bit before we get down to business."

The spider's parlor was grand indeed, grander even than she'd remembered it from the few times she'd been there. A burgundy-colored velvet couch sat against one wall, fronted by a long coffee table and opposite two overstuffed lounge chairs. Vases of gardenias, roses, and other fresh flowers filled the room. Mark sat on the couch, gesturing for her to join him.

They talked for about ten minutes, catching up on each other's lives and reminiscing about the past, before, as Mark said, "getting down to business."

"Now, as you already know, your grandmother arranged for most of this. All you really need to do is decide on the day and whether or not we're having a visitation."

She stared at him. "No," she said slowly, "I didn't know that she arranged for most of this. I knew she had a burial policy, but that's about it."

"Well, then, I'll catch you up to speed. Basically, she picked out her own coffin, purchased her plot at Moss Ridge Cemetery, and took care of a few other details. The coffin was special order. I've had it in storage for six months. It was almost like, well .."

"Like she knew she was going to die," Zara finished for him. "But how could she? She wasn't even sick. At least, not that I know of." There were clearly more than a few things she hadn't known about her grandmother.

"So, about the visitation," Mark prompted. "Your grandmother was much loved in Carthage, so I'd definitely recommend having the visitation. Ideally, we'd hold the visitation Wednesday night and the funeral Thursday morning, so the *Journal-Pilot* could run the announcement and the obituary Wednesday morning

In fact, I've already penciled all of that in and made arrangements with Moss Ridge, but of course we can switch any or all of it around if you want."

The *Journal-Pilot*, Carthage's one and only newspaper, was published once a week, on a Wednesday, so the timing made sense. She didn't like being away from Matt and Matilda that long, but it really couldn't be helped.

"No, that'll be fine. We should definitely have the visitation. I think Mrs. Olinger would skin me alive if we didn't," she said, allowing a small smile to flash across her face. "We'll do everything just like you said. I'm just...overwhelmed."

"I understand completely," he said, taking her hand in his. "But we'll get through this together. And Matt and your lovely little daughter will be here to support you soon, I'm sure."

"Not so little anymore," Zara said. "She just turned five today, and I had to miss her birthday. But, yep, they'll be here."

"Good, good," Mark reached out to squeeze her hand. "Now, are you ready to see your grandmother's body?"

Zara steeled herself, rising from the couch. "Ready as I'm going to be, I guess."

She followed Mark through one room into another, finally arriving at a viewing room in the back of the building.

"And here it is," Mark said, gesturing toward a wooden casket decorated in silver. "It's made of solid poplar wood with silver trim, just like Lucy specified. And notice the inlaid marble on the lid. That's what took so long. It had to be custom made."

She stared at the casket. There was a symbol carved into the marble, a silver star with a circle around it—a pentagram, it looked like—and on top of that three interconnecting, oblong circles. They looked like they were tied into a knot. The carving looked somehow familiar, but she couldn't place it. She shrugged, more to herself than to Mark.

Mark laid a hand on her shoulder. "Do you want to see her?"

"I suppose I'd better," she said, staring down at the coffin.

Mark unlatched the casket and opened the top half. There was her grandmother, eyes closed, arms crossed over her chest. She looked almost as if she were sleeping. Lucy Brennan was dressed in her favorite blue dress, a black belt cinched around her waist. Something was clutched in her hands, but she couldn't tell what.

"What's she holding?" asked Zara, inexplicably unable to tear her eyes away from the woman's hands.

"It's a necklace," Mark said. "I assume it held some sentimental value to her. Like everything else, it was specified in her final instructions. There was something else as well, but it's kind of strange…"

Matt didn't think he could take any more time off work than was absolutely necessary, so they agreed that he and Tildie would catch a flight out of Fayetteville early Wednesday morning. Zara had set the visitation for seven Wednesday evening and the funeral for ten Thursday morning, so that should give them plenty of time. He'd purchased return tickets for all three of them for Friday morning.

It was just nine in the evening on Saturday, and she desperately missed Matt and Tildie. Mark and his husband Christopher had taken her to the Taste of China, located on the north side of the town square, where they had dined on cashew chicken, broccoli beef, orange chicken, and a plate full of eggrolls. Zara had added a sweet chili sauce to everything she ate, helping to clear out her sinuses. The food was great and the company even better, but now she was alone again.

She had an appointment with her grandmother's lawyer Monday morning, but beyond that not much on her agenda until Wednesday. Zara looked through the DirecTV channel guide on the widescreen television but couldn't find anything interesting, finally settling on MSNBC, where she caught up on the latest news about Iran, Miley Cyrus, and whatever politicians had been caught with their hand in the cookie jar this week.

Zara leaned back on the couch and soon Oscar joined her, and she found herself almost unable to keep her eyes open. Deciding that sleep was exactly what she needed, she muted MSNBC and closed her eyes.

She knew that she was dreaming, but didn't care. Zara was in Merryland. She was walking through a meadow alongside Professor Plum, the floating, bulldog-sized purple dragon her grandmother had included in her countless stories of the made-up land.

"So let me get this straight, Professor Plum," Zara said, a little girl again, about the age she was when her grandmother had first started telling her the stories, "the queen has been kidnapped from the castle, and it's our job to get her back."

"Indubitably, dear one," intoned the dragon, in a highbrow British accent, "no one else can do it, but we'll need the Necklace of Tears if we are to have any hope of getting past the ogres that guard her."

"But how do we find this necklace?" she asked.

"The necklace is identical to one the queen wears and has been missing for many years," said the dragon, between puffs on the old-fashioned pipe filled with cherry tobacco that he smoked, "but if my sources are to be believed, it's hidden in a metal chest at the very bottom of Lake Pelagic."

Her grandmother had often spoke of Lake Pelagic, and the dangers that lie beneath its crystal blue depths: sea monsters, sirens, and, if the legends were to be believed, perhaps even the skeletons of the last army that had tried to wrest control of Merryland from the Popcorn Prince.

"So how do we get to the bottom," Zara asked, "without getting killed or drowning?"

"That is the question, is it not?" the dragon said, blowing blue smoke out of its nostrils. "Legend has it that a certain, extremely rare flower found only in this forest—the very forest that we find ourselves in right now—will enable anyone who drinks a tea brewed from its petals to breathe underwater for exactly sixty minutes. That should be long enough to recover the necklace, with little time to spare."

"What does this flower look like?" asked Zara, at once paying attention to the foliage on the other side of the path.

Something unusual caught her eye, something she'd never seen before. She knelt in front of a brightly-colored bush filled with tiny blue flowers, plucking one. She held it up to the dragon, whose eyes grew instantly and almost comically large.

"Zara, my dear, you're brilliant. You've found it! With that flower, we should be able to get the necklace from the bottom of Lake Pelagic!"

"But what will protect us from the skeletons and other bad things in the lake?"

"Why, that's easy. We'll just..."

"Do you hear that?" interrupted Zara, cocking her ear back toward the path they had come.

"What are you talking about, dear girl? I don't hear a thing."

"It's a loud buzzing sound. Or ringing. I think—"

She awoke with a start, her eyes darting around the room. It was her cell phone. She reached out blindly for the coffee table, grabbed the phone, and swiped the icon to answer.

"What?" she yelled into the phone.

"Whoa," Matt said, "did I interrupt something?"

She took a deep breath, and then another. Had she been dreaming? She thought she had, but couldn't remember anything other than perhaps being in a forest.

"Sorry," she said, meekly, "I guess I fell asleep on the couch again. The phone just startled me."

Zara glanced at the grandfather clock: it was half-past ten. She'd been asleep for maybe an hour.

"It's okay, I just wanted to tell you goodnight and that I love you. Tildie and her friends had an amazing time, and so did my folks. We're all exhausted but happy."

"Miss me?" she said coyly, as she wiped the sleep from her eyes.

"Of course I do, babe. So does Tildie, but I think we managed to distract her, at least for tonight. Spent way too much at Build-a-Bear and American Girl, but c'est la vie. Easy come, easy go."

They talked another ten minutes or so before saying their good-byes, and Zara promised to call on Sunday around noon. Tildie was fast asleep, of course, but Zara couldn't help feeling a little sad (and maybe even a little jealous) that she hadn't had the chance to talk to her daughter.

She didn't have a clue how she would survive the next few days without Matt and Tildie. Clue. Something about that word. And then she remembered. Clue had been one of her favorite games as a child, and she'd invented an imaginary friend—a flying purple dragon about her size as a seven-year-old—named Professor Plum.

Zara had been dreaming about Professor Plum before the cell phone had awoken her. Something about Merryland, and a quest to find some mysterious lost object, but the misty tendrils of the dream were rapidly evaporating and that's all she could remember.

Dreams are funny, she thought, combining fragments of memories. Professor Plum had never been part of her grandmother's stories about Merryland—had he? Her thoughts seemed muddled, and she let the dream disappear into the ether.

MSNBC was playing something about the life of prison inmates, the story of a two-time killer who had earned his law degree from the inside of a jail cell. Zara clicked the television off, turned out the lights, and headed up the stairs toward her old room, to get ready for bed.

Sunday

Zara awoke at eight in the morning from a refreshing, dreamless night's sleep. She yawned, stretched, and rolled over, staring straight into the inscrutable face of Professor Plum. She screamed, flung out her arms, and Oscar yowled and leapt off the bed.

It wasn't Professor Plum, only Oscar. Her heart pounding, she rubbed her eyes, blinked, focusing on the room. The gray tomcat stared accusingly at her from atop the dresser, hackles raised.

"Here kitty, kitty, kitty," she called, patting the bed. Oscar turned away from her and exited the room.

Was she going crazy? No, she realized, it was just stress. The stress from missing Tildie's birthday party, the stress of dealing with her beloved grandmother's death, and the stress of being in her childhood home alone for the first time in her life.

Why, then, did the distinctive aroma of cherry tobacco fill the room?

Zara sat on the couch in the living room, half-heartedly playing Candy Crush on her phone while looking through her grandmother's old photo albums. She'd spent hours looking through the volumes as a child and early teen, mostly at her mother, Sara Gold, wondering what kind of woman she had been.

This afternoon, her phone call with Matt finished and with nothing else to do, she delved deeper. She was amazed at the depth of her grandmother's collection. The photographs easily went back eighty years, and included photos of her grandmother's wedding.

Thomas Gold had been a handsome man, and a decorated veteran of the Korean War. He'd been a Major when he finally retired from the army, having earned a silver star, two purple hearts, and countless other awards. They'd lived in this house, of course, which had been in the family's possession since it was built by Zara's great-great-grandparents in 1899.

Her grandfather had died of a heart attack in the late 1970's, when Sara was just a teenager, and almost ten years later Lucy remarried. Her second husband's name was Michael Brennan, but he, too, had died, less than five years after they had tied the knot, right after Zara had come to live with them. He'd fallen down the basement stairs and broken his neck.

Zara flipped pages, coming across a black and white photo that stopped her in her tracks. It was Michael Brennan, the man who's name her grandmother had taken and kept, smoking a pipe. The pipe looked uncannily like the one Professor Plum had always smoked when she imagined him.

She released an uneasy laugh. Zara must have looked through the albums as a very young child and used the pipe as part of her tapestry when deciding what Professor Plum looked like. In fact, now that she looked closer, she realized her dragon also shared the kind eyes of Grandma Lucy's second husband.

Yes, it all made sense. Zara remembered now, she'd taken the character from her grandmother's stories and had given him life as her imaginary friend, a companion for a lonely little girl who had just lost her parents. Professor Plum was her grandmother's creation, not Zara's, but it had been Zara that had breathed life into him in such a way as only a seven-year-old could.

Zara thought back to yesterday, at the funeral parlor with Mark. She had complied with her grandmother's request, but it still freaked her out a little.

Mark had retrieved a small, blue cloth bag from his office, handing it to Zara. Inside it had been a silver coin about the size of a quarter. One side showed a pentagram, while the other contained the three interconnected, oblong circles tied into a knot. Put both sides together and you'd have the same symbol that was inlaid in marble on the lid of the coffin.

She'd kissed it, as per the instructions, and then slipped the coin into the old woman's mouth, just between her slightly parted lips, resting on her tongue. She shuddered thinking about it, and couldn't fathom why her grandmother had requested that such a thing be done. Mark just shrugged and said he'd seen stranger requests, and so she'd let it go.

Grandma Lucy has never been particularly religious, but they often say that people who are dying will sometimes latch on to whatever faith they can. Lucy had grown up Catholic, as had her ancestors in Ireland, so maybe this was some sort of ancient Catholic ceremony. She didn't think it was, but couldn't be sure.

Zara sighed and set aside the photo albums. She'd arranged for a late lunch with two high school girlfriends at Ruskin's Pizzeria, and it was time to get ready.

Monday

Zara's cold continued to get better, and in fact today she was hardly sniffling at all. Maybe the cool September Illinois air was doing her some good, or perhaps the cold had just run its course. Whatever the reason, she felt more alive than she had in days, and she even felt energized by the storm currently raging outside.

It was a little before nine, and her meeting with the lawyer was at noon sharp. Thank goodness. With almost all of the funeral arrangements already made in advance by her grandmother, Zara felt like she was spinning her wheels. She just hoped it would stop raining by then.

There were only so many friends that she cared to see, with their pitying gazes and words of condolences. She knew they meant those words, but it was exhausting hearing them after a while. She just wanted to get on with business.

Today she was in the basement, doing laundry. She hated the basement, had hated it for as long as she could remember, but she'd forced herself down the creaky wooden steps just the same. She'd already washed the clothing she'd worn for the previous two days, as well as all the bedding from her grandmother's bed. She wasn't yet sure if she'd keep or sell the house, but she certainly didn't want to keep the unwashed sheets that her grandmother had died in on the bed.

Several friends had offered to cook meals and bring them over to her while she was in town, but Zara had demurred. It was easier just eating out, and, if she wanted to eat in, well, Ruskin's Pizzeria delivered. Heck, she still had three slices of extra-cheese and pepperoni in the refrigerator from last night out with the girls.

In addition to feeling better physically, she hadn't had any of the crazy dreams last night and had slept the entire night through. Perhaps now that she'd figured out who Professor Plum was, he'd finally left her psyche. She enjoyed her memories of the imaginary dragon, who had seemed very real at the time, but was happy leaving him firmly in the past.

A bright streak of lightning was visible from the little basement window, and Zara was counting the seconds until she heard thunder when the lights went out. Thunder roared. The lightning was close. Heart racing, already on edge, she dropped the basket full of clothes she'd just retrieved from the dryer and screamed as something ran across her foot.

It was Oscar. It had to have been Oscar. She fumbled in the dark, trying to remember where the fuse box was. This house was over a hundred years old, and just about any fluctuation in the electricity would cause the circuit breakers to trip. She hoped that's all it was, and that the power hadn't gone out entirely.

Lightning flared again, illuminating the basement for half a second, long enough to see a face made of twigs and sticks staring at her. She screamed and leapt backwards, banging her hip against the dryer, scrambling to get away from whatever it was she'd just seen.

She stepped on something, heard Oscar hiss, and winced as teeth and claws sank into her ankle. She must have stepped on Oscar's tail. She quickly moved backwards, away from the cat. Fumbling in the dark for where she thought she remembered a box of candles and a book of matches, Zara jumped again as lightning struck and thunder boomed less than a second after.

"Zaraaaa," whispered something in the dark, just a few feet away, and she found herself praying, something she hadn't done in years, praying that she had misheard her name and that it was just the wind.

Her hand closed on something, but it wasn't a candle. It was a handle of some sort, maybe to a door. She tugged on it, but it wouldn't open. Throwing her shoulder against it, tears suddenly running down her cheeks, she yanked again, to no avail.

"We need you, Zara," whispered the voice, and it was then that she knew it was more than just the wind.

Forgetting the candles and matches, she ran full-tilt for the stairs. Her foot caught on something (the clothes basket, she'd later realize), and she went careening across the basement, her head and right shoulder slamming hard against a wall. She thought no longer as consciousness left her body and her thoughts turned as dark and barren as the room around her.

Zara lay at the bottom of the stairs, head throbbing and her shoulder feeling like it was split in two. Her eyes didn't want to open, but she forced them open anyway. They felt like sandpaper, and her mouth was dry. How long had she been lying here?

She pushed herself to a sitting position, every muscle in her body screaming. The lights were on again, and the storm had passed. Zara shook her head, instantly regretting it. A blinding pain in her right temple almost made her close her eyes again, but she fought against the urge to sleep and instead used the wall to climb to her feet.

It was 1:15 p.m., her Minnie Mouse watch said. Shit! She'd been unconscious for a little over two hours and had completely missed her meeting with the lawyer. Did she have a concussion? She took a step and instantly regretted it, dizziness rushing in at her. Steadying herself against the wall, she took a breath and surveyed the room.

Clothes were spread out all over the basement floor. They would have to be washed again. Oscar sat atop the pair of jeans she'd worn yesterday, staring at her. She smiled at the cat, wincing at the flare of pain the movement caused.

What had happened? She remembered the lights going out and fumbling for candles, and then nothing. No, scratch that, she remembered her hand closing around a handle, trying to pull it open and growing panicky when it wouldn't budge.

And there it was, a huge oak cabinet standing opposite the washer and dryer, on the east side of the basement. She remembered wondering what was in the cabinet as a child and being told it contained Grandma Lucy's things from childhood and not to touch it.

At the very top, above the door, was a symbol much like the one on her grandmother's coffin: a star surrounded by a series of interconnected oblong circles. Curious now, she made a mental note to Google the image and hopefully decipher its meaning.

But there was no time for that now. She needed to call the lawyer to see if she could reschedule, and was strongly considering a trip to Carthage Memorial Hospital.

She wished she could remember what had frightened her enough to run into the wall, but, try as she might, she couldn't coax the memory out of her aching head. And then she remembered stepping on Oscar's tail. She glanced down at her ankle, ignoring the throbbing in her head as she did so. He had bitten and scratched her, and her ankle was covered in blood. Mystery solved. It had been Oscar that has startled her into running headfirst into the wall.

Zara slowly climbed the stairs, using the railing to steady her still-shaking legs. She'd pick up and re-wash the clothing later, and maybe even try to find a way to get into that cabinet. Once she'd apologized profusely to the lawyer, that is, and dealt with her possible concussion. She no longer bemoaned having nothing to do, and regretted having ever had the thought in the first place. This was shaping up to be a busy day, after all.

Mr. Wang, the lawyer, had been completely sympathetic to Zara missing the appointment, and had rescheduled her for three this afternoon. Thanking the man, Zara hung up the phone, found a box of bandages in the downstairs bathroom, and tended to her ankle.

Feeling ravenous, she wolfed down the three leftover slices of pizza as she drove herself to the hospital in her rented Nissan Altima. The emergency room was, thankfully, all but empty on this wet Monday morning, so it took less than thirty minutes for her to be seen.

"You're a lucky young woman," said the gray-haired, sixty-something doctor on duty, identified by her badge as Dr. Vanessa Wages, M.D. "You knocked yourself out, all right, but it could have been much worse. Definitely no concussion."

"I felt silly even coming in," apologized Zara, "but I wanted to make sure."

"Better safe than sorry," Dr. Wages agreed. "The lights went out here too, you know. All over town. I'm surprised we haven't been busier, especially considering the storm."

Zara supposed not everyone was as clumsy as her. "Just lucky, I guess."

"Say," asked Wages, "you aren't Lucy Brennan's granddaughter, are you? You look familiar, and I heard she was coming into town for the funeral."

"I am indeed," Zara said. "I'm staying at her house."

"I'm so sorry for your loss. I was your grandmother's doctor, you know."

"No, I didn't know that. Was it a heart attack? No one seems to want to tell me what she died from, and they just skirt around the issue. Mark Wiseman said the coroner had ruled it as a heart attack."

Wages' face turned white. "Oh, my. I'm so sorry, Zara, I didn't know."

"Okay, now you're scaring me. Tell me, Dr. Wages, what did my grandmother die from?"

"Well," Wages drew the word out, "it was a heart attack, actually, just like you'd been told. But the medical examiner found a mass of tumors on her stomach, and that made us delve deeper. When we examined her body yesterday morning, we found stage IV non-Hodgkin's Lymphoma. It was everywhere, her entire body."

Zara felt her jaw clench. Grandma Lucy had been sick and hadn't even told her. "How long?" She found herself asking, tears clouding her vision. "How long was she sick?"

"That's the thing, Zara. Your grandmother came in for regular checkups, like clockwork. And not just routine, either. We did MRIs, blood tests, echocardiograms; the whole nine yards. She was obsessive about her health, to the point where I worried that she might have hypochondria or OCD.

"But I digress. Her last checkup was just about two months ago, and she was healthy as a horse, easily as healthy as a woman ten or twenty years younger. And she certainly didn't have cancer."

Zara was still reeling from the news. Lucy Brennan had, in fact, died from a heart attack, but one brought on by the cancer in her body weakening her entire system. But cancer didn't come on that quickly, according to Dr. Wages, let alone stage IV non-Hodgkin's Lymphoma.

She was sitting across from Mr. Wang, her grandmother's attorney, in his office on the north side of the town square. The office looked professional, if a little sparse, and his secretary had shown her right in.

Wang was Asian, looked to be in his early thirties, and had deep brown eyes and buzz-cut black hair. He'd apparently been Lucy's lawyer for years, but Zara had never known he even existed until after her grandmother's death.

"I, Lucille Eileen Lennahin Gold Brennan, of Carthage, Illinois, being of sound mind and body, revoke my former wills and codicils and declare this to be my last will and testament," Wang said, all in one breath.

"Hold on. Other wills and codicils?"

"It's just legal speak. She didn't actually have any other wills or codicils, at least not that I'm aware of. Your grandmother's will is fairly standard, simplified by the fact that you're her only living relative. I can skip the legal mumbo-jumbo and get right down to the nitty-gritty, if you'd like?"

"Yes, please do." said Zara, deciding she liked Mr. Wang. "I was never one for the legal mumbo-jumbo anyway."

"Me, either, to be honest. Okay, here we go. 'I leave the entirety of my estate, including but not limited to the house located at 1342 Locust Street in Carthage, Illinois, to my beloved granddaughter, Zara Grace Boone.' And that's pretty much it."

Zara felt disappointed. She'd hoped that the woman's will might hold some clue to the sickness that had apparently come on so suddenly.

"Of course," continued Wang, "there's also her checking and savings account at the Marine bank, which holds," he glanced down at a green piece of paper on his desk, "$3,542.17 and $53,318, respectively."

"Hold on. Seriously?" she heard herself say, wondering if she'd heard right. "The checking doesn't really surprise me, but Grandma Lucy had that much in savings?"

"Apparently so," smiled Wang. "And if I'd have known that, I might have increased my hourly rate. Just kidding, of course."

She smiled back, still a little in shock. In the long term it wasn't a huge amount of money, but it would certainly be a nice nest egg for Tildie's college fund.

"Thank you, Mr. Wang," Zara said, starting to get up, "and I really appreciate you rescheduling my appointment."

"There is one more thing," said Wang, gesturing for her to remain seated. "Your grandmother had a safety deposit box at the Marine bank. You know where that is, right? What the box might contain I haven't a clue, but I suspect perhaps an insurance policy or maybe jewelry or something. The key is now legally yours."

Wang handed her a small key, maybe two inches long with square cut teeth, sporting a circular brass tag hanging from the end with the number 1425 engraved into the metal.

She half-expected to see that strange symbol on the key, and was somehow relieved that she didn't. Maybe she'd make it through the week sane, after all.

"May I ask you a question?" Zara said, holding the key in her hand. "My grandmother…did you know she was sick?"

Wang gestured helplessly. "Not at all, Mrs. Boone. I wish I had. Though I suppose I might have figured it out when she came in to give me the key. Up until then, she'd always kept it with her."

Zara almost didn't ask the next question, because she feared she knew the answer. "And when was that?"

"Maybe two months ago? I can check my records if you'd like."

Zara assured him that wasn't necessary, then rose from the chair, shook hands with Mr. Wang, and promised to call him if anything involving her grandmother's estate came up that she needed help with. She tucked his business card into her purse, waving to the secretary as she exited the building.

Though her rental car was parked in front of his office, it was such a beautiful day after the storm and with the sun starting to peer through the gray skies that she decided to walk the five or so blocks to the Marine bank and Grandma Lucy's safety deposit box.

Zara's grandmother had gotten a check-up two months ago, around the time that she'd given the safety deposit box key to Mr. Wang. But her tests had all come back negative. There was nothing wrong with her then. Why had she given Wang her key? There was something here, she thought, something buzzing around in her brain, but she wasn't quite getting it.

She glanced at her watch. It was almost four. For a moment she was worried that the bank might already be closed, but a quick phone call on her cell confirmed that it stayed open until five. It hadn't always been that way. She remembered once rushing to the bank with her grandmother, only to find the doors locked at just one minute after three.

That thought almost stopped her in her tracks, and she thought back to another trip to the Marine bank. She was maybe eight or nine, sitting in the lobby with her stuffed teddy bear Willard, waiting while her grandmother was escorted to the back of the bank. She'd asked Grandma Lucy what she was doing back there, but the old woman had gruffly and uncharacteristically told her that it was private and none of her business. Had she been visiting her safety deposit box then?

Walking past the County Market grocery store, Zara spun around as she caught a reflection in the glass. Her heart beat staccato against her breastbone, but she was alone, save for an elderly man with a cane exiting the store. He stared at her, shook his head, and continued on down the sidewalk.

She remembered now what had so freaked her out during the storm. Between the flashes of lightning, she'd imagined seeing a face made of sticks and twigs. The very same face she'd just seen reflected in the glass. Was it her imagination? It had to be, unless someone wearing a mask was stalking her.

Something jiggled at her brain again, something about Merryland, but as soon as she tried to snatch at the thought it was gone. A minute or two later, she was entering Marine bank.

Ten minutes after presenting her identification and waiting for the bank manager to verify that she was listed on the account (something she didn't know until now), Zara was led to a room in the back. The manager, a Mr. Fitch, produced his key and together they opened her grandmother's safety deposit box. Inside was a long metal box, which Fitch carried for her to a small room just off the safety deposit room.

Zara sat at a long white table, shaking. She wasn't sure what she expected to find, or why the box made her so nervous, but she steeled herself to find out. With a deep breath, she dumped the contents of the box on to the table.

Three separate insurance policies for $250,000 each and one for $500,000 sat atop the table, as well as the details of a Swiss bank account containing just over two million dollars, $50,000 in cash, the deed to a house in London, a blue felt bag, and an antique-looking brass key. The key sported the same symbol that was on the cabinet in her grandmother's basement, and no doubt opened the door.

Zara felt lightheaded as she opened the felt bag, pulling out two objects: a silver chain necklace holding a deep blue sapphire shaped like a tear drop, and a folded piece of paper.

She unfolded the paper, instantly recognizing her grandmother's handwriting. It said: *Prepare to go on an adventure the likes of which you haven't experienced in a very long time. Love, Grandma Lucy.*

Refolding the letter, Zara slipped it, the key, and the other papers into her purse. She picked up the necklace with trembling fingers, staring at it, as she began to remember.

It was almost midnight, and still Zara couldn't sleep. She tossed and turned in bed for what felt like hours, finally giving in to her insomnia, trudging downstairs to boil a pot of tea.

The stories her grandmother had told her as a child…had they actually happened? No, that didn't make sense. There was no place called Merryland, and the creatures that resided there just simply couldn't exist in real life. There were no dragons, no faeries, and certainly no creatures made of sticks, at least not this side of sanity.

She resisted opening the cabinet in the basement, because now she remembered what resided there. It was a mirror, and the mirror was an entrance to Merryland. Or was that just in Grandma Lucy's stories? She felt like she were going insane and could no longer tell reality from fiction.

The tea pot whistled as she searched the kitchen for a snack, startling her. She whirled around, knocking the tea cup and saucer she'd planned to use to the kitchen floor. She watched helplessly as they shattered, littering the tiled floor with porcelain shards.

"God damn it all to hell," she yelled, grabbing another tea cup and dashing it to the floor, followed by another and still another, "and damn you, Grandma Lucy, and damn your crazy stories!"

She was breathing hard, staring down at the mess she'd just made, still listening to the teapot's incessant whistling. Sighing, she turned to the stove and removed the teapot.

"I really am going crazy," she mumbled to herself, avoiding stepping on the remains of the saucer and tea cups as she went to track down a broom and a dustpan.

Zara sat on the couch in the living room with the television off, sipping tea. She thought about calling Matt, but worried about waking up Tildie. Besides, what would she say?

Matt, dear, I'm beginning to think the stories my Grandmother told me when I was little were real. That, or I'm having a nervous breakdown.

No, thanks. She didn't need her husband thinking she'd gone off the deep end. There was only one solution to this: opening the cabinet.

It was at the bank where she'd remembered about the mirror and the key her grandmother had used to open the cabinet, as well as the necklaces they wore when entering the magical realm.

The necklace worked hand-in-hand with the key. The key opened the cabinet, but one couldn't enter without wearing the necklace. At first, she hadn't had her own necklace and thus had to enter Merryland holding her grandmother's hand, but when she helped Grandma Lucy rescue the good Queen Isabella—the Queen of Merryland—from the nefarious clutches of the evil cowboy Seattle Slim, she'd been given a quest of her very own, and the necklace was her reward.

She flashed back to her meeting with Mark Wiseman and the object that her grandmother's body had been holding in its hands. Mark said it was a necklace, but she hadn't really been able to see. Was it the twin to the necklace that had been in the safety deposit box? It almost had to have been.

In her adventure to rescue the Queen, Zara remembered brewing a sweet-tasting tea from a magical flower called the Blue Sapphire that she and Professor Plum had found in the forest. The concoction had properties that somehow allowed whoever drank it to breathe under-water, thus enabling them to brave the dangerous waters of Lake Pelagic to find the necklace that was hidden in a trunk at the very bottom.

But it was all just stories, wasn't it? Her grandmother's alternative to the tried and true fairy tales, using her granddaughter as the protagonist. Except…what if they weren't?

Zara stood up from the couch. There was only one way to find out for sure, and if she felt like a fool afterwards, so be it. She snatched up the key and the necklace from the coffee table where she'd left them, fastening the necklace around her neck.

It was now or never, because she didn't think she'd ever again work up the nerve to open the cabinet. She stomped over to the basement entrance, flicked on the light, and walked down the stairs.

She inserted the key into the keyhole in the cabinet. It was a perfect fit. Slowly turning the key clockwise, she was rewarded with a satisfying "click" as the cabinet door unlocked. Her hands were shaking as she pulled the cabinet open to reveal a floor-length, tarnished silver mirror. Above the glass, engraved in the mirror's frame, was a small recess that contained the very same strange symbol that adorned the key, her grandmother's casket, and the coin that she'd inserted into the dead woman's mouth.

Jesus, she thought, *it's real.*

She reached a trembling hand out towards the mirror, encountering resistance. She pushed, but the mirror wasn't going anywhere. It was just a mirror, not a magical entrance into another universe. It wasn't real, after all.

Zara felt somehow sad but relieved at the same time. And then she remembered something else, just a flash of memory, of her grandmother reaching above the mirror to press something into the recess above the glass. She stood on her tiptoes, but the recess was covered in cobwebs.

She ran up the stairs and into the kitchen, looking in the pantry where she knew her grandmother kept the cleaning supplies. She gathered up a feather duster, an old rag, a bottle of Windex, a small metal footstool, and an old yellow Black and Decker flashlight in case the power somehow went out again. She shoved all of this save the footstool into an old cloth bag from County Market that she found hanging from a hook inside the pantry, and then headed downstairs again.

Moments later she again stood before the mirror, using the feather duster to clear away not only the cobwebs but also the dust that the entire mirror and cabinet had accumulated over who knew how many years. Standing on the footstool, she could clearly see a hidden key hole at the back of the recess. She ignored it for now, instead shoving the feather duster back into the bag and using the Windex and the rag to polish the mirror to a bright shine.

Zara stared into the glass, and then climbed back atop the foot-stool. She inserted the cabinet key into the keyhole inside the recess, and this, too, was a perfect fit. She turned the key clockwise, but it wouldn't budge. Turning it counterclockwise, she heard a low hiss somewhere inside the mirror. The key would not come out.

Stepping off the footstool, her eyes inexplicably filling with tears and her pulse pounding in her temple, Zara stared at the mirror. All she could see in the polished surface was her own reflection, and the basement behind her. She placed both hands against the surface of the mirror, pushed, and fell through.

Zara found herself in complete darkness. Panicking, she threw herself backwards, crashing into what felt like the mirror. Thankfully, the glass didn't break. She forced herself to calm down, finally remembering the flashlight she'd shoved into the cloth bag that dangled from her left hand. She groped for the flashlight, clicked it on, and stared.

She was in a small cave, with little bits of what looks like diamonds sticking out of the walls. The gems reflected the light from her flashlight, illuminating the entire cave.

Zara couldn't believe it. She'd walked (okay, more like fallen) through a mirror and into somewhere else. Was Merryland real? Her memories battled against one another, and she was no longer sure what to believe.

She took stock of her surroundings. The mirror on this side wasn't tarnished at all, and only showed her own reflection. It stood on the backside of the cave and a small tunnel was carved into the rock opposite it. An unlit torch hung from a bracket to the right of the mirror, but she had no clue what to light it with.

As she began to walk toward the tunnel, the flashlight grew dim. Panicking, she quickly backed up to the mirror, and the beam of light grew brighter. What the hell? She walked back toward the tunnel, and the light dimmed again. Once again she traced her steps back to the mirror, and the beam grew stronger.

Apparently, she was trapped in this cave unless she wanted to stumble around without any light. She shone the flashlight all around the cave, but, save for the mirror and the unlit torch, it was completely empty. Frustrated, she finally grabbed the torch, nearly dropping it as it flared to life.

She looked at the flaming stick, slowly shaking her head. Other than the mirror itself, this was her first concrete proof that magic existed. Zara tucked the flashlight into the County Market bag, left it beside the mirror, and headed for the tunnel.

After walking about fifteen yards down the tunnel, she began to hear a low rumbling sound and finally saw light. The tunnel became brighter as she walked, and, inexplicably, wetter. The rumbling turned into a load roar.

She rounded a turn in the tunnel, finally realizing where the noise was coming from. Zara stared in awe as water rushed down in front of her. She was behind a waterfall. The sun shone bright through the water, casting moving shadows that danced all around her.

The tunnel widened here, leading out to a natural stone terrace. Plants and flowers sprouted from cracks in the stone, stretching toward the sun. A set of stone steps to the left of the rushing water led downward, and Zara took a tentative step toward them but stopped cold when she saw where they lead.

She was on the side of a mountain, several hundred feet in the air. Reaching out to steady herself against the rock, she stared past the water. It was amazing. A huge, sprawling castle was visible in the distance, and, beyond that, a large lake shaped kind of like the state of Texas. Lake Pelagic, perhaps. A pirate ship floated in the middle, sporting the Jolly Rogers as its flag. Between the two was a thick forest, and in the distance, off to the left of the castle, was a huge chasm in the ground that put the Grand Canyon to shame.

It was real. Merryland was real. A loud caw broke her from her reverie, and she looked up to see a huge bird swooping alongside the mountain. No, scratch that. Birds have feathers. This was an honest-to-God pterodactyl, with a wingspan of a good twenty feet, maybe longer. She pressed herself against the rock wall, unable to take her eyes off the creature flying in lazy circles above her.

She laughed out loud, startling herself. She wasn't insane, after all, and the things that she'd just recently started remembering had actually happened. Professor Plum, Queen Isabella and her son the Popcorn Prince, Meat Legs Johnson, Genghis Bill, Scottie...all of it was real.

Why had she stopped believing, and why had her grandmother stopped bringing her here? She wasn't sure that she'd ever know the answer to those questions, but there was only one way to find out.

Pushing down her sudden fear of heights and pterodactyls, she tentatively began walking down the stairs. The flying dinosaur didn't seem to take much notice of her, but she continued her descent as quietly as possible just in case.

The steps zigzagged back and forth across the mountain, like a switch trail. There were handholds carved into the rock here and there, but beyond that nothing to hold on to as the winds, which seemed mild at first, began to gust. She dropped to a crouch, knuckles turning white as she gripped the handholds, waiting for the winds to subside.

"You're silly, Zara," said a high-pitched voice behind her.

She almost fell off the side of the mountain as she whipped her head around to stare at a tiny pink faerie floating beside her. Her skin and hair matched the pink of her wings. The little creature was pink from tiny head to even tinier toes.

"Scottie?" Zara whispered, forgetting about the wind.

"You remembered!" the little faerie exclaimed, clapping her hands in delight. "Good! It's been so long, we were afraid you might have forgotten us."

"I did, for a while," she admitted, her heart rate slowing a little as the wind once again died down, "but I'm starting to remember again. You are Scottie, right?"

"Yes, I am! Oh! So exciting! Zara, you found your way back!"

"You think maybe we could talk once I get down these stairs?" Zara asked.

"Oh, silly," said Scottie. "You *have* forgotten things. You don't have to walk!"

Scottie grabbed one of Zara's fingers in her tiny hands, and tugged. Zara screamed as she toddled precariously on the edge of one stone step, finally falling. Only she didn't fall. She was floating. The faerie looked at her and winked.

Zara tilted her head back and laughed. This was absolutely amazing. She was flying. She was honest-to-God flying! She felt almost weightless as Scottie guided their descent, taking them in looping circles, twirling toward the ground.

She felt the blast of air from its beating wings before she saw the pterodactyl diving at them. She screamed and Scottie let go of her finger, zigzagging away from the flying predator. Zara felt gravity catch up with her as she plummeted toward the ground. But then the faerie was there again, touching her elbow, slowing her descent, until finally she landed on the ground as gently as a leaf falling from a tree.

"Oh my God," said Zara, sprawled in the grass. She wrapped her arms around her legs to stop them from shaking.

"When you laughed, you attracted its attention," said the faerie in a high-pitched voice, "You need to remember just how dangerous Merryland can be."

"I won't remember anything if I'm dead," she complained, as she tried in vain to rub out a grass stain on the knee of her jeans.

"I'm not so sure about that," the pink faerie said, "but there's no good reason to find out. I'm sorry I dropped you, I just had to get his attention on me instead of you. I won't do that again. But Merryland really can be very dangerous. Do you remember the time…?"

"I barely remember anything," Zara interrupted, "and most of what I do remember, I thought were dreams and stories until just a little while ago."

"But you remembered me," Scottie said, in a soft voice. "So there's hope for you yet, right?"

Zara had to laugh at that. "At least now I know I'm not going crazy. So, yeah, there's hope for me yet."

"Sooo," said Scottie, stretching out the word, "why are you here, after so much time away?"

"Well, I hate to tell you this, but my grandmother passed away."

"Passed away?" Scottie said, cocking a tiny eyebrow. "What does that mean, passed away? To where did she pass?"

"She died, Scottie. She died and I inherited her house, and I found the mirror and…why are you looking at me like that?"

The little faerie looked nonplussed. "Because what you're saying is impossible, Zara. I spoke to your grandmother just yesterday. In fact, she's the one that sent me to fetch you. She is most definitely alive."

Tuesday

Zara came awake instantly, sitting up, eyes wide and heart pounding. She was wearing the same clothes she'd been in last night, perched on her grandmother's stripped bed, back in the house. The last thing she remembered was Scottie telling her that Grandma Lucy was alive. Had she dreamed everything?

She felt around her throat. She was still wearing the necklace she'd recovered from the safety deposit box. Zara swung her legs off the bed, spying her boots on a wooden rocking chair on the other side of the room. At least she'd had the presence of mind to remove them before going to sleep, though she didn't remember climbing into her grandmother's bed in the first place.

Slipping the boots on, she padded downstairs, through the living room, past the kitchen and into the basement. The cabinet was still open, exposing the mirror that she distinctly remember falling through. Her bag, however, the cloth bag from County Market that she distinctly remembered leaving on the other side of the mirror, was leaning against the cabinet.

She walked over to the glass, reached out to touch it, then jumped as she heard the familiar trill of her cell phone ringing upstairs. She looked back at the stairs and again at the mirror, trying to decide what to do. Finally, she touched the mirror, feeling the smooth silvery surface. Ignoring the ring of the phone she pushed, but met resistance. Why wasn't this working?

Oscar mewed at her from the middle of the stairs, perhaps disturbed by the phone or maybe just craving her attention. Finally, the phone stopped ringing. Oscar stared at her for a second before meowing once, turning tail, and heading up the stairs.

Zara couldn't understand it. Was she batshit-crazy, after all? And her grandmother being alive, what was that all about? Wishful thinking, probably, the half-crazed and delusional mind of a woman in grief for the only parent she'd ever known.

She needed to get out of this basement, out of this house. Stepping on to the footstool she'd abandoned last night, reaching atop the cabinet, she felt for the key but it was gone.

Searching the rest of the cabinet and the floor around it, Zara became more and more frantic as she failed to find the key. When she'd gone through the mirror, the key was locked into place. It couldn't have just fallen out. Someone had to have taken it. But who, not to mention why and how? The doors to the house were all locked.

Zara caught the sense of movement reflected in the mirror and nearly fell off the footstool. She turned to face the room, but the basement was empty. Of course it was empty. This whole thing was making her paranoid. Other than Oscar and Mrs. Olinger, she'd been the only living being in the house since Grandma Lucy died.

Mrs. Olinger. She knew the old woman had a key to the house, but why on earth would she sneak inside, come down into the basement, and steal the key to the cabinet? It didn't make any sense.

The telephone began to ring again, echoing through the empty house. Zara climbed the stairs and made her way into the kitchen, where she'd left her phone charging.

"Zara, it's Mark," said a voice over the telephone, and it took her an instant to realize that it was Mark Wiseman.

"Hi Mark. Is everything okay?"

"Well, that's why I was calling. I called the *Journal-Pilot* this morning, and they said you haven't been in to give them the obituary yet. They really need it by three to be able to get it into the newspaper tomorrow."

Shit. Zara glanced at her watch. It said seven in the morning, while the grandfather clock claimed it was just past ten.

"Mark, what time is it?"

A pause. "10:07. You still have a few hours."

Her watch had kept perfect time for years. She wondered what was wrong with it, quickly winding it forward to the correct time.

"I'm on it," she said, though she hadn't even started the obituary yet.

Mark offered to help her write it if she wanted to come by the funeral home, but she declined. Instead she climbed the stairs to her old room to retrieve her laptop, determined to write the damned obituary herself. Thirty minutes later, it was finished.

Lucille Lennahin Gold Brennan, 75, of Carthage, passed away on Friday, September 19th, at her home. She was the beloved grandmother of Zara Boone and the great-grandmother of Zara's daughter, Matilda, both of Fayetteville, Arkansas. She was preceded in death by her daughter Sara. She was loved by many and will be missed by all.

She added the dates of the visitation Wednesday evening and the funeral Thursday morning and called it finished. It wasn't her best work but it would have to do, because she desperately needed to get out of this house.

Zara saved the Microsoft Word document to a flash drive, yanked it from the laptop, and was halfway down the stairs before the thought hit her that she hadn't bathed since yesterday morning.

Well, so what? She had also slept in the same clothes she'd been wearing last night. That's when she noticed that her jeans had a grass stain on the right knee.

She wanted to cry, scream, break things, do something, anything, to break the silence that surrounded her, but she couldn't even move, could barely breathe. She had stained her knee tumbling to the grass after Scottie had dropped her. But it couldn't have been real.

The last thing she remembered last night was talking with the little pink fairy, and her making the claim that Grandma Lucy was still alive. And then, poof, she'd woken up this morning, fully clothed, in her grandmother's bed. She had no memory of how she'd gotten there, and the key that had (or probably hadn't) allowed her to step through the glass into Merryland was missing.

Her mind was racing in circles. It wasn't real. It couldn't be. Places like Wonderland, Never Never Land, Oz, and her grandmother's Merryland were all fiction, made-up places filled with fantastical stories to entertain bored children. None of it was real.

Zara felt suddenly angry. Why was she letting her memories affect her like this? She really was going batshit crazy, cooped up in this old house with no one to talk to. Though she hadn't been drunk in six years—since she'd first found out she was pregnant—she desperately wanted to get plastered, to just forget about Professor Plum, Merryland, Scottie, and the whole damned thing, at least for a few hours.

The phone rang then. Matt, of course. She turned off the ringer and shoved it into her purse. She'd call him back later, after she'd dropped the flash drive off at the *Journal-Pilot*. Or maybe after she'd had a few drinks at the Peacock Inn, a local bar that she hadn't visited since the day she turned twenty-one.

She stomped through the front door, slamming it closed behind her, not even flinching as she heard a familiar voice calling her name from somewhere deep in the house.

Zara's mouth tasted awful, like bad beer and pretzels, and her eyelids felt like sandpaper. She struggled to open them, failed, and then tried again. The light gave her an instant headache but she forced her eyes open anyway, wondering exactly where she was.

"Are you awake, baby?" said a man's voice beside her.

Matt? No, Matt was at home, in Fayetteville. She was in a bed, naked, the stale smell of cigarettes in the air. Her vision cleared, and she stared across the room, at a black cat hanging on the wall. No, it wasn't a cat, not really. It was a clock that looked like a cat, its tail moving back and forth, back and forth, as it counted off the seconds.

She blinked. The clock said it was seven fifteen in the evening. She flinched as an arm encircled her waist, cupping her left breast, then spun to look into the face of a sleepy-looking man with pale blue eye and a beard. *Oh fuck. No, please. Please, please, tell me I didn't do this,* Zara thought, wanting to crawl under the covers and die. *Tell me I didn't cheat on Matt.*

She clawed at her memory, desperately chasing down the threads of the last eight hours. She remembered dropping the flash drive off at the newspaper, paying for the obituary with her credit card, and then following through on her stupid, moronic impulse to visit the Peacock.

Zara had been drinking alone at first, in a dark little booth in the corner. She'd started with a glass of white wine but quickly moved on to tequila shots and then vodka. She'd been pretty out of it by the time Brett, someone she vaguely recognized from high school, had asked if he could join her.

"I always liked you, you know," he said, scooting into the booth beside her, "but was just too damned shy to say anything."

"That's nice," she mumbled, sucking down her third vodka tonic. "I think I remember you."

"But here you are," he said, not even listening to her, "and I'm not so shy anymore. When did you come back to town, Zara? I thought you'd moved to Alabama or something."

"Arkansas," she slurred, angry that the alcohol seemed to have disappeared from her glass. "Where's my fucking drink?"

"Jim, can I get us a round of beers over here? Whatever you have on tap is fine. And a bowl of pretzels, too."

"Beer and pretzels," Zara said, steadying herself on Brett's shoulder. "I like beer and pretzels, and I think I like you, too."

The bartender deposited two beers and a bowl of pretzels at their table. "Miss," he said, his bald head glowing beneath the neon lights that lit the darkened bar, "I think maybe you've had enough."

"Why don't you mind your own fuckin' business, Jim?" Zara said, snaring a pretzel out of the bowl.

"Hey, just trying to be responsible," Jim said, his hands out in front of him. "But whatever." He turned to Brett. "Just make sure she gets home safe, okay?"

"Will do, buddy," Brett said, already turning back to Zara. "So, baby, let's say we down those beers and get outta here. I got an apartment over in Spencer Heights, and—"

"But I gotta get home," she protested, half-laughing. "I need to look for the key."

"Baby, I got a key for you, and I think it'll fit your lock just fine."

She remembered getting into his old, rusted red Mustang with him, kissing in the car. She almost threw up. Had she really kissed him? And then they were in his apartment, tearing each other's clothes off. His hands and mouth on her breasts, his hand between her legs.

Zara spotted a trash can half-filled with beer bottles a couple of feet from the bed. She sat up, swung her legs out of the bed, and barely made it to the trash can before vomiting a stomach full of alcohol and pretzels. She heaved and heaved until finally there was nothing left, and then she heaved some more.

"Baby, you okay?" Brett's voice called from the bed.

"Fuck you," she sobbed, her face awash in tears. "I am not your 'baby.' I'm nothing to you, and you're nothing to me. This did not happen. Okay?"

"Hey, Zara, chill out," he said, finally sitting up in his bed. He was shirtless, his chest covered in thick, dark chest hair. "We didn't do anything, all right? I was…well, I was too drunk, and you passed out."

"Bullshit!"

"No, really," he said, shrugging. "Look. You're still wearing your jeans."

She looked down to stare at her jeans, speckled in vomit but still very much buttoned and zipped.

"I mean, you wanted to," he went on, "and so did I. We made out a little, but then you fell asleep."

She started sobbing then, huge hiccoughs escaping her lips, hugging her arms around her naked breasts. She'd almost cheated on Matt, with this guy she only half-remembered from high school. What in the hell was wrong with her?

"Shh," Brett said, "it's okay."

Brett gathered the bedspread from where it had pooled on the floor at the end of the bed, walked over to her, and wrapped it around her shoulders.

Zara let out a grateful whimper and began crying again, as he held her against his shoulder. They stood like that for almost ten minutes as he let her cry it out. Exhausted and embarrassed, she finally pulled away from him.

He turned away while she slipped her shirt over her head, her bra so lost in the recesses of his apartment that neither of them could find it.

"Are you sure you don't want to stay?" he asked, smiling. "I don't usually get drunk before noon, you know."

She laughed. "I believe you, but, yeah, I'm sure. Thank you, though. For the offer and for...well...for not doing anything. Other than what we did, I mean."

Brett drove her back to the Peacock, where she picked up her rental car and headed back to her grandmother's house. He offered to follow her home to make sure she got back safely but she politely demurred, assuring him that she was all right to drive.

Zara sat on the couch, watching some old *Twilight Zone* rerun about a mannequin that thinks she's human, nibbling at the hamburger and fries she'd picked up from Dairy Queen on the way back to her grandmother's house. She couldn't believe what she'd almost done. Hell, what she *had* done was bad enough.

If she told Matt, he'd never forgive her. If she told Matt. She couldn't believe she'd just had that thought. Of course she should tell Matt. He was her husband and he deserved to know. Didn't he? She could justify it seven ways to Sunday, but even if she hadn't actually had sex, she'd been unfaithful just the same. She'd gotten drunk and almost slept with another man.

Matt. She looked at her watch. It was eight o'clock. She dug through her purse, looking for her cell phone. It wasn't there. She dumped everything out on to the coffee table, not even caring as a tube of lipstick, three quarters, and several dimes rolled off to clatter to the floor. The phone was shoved into the very bottom of the purse, sandwiched between her wallet and the rental car agreement she'd signed Saturday morning.

She typed in her four-digit security code, staring at the phone. Matt had called seventeen times. Make that eighteen. She almost dropped the phone as it started to vibrate. She'd turned the stupid ringer off. Matt was calling right now.

"I can explain," she said immediately after thumbing her phone on, without giving him the chance to talk.

"Explain what?" said Matt, his voice calm.

"Umm, where I was all afternoon, and why I didn't call."

"You were out with your secret boyfriend, weren't you? I knew it!"

She felt like she were going to be sick again. "I'd never cheat on you, ever. I love you so much, Matt." She started to cry.

"Hey, whoa, I know that, I was just being silly. Sorry, probably not a great way to be with you feeling the way you do."

Zara stared at the phone in her hand. "What do you mean, feeling the way that I do?"

"Your migraine," he explained.

"But…Matt, what are you talking about?"

"When I called earlier. Your friend told me that you had a migraine and were lying in bed."

"But my ringer was off."

"The house phone, silly. When I couldn't reach you on your cell I tried the house phone, and your friend answered and told me that you weren't feeling good and were lying down. That's why I called your cell this time. I figured when you felt better, you'd answer."

"My friend? Do you mean Mrs. Olinger?" So the old woman had been in here, after all, and had even been so bold as to answer the telephone.

"No, no, not Mrs. Olinger. Your friend…what's his name? Doctor…no, Professor. Professor Plum, just like in that game."

Wednesday

Zara thought back to last night. She'd confirmed the headache, lying to her husband once again, and then quickly got off the phone. She had also begged off talking to Tildie, and was disgusted with herself. She'd gotten drunk, came dangerously close to having sex with someone she only half-remembered from high school, and her husband had talked to someone who was either a figment of her imagination or who existed in a fantasy land accessible only by a magical mirror in her dead grandmother's basement.

It was six in the morning, which meant she'd slept a solid ten hours, and Tuesday night was just a blur. She had fallen asleep on the couch, half-starving and crying. Matt and Tildie would be here later this afternoon, and she wasn't sure she could face them. She'd turned from a fairly responsible mother and wife into a raving lunatic. And she'd almost lost everything with one stupid, drunken mistake at the Peacock Inn.

Correction: she could still lose everything. She had to tell Matt, if not tonight then tomorrow, or at the very latest Friday, after they'd flown home. He deserved to know who his wife really was, even if it meant losing him forever.

Zara knew she was ignoring the elephant in the room: Matt had spoken to someone, someone who had covered for her, and it obviously wasn't Professor Plum. Who, then, was it? And who else even knew about Professor Plum other than her dead grandmother?

She was filled with questions, but precious few answers. Something smelled rotten. She sniffed her armpit, wrinkling her nose. It'd been a full two days now since she'd last bathed, and she was still wearing the same clothes she'd had on since Monday.

She forced her sorry ass off the couch and up the stairs, heading toward the bathroom. She was in desperate need of a hot bath. Stripping off her grass-and-puke-stained jeans and her stinky blouse, she let both drop to the floor beside the sink. Zara turned the bath as hot as she could handle, added some bubble bath that vaguely smelled like roses, and slowly lowered herself into the mixture.

Her shoulders immediately relaxed, and she felt some of the tension begin to leave her body. Yes, this was exactly what she needed. She scrubbed hard at her face and her breasts and between her legs, wanting to rid herself of any possible trace of Brett that still remained. She realized just then that she'd almost fucked the guy and didn't even remember his last name. That thought made her scrub harder, until her skin felt almost raw.

"Zaraaaaaa," echoed a voice through the house, and this time she didn't even flinch.

"Come on in, the more the merrier," she yelled out, finally accepting the fact that she was going insane. "I'm done hiding."

Nothing came in, of course. The bathroom door remained closed. And yet she could almost feel something in the room with her. She shivered, hugging herself.

"Is anyone there?" she asked, without an answer.

Sighing, she leaned back in the tub and closed her eyes. Whoever or whatever it was could come in here and slit her throat, for all she cared. Let it do its worst. But nothing came.

Zara suddenly jerked awake. She couldn't believe that she'd fallen asleep in the bathtub. The previously scalding water had cooled to lukewarm at best, and the bubbles had all but melted away. She pushed herself out of the tub, wrapping a blue bath towel around her body as she stepped onto the bath mat.

Not yet secure, the towel fell to the ground and pooled around her feet as she stared into the mirror. There, written in the steam that clung to the glass and nearly evaporated, were two words:

Don't go

Professor Plum, the little purple dragon who had been her childhood friend, sat perched on the toilet, staring at her in the mirror's reflection.

She whirled around, but he wasn't there. Standing naked in the middle of her grandmother's bathroom, she slowly turned back around to see him watching her in the mirror. She crouched down, retrieved the towel, and wrapped it around her breasts.

"Professor Plum, how are you here?"

He said nothing, but nodded his head toward the mirror.

"Okay, I'm here, I'm not leaving."

The dragon slowly shook its head, pointing again at the mirror.

"I'm not sure what you want," said Zara. "I'm here now, but I'm going home on Friday. I can't stay here forever."

The dragon bobbed its head up and down vigorously, then jerked to the right as its eyes grew almost comically large. A crooked hand that seemed to be made from sticks and twigs and little bits of sap shot out from beyond her vantage point, grabbed the dragon by the scruff of its neck, and yanked Professor Plum out of view of the mirror.

Zara spun around again, hearing hurried footsteps slapping against wood. She pushed out through the bathroom door, turning her head one way and then the other, but no one was there. Peering back into the bathroom, she wasn't at all surprised to see that the words that had been written on the mirror just moments earlier had vanished.

Don't go. Truth be told, she couldn't wait to get out of here. It was just before seven in the morning, and she needed to leave the house no later than eleven to meet Matt and Tildie's flight at 12:15. Just two more days, and she'd be back in Fayetteville. Screw you, Professor Plum. She was counting down the seconds.

"Mommy!" Tildie positively screamed as she spotted Zara from across the airport, arms waving wildly as she ran toward her. She held a white stuffed owl dressed in Thor clothing in one hand, presumably the booty from her birthday trip to Build-a-Bear.

"Tildie-bear!" Zara screamed back, surprising herself by using the nickname they'd had for their daughter when she was a baby.

She scooped Tildie into her arms, hugging her tight. Zara felt hot tears running down her cheeks. Holding Tildie like this, she could almost forget the last few days. But then Matt, carrying Tildie's *My Little Pony* suitcase in one hand, Tildie's car seat in the other, and his own black duffel bag over his shoulder, caught her eye, and shame burned her cheeks. She had to fight not to turn away.

"Hey, don't I get some of that?" he smiled, stepping forth to pull both of them into an awkward hug.

Tildie giggled, then started chanting, "Kiss Daddy, kiss Daddy, kiss Daddy," until finally Zara gave her husband a quick peck on the lips.

"Sorry, the migraine," she offered by way of explanation at his raised eyebrows. One more lie couldn't hurt. She took Tildie's suitcase, relieving him of some of his burden.

"We've missed you," said Matt, taking Zara's hand in his own. "It's been a rough few days at the old Boone homestead."

Tildie took Zara's hand, the one holding the suitcase, and echoed the sentiment. "We missed you, Mommy."

"I missed you guys, tons and tons," she said, trying not to look at Matt. "It's been really lonely here without you, and I'm so looking forward to going home on Friday."

She realized just how true that was. The house, dealing with her grandmother's death, had turned her life upside down. If she could just get through tonight and tomorrow, she'd be all right.

They ate a quick lunch of loose meat sandwiches and fries at the Maid-Rite in Quincy, and were on the road back to Carthage by a little after one in the afternoon. The drive was pleasant, and Tildie fell asleep in the back hugging her new plushie while Matt drove and Zara rode shotgun. A jazz station played at low volume from the car stereo.

"Where did she get that name?" whispered Zara, between clenched teeth. According to Matt, their daughter had named her new stuffed owl Scottie.

"I don't really know," Matt whispered back, hands on the wheel. "It wasn't in any of the books they had. She said the name just came to her."

And what could Zara say about that? *Matt, dear, that's the name of one of the creatures my grandmother used to tell me about, creatures that might or might not actually exist.* No, she couldn't say that. Instead, she just settled for whispering, "That's a really interesting name."

He glanced over at her, taking his eyes off the road for just a second. He laid a tentative hand on her knee, and she had to fight not to push it off.

"Eyes on the road, mister," she said, flashing him a false smile.

"You just seem...I don't know. Different, somehow. Did something happen?"

She almost told him everything then, but instead bit her tongue. "I just don't feel good." At least that wasn't a lie. "Lucy dying, this whole trip...I just want it be to over and done with. I miss you and Tildie, I miss our house, and, hell, I even miss my job."

"Well, your job will wait for you, I tried to bring the house but couldn't fit it in the luggage, and Tildie and I are right here. That'll have to do for now." He squeezed her knee.

"You're sweet," Zara whispered, meaning it.

She laid her hand atop Matt's, squeezing his fingers. They'd shared everything since they first met in their last year in college seven years ago, and it was breaking her heart that she couldn't be honest with him now.

"Hey, what's wrong? You're crying."

"Nothing," she sniffled, pulling her hand away from his to wipe at her face. "Just thinking that I'm the luckiest girl in the world to have you and Tildie, that's all. The luckiest girl in the world."

"Wake up, Tildie," Zara said, gently shaking her daughter awake.

"Are we there yet, Mommy?" Tildie asked, eyes full of sleep.

"We are," she said, as she unbuckled the car seat. "Daddy's bringing the luggage in, so I'm responsible for bringing in the Tildie!"

She drew the little girl into her arms, eliciting a titter of laughter. Zara lifted Tildie onto one hip, bumping the car door closed with the other. Tildie suddenly threw her arms around Zara's neck, pulling herself tight against her mother, covering her face in little kisses.

Zara began to giggle uncontrollably, which only spurred on her daughter, and before long they'd tumbled to the brown September grass, laughing and rolling, forgetting the world and everything around them.

"C'mon, girls," said Matt, standing in the open doorway, "there'll be plenty of time for playing once we unpack."

"Grandma Lucy!" yelled Tildie, sitting up in the grass.

Zara felt a shiver run up her spine. She turned to follow Tildie's gaze, but it was only Mrs. Olinger.

"Oh, heavens," said the old woman, wearing a white apron. She had flour in her hair and had clearly been baking.

"Honey, Grandma Lucy passed away, you remember that," Matt said gently, walking over to lift Tildie off the ground. "This is her friend, Mrs. Olinger."

"Hello, Mrs. Olinger," Tildie said solemnly, from her father's arms.

"Why, hello there, Tildie," said Mrs. Olinger. "You probably don't remember because you were so little, but we met the last time you were here."

Zara quickly rose from the grass, embarrassed. "Sorry, we were just playing."

"I wish I could still play like that," Mrs. Olinger said, winking at Tildie. "These old bones aren't getting any younger. Enjoy it while you can."

"I will," said Tildie in a serious tone, making all three adults laugh.

"Now, I know you said you didn't need any food," Mrs. Olinger began, "but I get tired of cooking for myself, and so I decided I'm going to cook for you and your beautiful family. And you can't say no, because I'm mostly finished already."

"That's awfully sweet of you, Mrs. Olinger," Zara said, "and of course we accept."

"Good. I'm making you a tuna casserole, a baked ham, fresh green beans because I just can't stand that canned stuff, a nice green salad with homemade Italian dressing, and two pies. Apple and Banana cream. Now, I know it's a lot, but you can take whatever you don't eat back with you on the plane."

"Wow, Mrs. Olinger, that's very generous of you," said Matt, allowing a squirming Tildie to slip to the ground. "It all sounds delicious. Just tell us when you're ready and I'll come over and get it."

"Nonsense," said Mrs. Olinger. "You rest, get ready for tonight. My nephew will be stopping by in a couple of hours, and we'll bring it all over then. Enjoy some time with your family, I know how Zara's missed her handsome husband and her beautiful little girl."

Tildie beamed at the compliment, taking her mother's hand. "Come on, Mommy," she said, hugging her owl. "You can play with Scottie and me!"

Scottie, as it turned out, was actually Scotty, named after the character from the *Star Trek* movie they'd watched two nights before Zara had left town. She didn't realize the Scottish Star Fleet engineer had made such an impression on Tildie, but at least that was one mystery solved.

Tildie was playing on the floor by the grandfather clock with some of her action figures, while Zara was lying on the couch with her feet in Matt's lap. They were watching *Small Things*, one of Zara's favorite movies, as Matt massaged her feet and Oscar slept on her stomach.

She'd decided that she could never tell him about Brett. What would the confession do other than potentially break them up, destroying their tiny family? What's done was done, and besides, she hadn't actually done anything, not really. Some kissing and fondling, and that's about it. It could have been worse. Much worse.

Zara would just have to let it go. If she was going to keep this secret from Matt, it wasn't fair of her to keep him at arm's length without him ever knowing why. She pushed Oscar off her stomach and pulled herself into a sitting position, giving Matt a slow, lingering kiss.

"Mmm, that was nice," he said, looking into her eyes. "What was that for?"

"For being the best husband in the world," she whispered, snuggling into his arms. "I've missed you guys so much. And tonight, after Tildie's fast asleep, I think I'm gonna have to show you just how much you mean to me."

"I think I'd like that," he said, maneuvering his arm around her shoulder. "No, scratch that. I think I'd love it."

The screen caught her attention for a second: Shane Sullivan, the fifteen-year-old hero of the story, was beating up two school bullies at the Dairy Queen. She enjoyed the scene, but didn't like how the director had given Shane a background in martial arts. The book didn't have that, and the sudden, unexpected violence from Shane had seemed much more realistic as a result.

"Mommy, Daddy, look what I found!" yelled Tildie, running over to them on the couch.

"What is it, sweetie?" asked Zara.

Tildie held out a key, the very same key that had disappeared from the cabinet in the basement two days ago.

Zara bolted from Matt's arms. "Where did you get that?"

"Umm, I just found it when I was playing with my men." She called her action figures 'her men.' "Can I keep it, Mommy? Please?"

"I'm sorry, honey," she said, "but you can't. Mommy lost that and has been looking for it everywhere. Where did you find it?"

"Please, Mommy?" the little girl looked like she was about to cry.

Zara snatched the key from Tildie's hand. "I said no. Now tell me, where did you find it? Where?" Her voice was getting louder, and she felt powerless to stop it.

"Zara…" said Matt, tensing. "Are you all right?"

"Matilda Lorene, tell me this instant: where did you find that key?"

Tildie started to cry.

"Zara, for Christ's sake, what does it matter?"

"It matters," she said, "because I'm her mother, and I asked her a question. Now tell me, sweetheart, where did you find the key?"

"Under the…under the Grandpa clock, Mommy. I'm sowwy, Mommy." Tildie's upper lip was trembling and tears were rolling down her cheeks. "I'm sowwy. I won't play there anymore."

Zara felt sick to her stomach and immediately enfolded her daughter into her arms. "Shh, sweetie, it's okay. Mommy's sorry for yelling, it's okay. It's just an old key. It was Grandma Lucy's, and I thought it was lost forever. You didn't do anything wrong."

"Jesus, what was that all about?" asked Matt, once Tildie had gone back to playing. "I've never seen you so angry at her."

"Stress, I guess" she said, knowing it was a lie. "I feel awful about it, so don't make me feel worse, okay?"

She shoved the key into her jeans pocket, planning to just throw it away later. The cabinet hadn't taken her anywhere. Merryland wasn't real, and her grandmother was gone forever. There. No more wondering. No more going crazy.

"I'm not trying to make you feel worse," he said, "I'm just worried about you."

"Everything will be fine once we get home," said Zara. "We just have to get through tonight and tomorrow, and then everything is smooth sailing from here on out."

"I don't know about smooth sailing," he said, "but it will be good to have my wife home again."

She stood up from the sofa, taking his hand and pulling him to his feet. "Oh, I know for a fact that it'll be smooth sailing. Come with me into the kitchen, I need to show you something."

"Jesus Christ," exclaimed Matt, staring down at the insurance policies. "That's a million dollars."

"And that's not all," Zara said, pulling out the $50,000 in cash.

Matt's eyes grew wide. "Jesus, Zara."

"But wait, there's more," Zara added, doing her best impression of a game show host as she showed him the details of the Swiss bank account. "There's about two million dollars in there."

"But why didn't we know about any of this? Zara, your grandmother was filthy, stinkin' rich!"

"Apparently so," she smiled. "And she also has a house in London. I don't know what kind or what it might be worth, but...why didn't she tell us—why didn't she tell *me*—about any of this?"

"You're asking me?" he laughed. "Maybe your British friend knows something, at least something about the house in London."

She stared at him blankly.

"You know, Professor Plum. The guy who I talked to yesterday. He's British, and she has a home in London. It couldn't be a coincidence."

"Oh, yeah, him," she said, looking away. "I'll ask. But right now, we have," she glanced at her watch, "about an hour and a half before the visitation. I say we get ready and then get this thing over with. I'm sure Mrs. Olinger will have brought over her food by then, and we can eat after."

"Sounds like a plan," Matt agreed. "I'd like to take a shower anyway. Bathroom still up the stairs and to the left?"

"You got it, Mister," she said, standing on her tip toes to kiss his nose.

"No, I won't say that," yelled Tildie from the other room. "Now, stop bothering me."

Was someone in the house with Tildie? Zara and Matt raced through the door to the living room, but it was only Tildie, holding Scotty, staring into the corner of the room to the right of the grandfather clock.

"Tildie, honey," Zara asked, "what's wrong?"

"He wants me to tell you not to use the key, Mommy, but I won't. I won't do it. I told him it's your key now, and you can do whatever you want with it."

Zara felt her stomach go sour. "Who's telling you this, sweetie? There's nobody in the room but you."

Tildie turned to stare into the corner, then spun around, eyes darting all across the living room. "Well, he was here just a minute ago."

"Who, Tildie?" asked Matt.

"Professor Plum," she said.

Zara felt delirious and leaned against the door frame. It was all she could do not to pass out.

Matt let out a laugh. "You were listening again at the door, weren't you, honey? Professor Plum is a friend of Mommy's. We'll probably see him tonight at the visitation."

Tildie started giggling.

"What's so funny, Tildie-bear?" asked Zara, almost scared to find out.

"I was just thinking," she said earnestly, "about what kind of suit a little purple dragon might wear."

There were no little purple dragons in suits at the visitation, just a lot of adults in black clothing that wanted to hug Zara or shake her hand. She, Matt, and Tildie stood near Grandma Lucy's coffin, greeting a near-endless procession of well-wishers.

"I'm just so sorry for your loss," said Irene Gilpin, herself a widow, simultaneously hugging Zara and ruffling Tildie's hair. "I know how proud she was of you, and how much she loved all of you."

"Thank you, Mrs. Gilpin," Zara said automatically, a variation of the same phrase she'd already said at least fifty times this evening. "We really appreciate your support."

"How're things going, guys?" asked Mark Wiseman, coming up to Zara just as soon as Irene Gilpin moved on. He glanced at his watch. "Just another hour and this'll be over."

"Good," said Tildie, dressed in a little black dress with a bow around the waist.

Mark smiled, then dropped to a crouch. "Your Grandma Lucy loved you very much, you know. And you're being so patient, and so good. I know she'd be proud of you."

That brought a smile to Tildie's face, not to mention to Zara's and Matt's. "Thank you, Uncle Mark."

Zara and Matt were dressed in black, too, of course, as were most of the visitors. And here came Mrs. Olinger, with a man in dark clothing sporting a beard. He looked familiar and Zara couldn't place him for a second, but when she did she felt like her world was crashing down around here.

"Zara, dear," said Mrs. Olinger, "Matt, Tildie, this is my nephew, Brett Nielson. We just dropped off the food in your kitchen. The pies are on the counter, and everything else is in the refrigerator. I left little Post-in Notes on everything with directions for heating it up."

"Nice to meet you," said Brett, first shaking Matt's hand and then Zara's. "I'm sorry for your loss. You too, Tildie. I've heard a lot about you."

"Nice to meet you, too," Zara said automatically, staring into the eyes of the man she'd almost slept with yesterday.

"I left something for you in the pantry," he whispered to Zara as Mrs. Olinger chatted with Matt.

She blushed, nodded her head, and pulled away from him. "I'll be back," she said to Matt. "Give me five minutes. I need to find a bathroom."

Zara pushed past a group of elderly women staring down at Grandma Lucy in her casket, weaved past a surprised Mark Wiseman and his husband Christopher, and almost bumped into a silver-haired old man with a cane.

The funeral home was huge, and soon she became lost among the various rooms in the house. She hadn't really needed to use the restroom, thank God, but now she wondered where it was. Instead she found herself in a showroom filled with nearly two dozen various coffins. About half were open and empty, but she wondered about the other half.

Glad to be away from the crowd and, more importantly, Brett Nielson, she wove her way among the coffins to the back of the room and the wide elevator that took up half of the back wall. Curious, she pressed the red button beside the elevator and stepped inside when the car opened.

It was very industrial looking and only had two buttons: "Up" and "Down." She pressed "Down," and the doors closed. A moment later, she felt the elevator began to descend, and a moment after that the door opened.

Zara pressed the "open door" button and stepped into the room, instantly struck by the strong aroma of formaldehyde. She knew where she was. It was the room where Mark readied the bodies for burial. She looked around despite herself but, thank God, there were no bodies here.

Tools for which she had no name lined the walls, along with various colored tubing coming out of vats of differently-colored chemicals. There was an entire chest filled with make-up against one wall, used, Zara supposed, to give corpses the illusion of life.

She almost turned around to get back on the elevator, but movement in an open closet at the far end of the room caught her eye. She slowly stepped across the floor, squinting at the shadows that danced across the room like manic ballerinas.

Something stepped out of the closet just as she approached and she jumped back, smashing into one of the counters that ran along the edge of the room, sending a blue toolbox crashing to the floor.

"I know you might have forgotten me, Zara, but I haven't forgotten you," said a man made entirely of sticks and twigs, with some sort of glowing red berries for eyes.

He wore nothing save a white, ten-gallon hat, a pair of cowboy boots with silver spurs, and an old-timey western gun belt complete with a pair of black-handled silver six-shooters.

"Who…what are you?" gasped Zara, backing away.

"Seattle Slim, at your service," he performed a mock bow. "You really don't remember me, do you?"

She did now, sort of. Seattle Slim was one of the villains in her grandmother's Merryland stories. He'd kidnapped Professor Plum once, and she and Scottie had been forced to enter the Chasm of Doom to find and rescue him.

"You're not real," she said, trying to still her racing heart.

"I'm here, aren't I? I'm real enough."

"What do you want?"

"I'm here to tell you to stay away from Merryland. I have your grandmother now, and you'll never rescue her, so don't even bother trying."

"Grandma Lucy is dead, you twisted fuck."

"Here she is, you're right, Zara, but there…there, she's very much alive. But I've got her, and neither you, Plum, nor that pink faerie bitch can do anything about it."

The characters in her grandmother's stories never talked like this. "What are you going to do with her?"

"Kill her, of course. But she won't die of some silly heart attack, not like her body did here. She'll die my way, and she'll die slow. And once she's dead, Merryland will be mine forever. And then I'll come for your world, my not-so-little Zara."

"She didn't die of a heart attack," Zara said, surprising herself. "She was in perfect health."

"Very good, my dear," said Slim, his stick mouth moving in impossible ways. "What else have you figured out?"

"She killed herself, somehow gave herself cancer."

"Exactly. She killed herself to prevent me from coming out into your world, but she had it all wrong. She was the only thing keeping me in Merryland. Once she's dead in there, too, then I'll be free to do whatever I want. Maybe even play with that beautiful little daughter of yours. Tildie would love to play with me, wouldn't she?"

"No!" Zara screamed, launching herself at the man made of sticks. "No, you leave Tildie alone!"

She ripped at his eyes, clawing twigs from sap, snapping sticks in half, breaking him into smaller and smaller pieces until nothing was left. His hat tumbled from his ruined head, hit the floor, and vanished. There was nothing left of him, and yet still she pounded the floor where he'd been, screaming.

"Zara," Matt yelled in her ear, shaking her, "snap out of it!"

Her eyes snapped open and she stared up at her husband, crouched over her, concern written on his face. Mark and Christopher stood uncertainly beside him, eyes big.

"Where's Tildie?"

"She's fine, she's upstairs with Mrs. Olinger. We heard you screaming, and it took us a while to realize you were down here. We ran down the stairs and found you thrashing around on the ground. It looked like you were having a seizure."

"Stairs?" she said blankly. "But I took the elevator."

"Which is why we took the stairs," said Mark. "I guess you pressed the 'open door' button, because we couldn't get it to come up."

Zara looked around for signs of the destroyed Seattle Slim, but couldn't find even a twig. Her hands, however, were bloody and scratched, and beside her lay the broken remains of a mop.

"You were taking it to that mop pretty good when we came down," said Matt, as he helped her up to a sitting position.

"Matt, should I call someone?" asked Mark, trading glances with his husband.

"No, I'm fine," said Zara, not giving Matt a chance to reply. "I just...I got lost, looking for the bathroom. I wound up here, something spooked me, and I guess I took it out on your poor mop. I'll pay for a replacement, Mark."

"I don't care about the fucking mop," Mark barked, causing her to jump. "Sorry, sorry. We're all just worried about you, Zara."

"Your voice carries," Matt said, smiling. "We couldn't hear what you were yelling about, not until we got down here."

"And what was I yelling?" Zara asked, half-dreading the answer.

"'Leave Tildie alone,' you were saying. Over and over. 'Leave Tildie alone.'"

Zara shuddered as she remembered the stares and pitying shakes of the head she'd received upon walking into the visitation room. Everyone had heard her screaming at the top of her lungs, beating the crap out of some old mop, but thank God they hadn't heard anything more than that. If they'd heard her arguing with an imaginary stick cowboy her grandmother had made up, they'd have called the men in the white coats for sure.

Tildie had been scared, at first, but she'd quickly gotten over her fear, breaking from Mrs. Olinger to run into her mother's arms the moment she stepped into the room. They'd excused themselves without so much as an explanation after that and had walked home, Zara holding Tildie, who fell asleep in her arms before they even reached the front door.

Tildie was asleep now in Zara's old room, with Scotty tucked safely in her arms, while Matt and Zara lay spooning under the covers in the master bedroom. It was just before eleven, but Zara hadn't argued when, after dinner, Matt insisted that what she needed most was to fall asleep in her husband's arms.

Try as she might, however, she couldn't sleep. She hadn't had a seizure, damn it, and she hadn't beat up a mop. There was something down in that funeral home basement, something that had followed her there, and she was determined to find out what it was.

Her hands hadn't been bloody, after all. They were covered in berry juice from the very same berries that served as Seattle Slim's eyes, she was sure of it. Neither Matt, Mark, nor Christopher had been able to explain where the berry juice had come from, finally deciding that Zara must have accidentally touched one of the chemicals in the basement. She'd gone along with the idea, all the while knowing that wasn't what had happened but just wanting them to stop talking.

She wasn't crazy, she knew that now. Something was behind that mirror, something evil that had gotten out, and she was determined to find out what. And, if her grandmother truly was alive, she intended to rescue her or die trying.

Zara carefully extricated herself from her husband's arms, going still when he mumbled something in his sleep. She managed to slip away from his grasp, watching as he grunted, said something unintelligible, and rolled over to face the wall.

Letting herself out of the room, she carefully danced down the stairs, avoiding the steps she knew squeaked from her teenage years of sneaking out of the house.

Finally, she reached the living room. Leaving on her *Hello Kitty* nightshirt, she stepped into a pair of jeans she'd grabbed from her suitcase and then slipped on her old leather boots. She wasn't exactly dressed for adventure, but it would have to do.

And then she remembered Brett whispering to her at the visitation. She walked through the kitchen to the pantry, and there it was: her black bra, hanging from the hook that had once held the County Market bag that lay on the floor beside the mirror in the basement. She slipped the bra on under her shirt, but felt something scratch her right breast.

Zara reached into the cup and pulled out a yellow Post-It Note. Scrawled on the note in blue ink were the words "call me" and a number, presumably belonging to Brett.

"Asshole," she whispered, crushing the paper in her fist.

She started to throw it away, but then thought better of it. What if Matt found it? Instead, she shoved it into one of the pockets of her jeans, and then began scouring the kitchen for a weapon.

All she could find was a particularly wicked-looking kitchen knife. She didn't like going into Merryland without a weapon, but then she didn't remember her grandmother taking anything along on their adventures other than her wits. Still, she felt more comfortable with the knife.

Taking a deep breath, she opened the door to the basement. Zara stealthily scaled the steps downward, avoiding every little creak that she possibly could. The light was still on in the basement, and the cabinet door stood wide open. She crouched to retrieve the County Market bag, shoving the knife inside.

And then it was time. She stepped up on to the foot stool, inserted the key into the niche, and turned it. It made a satisfying click. She took an old bottle of Elmer's Glue she'd found in one of the drawers in the kitchen and carefully glued the key into the socket. If someone was determined to steal the key again, the glue wouldn't stop them, but, once it hardened, it would make it a damn sight more difficult.

She was ready. Zara felt her neck, reassuring herself that she still wore her grandmother's necklace, then took a deep breath and stepped through the mirror.

"Finally!" said Scottie, as Zara walked into the cavern on the other side. "We've been waiting for you since, well, forever. Where did you go?"

"I have no idea," said Zara, squinting against the light.

She felt disoriented, but knew from her prior trip that the feeling would pass in a minute or two. The torch hanging from the wall beside the mirror was blazing with fire, reflected in all of the tiny gems that were part of the walls surrounding them.

"You were here one moment and gone the next," said the faerie, eyebrows raised. "Poof. You just vanished."

"I'm here now," Zara said grimly. "You said my grandmother was alive."

"Seattle Slim," whispered Scottie. "He has her now, and he plans to sacrifice her to the elder Gods of Merryland, to trade her for access to your world. And once he has that, he will be unstoppable."

"But why wait? Why hasn't he done it already?"

"He can't," said the faerie, floating inches from Zara's nose. "Not yet. The three moons align tomorrow at midnight, like they do every month, and that's when he'll need to do it. And once he does…it'll all be over."

"You said 'we,'" Zara reminded the little pink faerie. "Have you found help?"

"I'm back," said a British voice from the opposite end of the cavern as if on cue, its owner cloaked in shadows. "He still has Lucy, and…Zara!"

Professor Plum flew out of the shadows, his purple wings beating the air to keep him aloft.

"Professor Plum," she said, tears forming in her eyes. "I've missed you so much. But thank you, thank you for coming to me on the other side, for trying to help."

The professor arched an eyebrow. "My dear Zara, I've missed you too. But this is the first time I've seen you in a very long time. I can't travel through the mirror. None of us can, save you and your grandmother and now apparently Seattle Slim."

"But...you came to me, you wrote things in my mirror."

"It wasn't me, Zara. Perhaps it was Slim, trying to trick you."

She thought back to her bath, staring into the mirror as a hand of twigs and sticks pulled the little purple dragon from her sight, and the dragon's kind eyes when she'd rolled over to face him that first morning. What would Seattle Slim have to gain by such a ruse? Or had she imagined that part, after all?

"We can't worry about that now," said Scottie, buzzing between Zara and Professor Plum. "We need to rescue your grandmother, before it's too late."

"Lucky for us," Professor Plum started, lighting his pipe, "some more of your friends have come to help us."

"Friends?" Zara asked.

As if on cue, three figures stepped forth from the tunnel opposite the mirror. One was so tall that he had to stoop. Standing at least eight feet high and made of nothing but rocks, she immediately remembered his name.

"Feldspar!" she yelped, running over to hug him.

Feldspar had once helped her rescue Scottie when the little faerie had been kidnapped and ransomed by the mysterious Masked Highwayman and his motley crew of thieves. He was a brave soul with a gentle touch that belied his massive frame.

"Hello, Zara," he said, the deep gravely bass of his voice rumbling from somewhere deep in his chest.

Another figure stepped out of the shadows, a small, lithe woman with long blonde hair hiding pointed ears. She was dressed from head to toe in green leaves, and carried a long bow nearly as tall as she was. On her back she wore a quiver of arrows. If Zara remembered correctly, her name was Elwin. She bowed at Zara, who returned the bow in kind.

"Zara Gold," said Elwin, using Zara's maiden name. "It has been such a long time. I'm truly pleased to see you, despite our current circumstances."

Zara looked past her, to the third person standing in the shadows. But of course it wasn't a person at all. Out stepped Target, the psychic bulldog. She'd had many adventures with Elwin and Target, and they had even once worked together to stop the invasion of the mole men from deep within the great Chasm of Doom.

"Hello, Zara," he whispered inside her head, *"I've missed you."*

"I've missed you too, Target," she said, dropping to her knees to give the black and white bulldog a hug. "I'm sorry I was gone for so long. I just...I just forgot. I thought Merryland was just a story my grandmother told me. I didn't remember that it was all real."

"It was as it was designed," the bulldog said. *"It's only the most blessed of adults that can remember Merryland, and keep it in balance with your own world. So blessed is your grandmother and, as it now turns out, are you."*

"Target is right," said Professor Plum, flying to her side. "You had to forget us then in order to remember us now, when it truly mattered. Together, we will save your grandmother and defeat Seattle Slim and his army."

"Army?" asked Zara, eyes wide in surprise. "Well, if he has an army, we should have an army. Professor Plum, fly straight away to the good Queen Isabella and the Popcorn Prince and..." They all looked away from her, eyes downcast. "What's wrong?"

"Things have changed since last you were here, my dear," Professor Plum said gravely. "Queen Isabella, the Popcorn Prince, the

Knights of the Good…they're working with Seattle Slim. The Masked Highwayman and his band of thieves, Meat Legs Johnson, Kabuki, Genghis Bill, the trolls, the Ogre King, Brownbeard the Monkey Pirate…they've all come to an accord, with their hearts set on taking over your world."

Zara's mind was reeling. "So... it's just the six of us? Us against all of them?"

"Yes, Zara," intoned Target, in her mind, *"but we have something that they don't, that they'll never have."*

"And that something," Feldspar growled, "is you."

Grandma Lucy was being held in the Merryland Castle, the very same castle she and Zara had shared tea and broken bread with the Queen and her son, the Popcorn Prince, countless times in the past. Zara and her band of heroes were hiding in the south side of the forest, using an old telescope Professor Plum had procured from somewhere to watch the castle.

Things didn't look good. The trolls and ogres had joined forces with the Merryland Knights, patrolling the castle. Giant men twenty feet tall made of earth and stone guarded the drawbridge and parapets, while dark elf archers, bows ready, lined the battlements.

"How on earth are we going to get past that?" whispered Zara.

It had been difficult enough simply getting to their spot in the woods. Their group had been forced to sneak along the south side of the chasm to avoid the centaur patrols, and from there they circled around to the north and entered the forest to the east. They'd been walking for hours, and Zara's feet felt like stone.

"Do you remember that flower, Zara?" said Professor Plum, "The one that allows a person to breathe under water. That is the key. I've brewed enough tea from its petals for each of us to have a cup."

"But how will that help us get into the castle?"

"Patience, dear," whispered Scottie. "I think he's about to tell us."

Professor Plum smiled. "There lies a secret doorway at the bottom of the lake, to another world entirely. And from that world, just across a bridge, another doorway into the southeast turret of the castle."

"Another world? But how many worlds are there, Professor Plum?"

"No one really knows," Plum said, "and for our purposes today, it doesn't matter. What does matter is that we'll have to be quick. Though time in your world and time in Merryland moves at roughly the same pace, time on that world does not. For every three minutes spent there, an hour will pass here. We have to get in and get out as fast as we can."

"And that's where we come in," said Elwin, slapping Feldspar on the shoulder.

"Slim and Isabella," continued Plum, "know about the doorway in the tower, of course, and keep it guarded, but not heavily. They don't think that *we* know about it or can use it, because they cannot, but of course we do and can. Feldspar and Elwin will make an assault on that side of the castle and hopefully draw them away from the turret, thus enabling us to gain access to the castle."

"But how can we use it, if they can't?" asked Zara.

"*You* can, my dear," added Plum, "and, with you, so can we."

"Okay, then, how can *I* use it?"

"Your necklace," explained Plum. "It's just like your grandmother's, and enables you to walk through worlds. Because you've unlocked one doorway all other doorways will be open to you until that first doorway is closed."

Zara shook her head. This was getting complicated. "Do you know where they're keeping Grandma Lucy?"

"*In the dungeon, more than likely,*" said Target. "*She'll be safe enough there until the moons align.*"

"All right, then," Zara said, "let's get going."

The hike to the lake didn't take long at all, and through stealth and cunning they were able to avoid being spotted by any of Brownbeard's pirate crew.

She hoped Feldspar and Elwin would be all right. Target would connect with Elwin telepathically when they were ready to enter the tower, and then they'd begin their attack. They intended to draw the lion's share of Slim and Abraham's forces out of the castle, creating as much of a distraction as they could.

"Are you ready?" asked Professor Plum, having prepared the tea.

"As I'll ever be," answered Zara, downing a cup of the sickly sweet mixture.

The others quickly followed suite, and then they slipped into the water. Target would be their leader through this leg of their journey, using his psychic abilities to not only allow the team to communicate but also to help them steer clears of the sirens and other dangerous denizens of the deep.

It was amazing. At first Zara felt like she might gag, but then she was actually breathing the oxygen in the water. She swam down deeper, enjoying the feeling of freedom, but a warning from Target stopped her descent.

"Be careful, Zara," he buzzed in her head, *"don't get too far ahead. There might be traps."*

Why would there be traps, she wanted to ask, if Seattle Slim and the formerly-good Queen Isabella didn't think they could access the door? But she obeyed the bulldog, slowing so the others could catch up.

It didn't take them long to reach the bottom, where they found a sunken navy ship. Target entered, then signaled for the others to follow. Zara went first, then Scottie, and finally, bringing up the rear, Professor Plum.

They followed Target through the entrance into the lower deck, past the crew quarters, and finally to the room the Navy captain had once called his own. And there it was, a glowing blue triangle set into the floor of the cabin.

"Not all doors are actual doors," said Target, responding perhaps to Zara's look of confusion. *"One door might be an actual, physical door, while the other could be, well, a glowing blue triangle."*

She nodded, tentatively reaching out to touch the door. The glow changed, began pulsing, dot-dot-dash-dash, like Morse code. A few seconds later, the door disappeared entirely, and they were being sucked through the portal. Zara grabbed at the edge, but to no avail. In a moment, she was through.

Zara blinked her eyes, staring around the room where she now found herself. The others stood beside her, equally flustered. The room wasn't so much a room as a space, and all around them, above and beneath as well as in all the cardinal directions, were stars. It was like being in a dark room filled with black light posters, and she found it terribly disorientating.

"That felt like going through a drain," Zara said, glad to be able to speak again. "Is everyone all right?"

"Indeed," said Professor Plum, puffing on his ever-present pipe. "I think we all survived the trip. Now, look. Do you see the bridge?"

Darkness surrounded them, save for the stars. She stared in the direction where he'd gestured, and it took a while but she was finally able to separate out a bridge spanning a huge chasm from the rest of the room. It was dizzying and difficult to tell which direction was up.

She had abandoned her County Market bag in the forest, but had slipped the kitchen knife into one pocket of her jeans and the magical torch into the other. She reached now for the torch, but it was gone.

"Where's my torch?"

"It must have fallen out on the swim down," Professor Plum said. "But don't worry about that, we can see enough to cross."

She pulled something out of her pocket. The Post-It Note from Brett. It looked somehow different, though, and then she realized that where once it had been yellow now it was purple. She unfolded the note, but it didn't say what she remembered it saying.

The words swam in her vision at first, and she couldn't make them out. She blinked, staring hard at the note, and was finally able to read the words:

Don't do it, Zara-Bear.

Zara shook her head, looked again, and it was just a random series of letters and numbers. Zara-Bear? That was like "Tildie-Bear," the nickname she'd given her daughter, but no one had ever called Zara by the appellation. Had they? And yet it felt familiar, somehow, like an old book that you read many years ago but couldn't quite remember.

"Don't worry about Brett's note," Professor Plum said, little ringlets of cherry-smelling smoke rising up from his pipe. "This world will play with your senses."

"But…" Zara started helplessly at the purple piece of paper, and in an instant it was yellow again. "Hey, did you see that?"

"I'll guide us," whispered Scottie, taking Zara's hand.

"But the paper. It means something."

"Forget it," said Scottie, pulling her along toward the bridge.

Zara began to float, letting the yellow piece of paper drop to the darkness at her feet. She was enjoying the feeling of weightlessness. "Just be careful, Scottie, and don't drop me in that hole."

"Zara," echoed a far off voice. "Are you okay?"

"Did you hear that?" asked Zara, looking first to Professor Plum and then to Scottie.

She pulled away from the pink faerie, settling back to what served as the ground in this strange dimension.

"Hear what?" Plum said, looking perturbed. "We don't have time for this. We're only going to have one chance to save your grandmother."

"Please, Zara, wake up," the voice said. It sounded familiar, but she couldn't place it.

"I didn't hear anything," said Scottie, floating now beside her shoulder.

"Nor I," whispered the bulldog's voice inside her head. *"It's probably just the wind."*

The wind? There was no wind at all here. What was he talking about? She strained to hear, shushing Scottie as she tried to speak again.

"Zara, you're scaring me. Snap out of it! I'm this close to calling 911."

Matt! The voice belonged to him, she was sure of it. But how could she be hearing her husband?

"We're almost there," said Scottie, alighting on Zara's shoulder, causing her to once again float with the faerie.

Professor Plum took her hand and began to pull her across the bridge, while Target nudged her from behind.

"Zara, God damn it. Don't do this to me!"

"Matt?" she murmured, looking around uncertainly.

"Your husband isn't here, Zara," barked Plum, for once losing his famed British cool. "Just ignore it, it's one of Slim's tricks. Now come on, one foot in front of another. We're almost there."

And then they were over the bridge, standing before an old wooden door decorated only with a brass doorknob.

"Open the door, Zara," urged Scottie, "only you can do it."

Her fingers closed around the door knob, twisting it, pulling.

"Zara, come back to me!" Matt yelled, and suddenly she felt his hands on her shoulders.

"Inside, Zara, inside," ordered Plum, but the door was becoming hazy, almost transparent.

Zara felt herself somehow tumbling backwards as she stepped forward, through the door, and everything went black. She opened her eyes to stare into the face of her husband, brow creased with worry.

"Matt?" she said, reaching up to touch his cheek.

"Thank God," he said, and she could see that he'd been crying. "What's wrong with you?"

She was lying on the basement floor, the County Market bag beside her. The cabinet door was open, the key was still in the niche, but she was no longer in Merryland.

"Grandma Lucy!" she exclaimed, trying to scramble to her feet.

Matt held her tight against him, and wouldn't let go. "Baby, your Grandma Lucy's dead. We're in Carthage, and tomorrow is her funeral."

"But I have to save her, Matt. I'm so close, I can't give up now. I have to go back."

"Zara, you're not making sense," he said, still holding her arms. "I woke up, wondered where you were, and found you down here, staring into that damned mirror."

"I was in Merryland," she insisted, "and you pulled me out."

"No, sweetie, you weren't anywhere, just here. Just standing in front of that mirror, and you wouldn't answer me. You scared the hell out of me."

She felt like someone had thrown a glass of cold water in her face. "I was just...standing there? I wasn't inside the mirror."

Matt laughed nervously. "I have absolutely no idea what you're talking about, Zara, but I'd like to know, if you'll tell me."

And so she did. She told him about the stories her grandmother had told her as a child, the stories that weren't really stories but real adventures on the other side of the mirror, and about seeing Professor Plum and Seattle Slim on this side of the mirror. She told him everything, leaving nothing out other than her near-indiscretion with Brett.

She told him about the voices calling her name, the writing in the mirror, about attacking Seattle Slim in the basement of the funeral parlor, and about the berry juice that even now still stained her fingers.

"You think I'm crazy, don't you?" she asked, when she was finished.

"No, I don't, but I do think you've been under an incredible amount of stress, and we both know that stress can play havoc on the mind. Hell, look at what happened to my brother."

Matt's brother Paul had been in the military, had seen combat in Iraq, and was still messed up over it. For the first year after he'd returned home, he'd woken up in the night—every night—screaming about the bombs and the blood and the dying little children.

Zara felt hot tears trailing down her cheeks, and knew she was crying. "Well, there's one way to find out whether or not I'm crazy."

"First of all, you're not crazy. Second of all, how?"

She climbed to her feet and this time he let her, but wouldn't let go of her hand.

Zara began walking toward the mirror, but Matt spun her around to face him. "Uh-uh, no way. Stay away from that thing."

"It's an entrance into another universe," explained Zara, "or at least I think it is. Keep holding my hand, it's all right. If we step through to another universe, then I'm completely sane. If not…lock me up and throw away the key." She tried to smile, but began to cry again.

Reaching out her hand, Zara pressed fingertips against the cold, hard surface of the mirror. She pushed harder, but the surface wouldn't give. Standing on her tip-toes, she checked to see if the key was still in the niche: it was. She couldn't understand it. Was it because she was holding Matt's hand? She felt for her necklace, and it was still there.

"Hey!" he yelled, as she suddenly pulled away from him and slapped her palm against the mirror.

Her hand bounced off the glass, instantly in pain. She held her hand, looking insolently into the mirror. "It didn't work. I'm fucking nuts. It didn't work."

Matt pulled her to him again, and this time she didn't resist, instead sobbing hysterically into his shoulder.

"Shh, Zara, it's all right," he whispered, stroking her hair. "Everything's gonna be all right."

"What's wrong with me?"

"We'll get through tomorrow and fly home Friday, just like we planned. In the morning, before we go to the funeral, I'll call your doctor and try to set something up."

She tried to squirm away, but he held her tighter.

"Shh, I know, babe. You're not crazy. But stress really can cause a lot of problems. You know it can. We'll call Dr. Andrews, and she'll give you a referral to a good therapist. Just someone to talk to, no judging, no medicine. It'll all be okay."

"I hope so," she murmured into his white t-shirt, staring over his shoulder into the malicious eyes of Seattle Slim.

He was mocking her, making little circular motions with his finger beside his twig and stick-filled head. The universal sign for someone who was certifiable. She blinked once, looked away and then back, and finally the evil stick cowboy was gone.

Thursday

The funeral went well, at least as well as a funeral can go, considering that you're putting someone you love deep in the ground. Zara sat on a metal folding chair at the cemetery with Tildie between her and Matt, half-listening to the minister talk about what a wonderful woman Lucille Brennan had been.

Though not as many had showed up for the funeral as had attended the visitation, it was still well attended. Mrs. Olinger had come, of course, but thankfully Brett hadn't. Most of the attendees were closer to her grandmother's age than they were Zara's, friends that she'd played Bridge with or just people whose lives she had touched over seventy-five years of living in the same small town.

Tildie's tiny hand found her own and she leaned over to kiss her daughter on her forehead. The thought of losing Tildie and Matt was almost more than she could bear, especially on top of losing Grandma Lucy, but if she didn't get help soon, she feared that's exactly what would happen.

How long had she stood in front of that mirror last night, imagining that she was in Merryland? It had felt so damned real. She wondered how long she might have stayed there, staring at her own reflection, had Matt not awoken her from her trance.

Something caught Zara's eye, about twenty yards away, next to an old, freestanding crypt. What in the world? It was someone waving, but they were mostly hidden by the shadows thrown by the angel that decorated the top of the shrine.

Her heart sank as she stared at the fingers: they weren't actually flesh, but sticks instead. Seattle Slim. She instinctively clenched her fingers, eliciting a yelp of pain from Tildie.

"What's wrong, Mommy?"

"Sorry, sweetie," she said, trying to still her rapid heartbeat. "Say, do you see that bunch of sticks over there, right in front of us, waving like a hand?"

Tildie squinted, staring at the point Zara indicated, then shrugged. "I don't see anything. Where, Mommy?"

"See that little building with an angel on top of it? Yes, right there. It's called a crypt. Don't you see some sticks that look like a hand, waving at us?"

"I don't see anything," she repeated, shrugging her little shoulders.

Seattle Slim's grinning face shot out from the shadows just then, and he threw them a kiss. Zara jumped back in her seat, pulling a screaming Tildie on top of her.

"Did you see that?" she whispered to her daughter.

"See what? Mommy, you're scaring me," Tildie said, starting to cry.

Zara looked around to see all eyes on here. Even the minister had stopped speaking.

"What's wrong?" Matt whispered, leaning over Tildie.

"Just a spider," she apologized to everyone. "Sorry."

Seattle Slim was out from behind the crypt now, dancing a strange little jig and grinning like a fool, but no one else could see him. Zara squinched her eyes shut, listening as the minister resumed his speech, but every time she opened them the evil stick cowboy was still there.

It was late in the afternoon and the funeral had been over for hours, but still Zara couldn't relax. She'd been in a lot of stressful situations in her life—heck, her job at the newspaper would stress most anyone out—and she'd never before had any sort of hallucinations, visual or auditory.

Zara sat in the living room, watching Tildie play with Oscar. Her daughter had a long piece of string and had spent the last thirty minutes dangling it in front of the old tom, giggling like a maniac when he chased after it.

It was a good thing that they'd decided to take Oscar back to Arkansas with them, because she didn't think Tildie would accept anything less. And now they could certainly afford for Matt to get all the allergy shots he'd ever need in order to get used to the cat, and then some.

"Hey you," said Matt, walking down the stairs. "How are you feeling?"

"Right as rain," she lied, using an expression her grandmother always used to say. "Everything is over, and tomorrow we go home. And we're rich! What could be better than that?"

He cocked his head, looking at her. "So no more seeing wooden stick figures waving at you?"

She'd told him about the incident at the cemetery, and immediately wished she hadn't. "Nope." At least that wasn't a lie.

"Good. I called Dr. Andrews, just like I said I would. She's gonna talk to a friend of hers, someone named Angela Wayne, who's supposed to be a great psychologist. Hopefully, we can get you an appointment next week."

"Yippee," she said, twirling her finger in the air. "Head shrinkers."

Matt frowned.

"Really, Matt, I'm fine. I'll go see this doctor, and maybe she'll put me on Xanax or something, and it'll be no big deal."

His face softened. "It's a deal. But in the meantime, stay away from the basement, okay?"

"I promise," she said, smiling, all the while knowing this was just one more vow she intended to break.

She knew it was crazy, but in her heart of hearts, Zara really felt that her grandmother only had a handful of hours left to live. After midnight struck, she'd be dead for real. She had to get to the mirror.

"So, want to watch some TV?" Matt asked.

"Actually, what I really want to do is go for a walk. I've been around too many people, both last night and at the funeral. No offense."

"None taken. But I get the couch. Time to channel surf."

Wrapping her arms around his neck, she pulled him in for a deep, lingering kiss.

"Hey, what was that for?" he said, when they finally came up for air.

"Just for being you," she said, "and for loving me. Now, go on. Get some TV time in, mister. I'll be back in 30 or 45 minutes, tops."

She kissed Tildie goodbye, ruffled Oscar's fur, and left by the front door. And then she circled the house and snuck back inside via the back door, which she'd left unlocked. Zara slipped off her boots, padding through the house as quietly as possible.

I'm turning into a career criminal, she thought, as she reached the basement door. She'd carefully oiled the hinges earlier today so that the door wouldn't squeak when she pulled it open.

She wrapped her hand around the door knob, pulled, but it was locked. Shit. Matt must have found the old skeleton key and locked it. So much for her career as a criminal.

Zara crept back through the kitchen, moving to the key hook beside the pantry. It wasn't there. Where had he put the damned thing? And then she had an idea. She slipped back out of the house, crouched behind a clump of bushes, and called Matt on her cell.

"Zara, what's up? You haven't been gone five minutes."

"I know, baby. But listen. I suddenly got nervous about Tildie and the basement. There's a skeleton key by the pantry in the kitchen. Could you grab it and lock the basement for me?"

Silence. "Well, I already did that. I locked it last night, after...after I got you into bed."

She feigned surprise. "Really? Wow, you were all stealthy, I guess. But could you make sure it's locked? Please, for me? That door is notoriously tricky, and sometimes it sticks and you think it's locked, but it really isn't."

"Hmm. Okay, sure. Do you want to hold on a second?"

She heard the sound of him walking, and then he came into view from the kitchen window. She crouched lower into the bushes, watching as he tugged on the basement door.

"Seems secure to me," he said, starting to walk back toward the living room.

"Wait," Zara almost shouted. "Can you move the key? She could easily reach it, hanging in the pantry like that."

"I already did," he said. "Please don't get mad. I just don't want you in that basement again."

"I understand. Really, I do. Hide the key, I don't care. But wherever it is, can you just check to make sure it's still there? Just the thought of Tildie finding it and going down there is stressing me out."

Yes, she'd used the stress card. She felt like a bitch, but she had to get into that basement, had to try one more time to walk through the mirror. And if it didn't work, she'd admit defeat and spill her guts to Dr. Wayne once they were back home in Fayetteville.

"Sure, if it'll make you feel better," he finally said. "But I promise you, it's somewhere safe."

"Thank you."

She watched through the window as he walked across the kitchen, lifted up a blue sugar bowl, and put it back down on the counter again. Clever. While Zara normally drank a ton of coffee, she drank it black, and rarely if ever put sugar on anything.

"Okay, it's safe now, and far from the hands of a curious little girl."

"Great. Thank you so much. That's such a relief."

Zara nearly jumped out of the bushes when Mrs. Olinger tapped her on the shoulder. "What're you doing down there?"

"Who is that?" asked Matt.

Zara thought quickly, glanced back at Mrs. Olinger, and then said, "Sorry, talking to an old friend. I'll see you soon, okay. Love you. Bye."

She hung up without giving him even a chance to respond.

"Who talks to their friends while hiding in the bushes?" asked Mrs. Olinger, raising a gray eyebrow.

Zara slipped the phone into her purse. "I was looking for something I'd lost when she called."

She stood up, taking the old woman's arm and purposefully walking towards Mrs. Olinger's house. Though it was slowly changing, many of the houses in Carthage still didn't have fences that separated neighbor from neighbor, and Mrs. Olinger and Grandma Lucy's house shared a backyard.

"What was it?"

"What was what?"

"The thing you lost," explained Mrs. Olinger, like she was talking to a little child.

"Oh! Well, I didn't find it."

"Do you want me to help you look?"

"It was my wedding ring," she said, surreptitiously slipping the ring from her finger. "But, actually, I think I left it on the sink when I took a bath last night. I'm going to go check."

She started to leave, but was stopped when Mrs. Olinger put a hand on her shoulder. "Are you sure you're all right, Zara? I know your grandmother's passing has been awfully hard on you."

Lady, you don't know the half of it, she wanted to say, but instead what she said was: "I'm okay, I promise. Now that the funeral is over, things will slowly get back to normal."

She gave Mrs. Olinger an impromptu hug, excused herself to go in search of her ring, and headed again to the back door. She hoped that Matt was still watching television. Glancing at her watch, she was disheartened to see that it had been almost twenty minutes since she'd left for her supposed walk.

Luck was on her side this time, as she quickly retrieved the key from beneath the sugar bowl, crept over to the basement door, and unlocked it. From the sounds coming from the living room, it sounded like Matt was watching soccer. Good. He usually got so engrossed in the game that a tree could fall and he'd probably never hear it.

"Daddy," she heard Tildie's little voice from the living room, "when will Mommy be home?"

"Probably in ten or fifteen minutes, honey. Why?"

"I just miss her, that's all. I love you, Daddy."

"I love you, too, Tildie."

Zara felt tears pushing at her eyes, and blinked several times to stop the flow. She cracked open the door just enough to squeeze past, then let herself into the basement, locking the door behind her.

Everything was just as she'd left it. She walked to the mirror, snatched up the County Market bag, and pressed her hand to the surface. She gasped as her hand immediately went through, yanking it back like she'd been burned.

She didn't understand. Why hadn't it worked last night? Was it because Matt was there with her? Or maybe she really was batshit, after all. She glanced at the niche above the mirror. The key was still there, glued into place courtesy of Elmer. Okay, it was time to go.

Zara stepped through the mirror, immediately finding herself in a small stone room with Professor Plum, Target, and Scottie.

"Zara!" yelled the little faerie, flittering through the air to hug her chest. "You're back, and just in time, too."

"We're almost to your grandmother's cell," said Professor Plum, nodding toward her.

"But…why aren't I in the cavern?"

"One of the many inconsistencies of inter-dimensional travel," said Target. *"You left without exiting the door in the cave, and so your essence, your true self, stayed anchored to us. So it only makes sense that you'd come out wherever we happened to be."*

"Precisely," agreed Professor Plum. "It makes perfect sense."

It made absolutely no sense to Zara, because it hadn't worked that way before, but she decided to let it go. "How close are we?"

"We're here," whispered Scottie.

They pushed through a scarred metal door, revealing a row of tiny jail cells. An old woman wearing dirty rags sat huddled in the corner of one cell, shivering against the dank coldness that pervaded the dungeon. She looked up, her eyes sparkling as they found Zara.

"Grandma Lucy," Zara whispered, her eyes filling with tears.

"Zara, you came for me," coughed the old woman, struggling to rise to her feet.

She couldn't believe it. Her grandmother, the woman who had raised and cared for her since she was seven years old, the woman she had just buried at Moss Ridge Cemetery, was alive.

"I can pick the lock," Scottie offered, "if anyone has any wire."

Zara immediately thought of her underwire bra. She slipped it off underneath her oversized Hello Kitty t-shirt, then removed the kitchen knife from her jeans pocket and cut out a section of the wire. She cut that in half, leaving her with two equally-sized pieces of wire.

"Will this do?" Zara asked, offering up the wire.

"Zara, you're a genius," said Scottie, snatching the pieces of wire from her hand.

"Hurry," intoned Target into all their minds. *"I can hear guards coming, we don't have much time."*

"I almost have it," mumbled Scottie, maneuvering two small pieces of wire into the jail cell door. "Almost, almost...there!"

Something inside the lock clicked, and the door swung open a few inches. Target head-butted the door open the rest of the way, and Zara ran inside, falling to her knees beside her grandmother.

"Zara-Bear, don't," said Professor Plum, and Zara turned to face him.

He began to flicker, almost as if shuttling in and out of existence, and for a moment was replaced by a little purple dragon almost identical to the one that had been there before. But the eyes were different, kinder somehow, and in that instant she recognized him.

"Grandpa Michael," she whispered, looking into the eyes of the British expatriate who had briefly been her step-grandfather.

She remembered now. She remembered everything. She remembered Grandma Lucy's friends, Mr. Kingfisher and Mr. Quarry, who would take Zara down to the basement with them. Kingfisher was huge, nearly seven feet tall, and resembled stage magician Penn Gillette. Quarry was short and didn't talk much, and looked an awful lot like Penn's partner Teller.

They had done...things to her. Not sexual things, but things almost as bad. They had taken blood from her, using it to cover her little girl body with strange and arcane markings, and, once, forced her to sleep outside during a full moon, naked, staked to the ground.

She remembered the drawing beneath the rug in the basement, the one that matched the symbol on the cabinet and on her grandmother's casket. They would place her in the middle of that circle, purifying her, Mr. Kingfisher had said, getting her ready to someday...to someday do what? Either they had never told her, or she simply couldn't remember.

Worst of all, she remembered her grandmother, there for all of it, sitting quietly, observing as Mr. Kingfisher and Mr. Quarry talked in a language that Zara had never before heard. Her grandmother, smiling, joking with the two men, and later, in front of Zara, stripping herself of her own clothing and allowing her friends to cover her in the same drawings and words that covered Zara. Her grandmother having sex with them in that very same basement.

"Run," the dragon whispered, before blinking out of existence and being replaced once again by the other Professor Plum, the Plum with nothing behind his eyes: no intelligence, no warmth. She saw that now, and couldn't believe she had failed to see it before.

"That stupid man," said Lucy Brennan, standing fully erect now, letting the rags fall from her shoulders. "If he'd minded his own business, he might still be alive."

Zara backed up from her grandmother, but they were all there, forming a half-circle around her, blocking her way. Seattle Slim, Scottie, Feldspar, Queen Isabella, the Popcorn Prince, Brownbeard the Monkey Pirate, Target, Meat Legs Johnson, Elwin, Genghis Bill, and, of course, the soulless Professor Plum.

"You're not going anywhere," said Seattle Slim, drawing both of his six-shooters and aiming them at Zara.

"You're not real," Zara said, walking toward him. "I know that now. You can't hurt me."

"But I can," Lucy Brennan said, from behind her.

She snaked out a hand to encircle Zara's wrist, and a thick, red energy traveled down her arm, enveloping her, choking her, and in an instant everything changed.

She was back in the cavern, staring at herself in the mirror. Only it wasn't really her, it was her grandmother in her body. Her double smiled.

"I don't understand," Zara whispered, staring at herself.

"Oh, I think you do," said her doppelgänger, stretching her arms and arching her back. "This feels good."

"You…killed him, didn't you? You killed Grandpa Michael, when he came home early from work and found us in the basement. You and me, and your friends."

The mirror Zara ran her hands over her breasts, sighing almost inaudibly. "Oh, this feels so very good. I'm young again, with so many years ahead of me, and so many possibilities."

"Answer me," Zara shouted, banging her fists against the mirror. "You killed Grandpa Michael."

"Very good," her face said back to her, nodding. "You know everything now, my darling granddaughter. You've served your purpose well, and I'm so proud of you."

"I remember him running down the stairs, tackling Mr. Quarry and trying to pull me from his arms, and Mr. Kingfisher reaching out to snap his neck like it was a stick. Oh, God, I remember it all."

"A messy affair, easily avoided had he just minded his own business. I loved that man, and it wasn't easy letting him go."

"You loved him, but you still let that monster murder him. How did I ever think you loved me? You're incapable of love," cried out Zara, as the light around her began to dim.

"I did love you," said Lucille Brennan, looking through the glass from Zara's eyes, "and I still do. I love you in the way that one loves a kitten, knowing full well that someday that kitten will grow into a cat and no matter how well you take care of it, will age and die long before you do."

"But I'm not dead," Zara countered, slamming her hands into the mirror that divided her from her own body.

"No, you're not dead, not yet," smiled her grandmother, as the lights around Zara grew dimmer still, "and this way, you, or at least a part of you, never will be."

Lucille moved to close the cabinet.

"No, not yet," Zara screamed, dropping to her knees. "Don't leave me, Grandma. Please."

"Dear child," she said, "I've had many grandchildren, and grand-children of grandchildren, all of them female, but none have whined quite as much as you have. You're almost as willful as your mother was."

"My mother? But...what's she got to do with this?

"Everything. It was supposed to be her, my dear. But then she ran off to Canada with your father and everything changed. You were al-most five before I first met you, Zara. Did you know that?"

"I don't remember much of my life before you took me in," Zara admitted.

"Well, she finally came back from Canada, and there was still time, still time to prepare you and to take her, but she grew suspicious, had probably always been suspicious, I suspect. She would never let me near you without her or your father present. Willful child. She figured things out, and plans went awry. Plans changed, which is how I ended up getting stuck in that old body for as long as I did."

Zara stared at her face looking down upon her. "How...how old are you?"

"That's not important. What is important is that your mother ru-ined my plans. She called your father at work and he swooped in to make the rescue. Only things didn't quite work out like they planned, now did they?"

She stared at her own body through the mirror. "That was the night of the accident, wasn't it?"

"How perceptive of you. Indeed it was, my dear."

"And you...you murdered them. You killed my parents."

"I didn't want to," Lucy Brennan said, shrugging. "I loved your mother and was quite smitten with Zachary, actually, but in the end they left me with no choice."

Lucy was smitten with her son-in-law? "But why didn't they take me with them?"

"Oh, they did. But I made sure you were safe, protected by a pair of dear old friends. You were thrown clear of the wreck, and never remembered a thing."

"Kingfisher and Quarry."

"Precisely. They visited often during those first few months. Surely you remember all of it by now."

"I remember, all right." She remembered the awful things that they did to her, every single one.

"All part of the ritual," Lucy said, as if reading her mind. "Your mother went through the same thing, bless her soul, as did her mother and her mother before her, and her mother before that, but all much earlier than you did. And that was why I required the help of Mr. Kingfisher and Mr. Quarry. The preparations should ideally start within five days of the fifth birthday, and you were nearly six.

"Think of it this way, dear Zara: you're about to join a long tradition, a proud sisterhood dedicated to keeping me alive."

"But what will happen to Matt and Tildie? Please don't hurt them."

"Oh, I wouldn't dream of it, my dear. They'll know me as you, and we'll spend your 'inheritance' with gleeful abandon. And, someday, dear little Tildie's body will carry me, just as yours will now."

"Leave her alone!" Zara gasped, as she felt her life draining from her body. "I'll kill you, you bitch! I'll kill you."

"No, you won't, and I can't leave her alone," mirror Zara said, "I've become way too fond of living."

"How old *are* you?" she repeated the question that had gone unanswered minutes earlier.

"Old enough to know when to stop talking," she said, and closed the cabinet door.

Thursday Evening

"Oh my God," whispered Matt, drenched in sweat, "we haven't been like that since before Tildie was born. What's gotten into you?"

He and Zara were naked in the master bedroom—Lucy's bedroom—and had just finished making love. She had ridden him until he came, and she'd come with him, screaming at the top of her lungs. He'd been worried for a moment that they might wake Tildie, but she'd silenced him with a quick thrust of her hips.

"You, for one thing," smiled Zara, playfully licking her lips. "And…well, the funeral, for another. It's over, Matt. I'm not going crazy, Grandma Lucy is finally in the ground, and we're rich beyond our wildest dreams. Who could ask for anything more?"

A thread of fear burned for just an instant in his thoughts, unasked for and not understood, but it was quickly forgotten as she mounted him again, ready for round two. His eyes rolled back in his head as her hands deftly brought him back to full erection, and then he was inside her again.

After that, whatever moment of intuition or superstition or whatever that uneasy feeling he'd had was gone.

* * *

Tildie lay awake in her mother's old bedroom. She didn't like this house, and really wanted to go home. Tomorrow, said Daddy. Tomorrow they'd fly home, back to her room and her plushies and all her friends. Tomorrow everything would be okay again. She hugged Scotty tight, hoping he'd protect her.

Her Mommy was no longer her Mommy, not really. She didn't think Tildie knew, but of course she did. All daughters knew their mommies, didn't they? She was still her but somehow not her, and that confused Tildie, but everything would be better when they got home.

Mommy/Not-Mommy and Daddy had stopped screaming hours or minutes ago, their fight, or whatever it was, finally finished, and now Tildie could hear only the beat of her own heart along with the tick-tock, tick-tock of the grandfather clock from downstairs.

She knew she should be sleeping, but she was afraid of what she might see when she closed her eyes. Last night it was the floating purple dragon again, smoking his pipe, and he had warned her to get out of the house while she still could. She'd tried explaining that they were leaving tomorrow, going home to Arkansas, and hoped that would be soon enough.

The dragon called himself Professor Plum, and he had been very nice, but somehow he still scared her. There was a sadness about him that made her think bad things, and she didn't want to see him again anytime soon.

"Silly Matilda," said her Mommy/Not-Mommy from the doorway, wearing a long white terrycloth robe. "Why aren't you asleep?"

"You aren't really my Mommy," she said, surprised as the words came from her lips.

"Out of the mouth of babes," Mommy/Not-Mommy said. "That's okay, Matilda. I'll be your Mommy soon enough. Now we need to get you to sleep. How about I tell you a story? You'd like me to tell you a story, wouldn't you, Matilda?"

The Mommy-thing stared at Tildie in a way that made her feel funny, sleepy, and scared, all at the same time. Tildie blinked, suddenly feeling happy. Of course this was her Mommy. Silly Tildie. Why had she thought anything different? And she loved stories, though usually it was Daddy reading her stories out of the big Mother Goose's Fairy Tales book at home on the nightstand beside her bed.

"I'd like that very much, Mommy," she said, as her mother gestured for her to scooch over. She loved her Mommy, and she really wanted to hear a story.

Mommy settled into the bed, with Tildie in her arms. "All right, Matilda, get ready, because you've never heard a story quite like this before. Let me tell you about a place called Merryland."

Mommy's Favorite

I was always mother's favorite. Even after my little sister Samantha was born, it was me who got all of the attention. Samantha came to hate me for it, and who could blame her? She was the baby, and yet I was the one constantly in the spotlight.

"Shouldn't we wait for Samantha?" I asked for the second time, as we began to open gifts on Christmas morning.

I always received the lion's share of the presents for birthdays and holidays, something my dear sister never tired of reminding me. The latest and greatest action figures, video games, Blu-ray players, and, later, a brand new car for my 16th birthday. I got it all, and Samantha always had to settle for my hand-me-downs.

My little sister was currently upstairs, changing clothes after Mother complained that her attire (pink pajama bottoms and an *Attack on Titan* spaghetti-strap top) was inappropriate for company. Never mind that the only "company" here was my girlfriend Jordyn, who often dressed similarly in her dorm back at college.

"Nonsense, Alex," Mother said, for the third time pushing a red and green wrapped present with a white bow into my hands. "If she can't dress appropriately, she doesn't deserve to participate in family activities."

Samantha was a junior in high school and hated me more than ever, but I didn't care. I was madly in love with Jordyn, a beautiful and brilliant young woman who was studying to be a veterinarian, and I'd brought her home to meet my parents. Everyone adored Jordyn save for my mother, of course, who never seemed to approve of my girl-friends. She had, in fact, given me a quick look of disapproval as I took advantage of the mistletoe in the hallway to give Jordyn a lingering kiss.

The house was decorated beautifully, as it always was for Christmas. The tree was strung with silver garland and sparkling white lights ("No colored lights on *my* tree," Mother always said) and yuletide trimmings filled the house, including a little baby Jesus manger set on top of the mantle that overhung the fireplace. The lights from the tree reflected off the maple wood floor and the metal surrounding the fireplace, giving the baby Jesus an unearthly glow.

"No need to wait for me, *Alexander*," said Samantha, using the long form of my name as she stomped down the stairs. "Go ahead and open your gifts. You'll still be opening them long after I'm finished anyway."

It was always a sure sign that she was angry with me when she used my full name, and it didn't seem to matter whether or not I actually did anything to deserve it.

I sliced off another thin piece of the coffee cake that sat atop the coffee table. Four matching mugs of cocoa with our names on them and a fifth, unmatched one, also sat atop the table. I felt bad that Jordyn didn't have a matching mug, but she'd assured me that her feelings weren't hurt in the slightest.

"Well, she's here now," said Father, trying to broker peace as usual. "Come on, honey, let's open the presents."

Jordyn snuggled close to me, whispering in my ear, "Is it always like this?"

"Pretty much," I whispered back, taking her hand in mine.

It was pretty much always like this, though Christmas was usually the worst. I got all of the attention, regardless of whether or not I deserved or even wanted it. Why, then, did I always feel that I could never live up to the attention that was lavished on me?

Alexander is a nice name, as far as names go, but I never felt it suited me, not even the nickname Alex. My sister was born when I was six, and from then on I coveted her name. I even went so far as to create an imaginary friend—a boy, just like me—named Sam. If I couldn't have the name, at least my imaginary friend could. My sister hated *my* Sam almost as much as she hated me, once she found out about him.

She complained to mother once, who spanked her and then grounded her for a week. My father tried to intercede, but she shut him down immediately. That's how it was in my family. Mother was the boss. I was her favorite, and everyone else a distant second or third, depending upon what sort of mood she was in that day.

Where my mother ruled the house with an iron fist, my father, in counterpoint, had the spine of a jellyfish. She'd worn him to a nubbin by years and years of constantly telling him how to think, what to do, and how to go about doing it. I felt badly for him, but, at the same time, could never understand why he put up with her.

"Go on, Alex," beamed Mother, once again pressing the gift into my hands. "It's a tradition, the eldest child always opens the first present. You know that."

And thus it always had been, as far back as I could remember. Mother, Father, and Samantha, always taking a back seat to me. The gift tag didn't even say from Mom and Dad but instead just from Mom. I sighed and unwrapped the present.

It was a brand new 5th generation iPad with 4k Retina Display and 128 gigabytes of memory. Just last week I'd mentioned to Mother in passing that I'd dropped my old iPad 2 between classes and cracked the screen. This replacement had to have cost at least $600, possibly more considering the black leather case it sported.

"Thanks, Mom," I said, avoiding Samantha's eyes. "This is really generous of you, but I've already sent my old one off to be repaired. I should have it back next—"

"Never mind that," she said, interrupting me. "You'll be graduating next year, and you need something reliable. You can sell the old one on eBay or something."

"Or, I don't know, give it to me," said Samantha. "Hell, I don't even have a tablet, broken or otherwise."

"Language, Samantha," Mother reprimanded her. "Or you can spend the rest of Christmas in your room."

"In my room? Jesus, Mom, I'm 17, stop treating me like a little girl."

"Then stop acting like one," said Mother, knuckles whitening as she gripped the cup of hot cocoa she'd been sipping from just minutes earlier.

"How about Samantha opens my present next?" I said, trying to circumvent the war that was starting to brew.

I stood up from the brown overstuffed couch where I'd been sitting with Jordyn, walked over to the tree, and found the present I'd wrapped for my sister. I had placed it beneath the little ceramic white owl ornament Samantha made one year, the one my mother had threatened to throw away on more than one occasion. My sister met me beside the tree, taking the gift from my hands.

"Hmm," she said, pretending to shake the package. "Sounds like a book, big brother. Looks like a book, too. Wait, I know, don't tell me. It's a book!"

"Don't speak to your brother that way," warned our Mother. "I won't have sarcasm in my home."

Samantha started to say something, but I cut her off. "Just open it. Who knows, you might even like it."

Samantha sighed, unwrapping the present. It was a copy of *Small Things*, her favorite novel. She rolled her eyes, then started back to the arm of the couch where she'd been sitting, next to Jordyn. She already had the book, of course.

"Look inside," I said, smiling. I knew she already owned the book, but this copy was special.

Her eyes caught mine, and for a moment I could see the little girl she once was, the little girl who'd adored her big brother and followed him everywhere.

She opened the book, her eyes widening. "'To Samantha, my #1 fan. Best wishes, Shawn Spencer,'" she said, reading the inscription on the title page, her voice filled with awe. "Oh. My. God. He never does signings, *ever*. Is this really him?"

"Yep," I said, glad to have surprised her. "It's really him."

"This is the best present, ever! Thanks, Alex," she said, staring down at the book. "This is awesome!"

"But wait, there's more," I said, in my best imitation of a game show host. "Flip a couple of pages."

She did, and soon found the $100 Best Buy gift card I'd stuck inside. "You remembered."

"Of course I did."

Sam was saving up for a new car stereo for her 2008 Honda Accord, another of my hand-me-downs after Mother had gifted me with a brand new Dodge Dart for last year's birthday.

She gave me an awkward hug, surprising us both. My sister hadn't hugged me in a very long time. I maneuvered my body between Samantha and the woman who'd given birth to both of us, so my little sister couldn't see our Mother's scowl at this all-too-rare display of affection between her two children.

The rest of the gift exchange went surprisingly well, and Jordyn absolutely loved the diamond stud earrings I gave her. It was almost one in the afternoon and I was looking forward to the ham that had been cooking in the kitchen since early this morning, when Mother pulled one last gift from the tree. It was wrapped in snowman gift paper, tied with a blue bow.

"'To Alex, from Samantha,'" she read off the tag, handing it to me. "I don't think there's an iPad in this one."

"Shit," yelped Samantha, standing up from the couch. "I forgot about that. Umm, I think I got the wrong thing. Don't open it."

"Language, young lady," admonished mother, eyes flashing anger. "How many times do I have to tell you, we don't talk like that in this house?"

"Samantha, whatever it is, I'll love it," I said, ignoring Mother's admonishments.

"Seriously, Alex, give me the package." She had an odd, almost desperate look on her face.

"Why?"

"Because I said so. Just give me the fucking package, all right?"

Mother was up in an instant, slapping Samantha hard across the cheek, raising an angry, red welt. "No more, young lady. No more! Up to your room."

"Jesus," muttered Jordyn under her breath, earning a shake of the head from Father. He knew better than anyone that you never took the Lord's name in vain in this house.

"Mother, stop it," I found myself saying. "She's seventeen, almost an adult. A few curse words never hurt anyone."

She whipped her head around to stare at me, took a deep breath, and lowered her eyes. "I suppose you're right, Alex."

Samantha stared at her, mouth open. "He really is the chosen one, isn't he, Mom? Whatever Alex says, goes. And you know what, Mom? It's not his fault. It's yours.

"Go ahead, Alex, open the present. Please, though, please…don't hate me. Just don't hate me, okay?"

"Never, not in a million years," I said, though something inside me trembled. What was in this small square box that had gotten Samantha so upset?

I ripped open the paper, letting it flutter to the floor, then opened the box inside. It was a picture of a small boy, maybe four or five, along with another boy a couple years younger. Both had blonde hair, and both looked a lot like me.

"What is this?" I asked, eyebrows raised.

"It's us," whispered a voice inside my head. It was my imaginary friend Sam. He hadn't spoken to me in years. *"I never thought I'd make it into a family picture, though."*

Mother's hand flew to her mouth as she saw the photograph. She stuttered and stammered, seemingly unable to form words. Finally, she lunged for the picture, but I stepped away.

Turning the photograph over, I saw two names with ages in parenthesis and a date. But it was all wrong. The names belonged to me and my sister, and for a moment I thought she'd had a sex change. But while my age proclaimed me to be three, hers said five. And the date was before she was even born.

"Uh-oh, buddy," whispered Sam, echoing in my head. *"The shit's about to hit the fan. I never wanted you to find out like this."*

"Margaret," said Father, rising from the Lazy Boy recliner he'd been seated in all morning, "why did you keep that?"

"Where did you find that picture, you little bitch?" Mother roared, hands suddenly around Samantha's throat. "Where?"

I couldn't move. I just stood there, numbly staring at the names on the back of the old photo. Jordyn, thankfully, had no such handicap. In an instant she was pulling Mother's hands from around my sister's throat, Samantha coughing and gagging as she recoiled from them both.

"Jesus Christ, what's wrong with you?" Jordyn screamed, standing between my mother and sister.

"In the basement," Samantha said, tears in her eyes. "I found your little hidey-hole, Mother. I know everything now. And I wanted to hurt him, hurt him so bad, but I was wrong. It's you I want to hurt. You!"

"I don't understand," I said, though I was beginning to put it all together.

Mother fell to her knees, huge, wracking sobs overtaking her body. We all just stood there, not even Father moving to the side of the woman he'd been married to for 27 years.

"Alex…" Father began, but fell silent as our eyes met.

"I struggled in school for the first few years," I said, talking to myself more than anyone else. "I was small for my age, and it took me longer to learn to read than it did most of the other kids. Hell, I was even late hitting puberty."

"I'm so sorry, son," said Father. "We just didn't know what else to do, and your mother…she loved him so much. He was her baby boy."

"I'm Sam, aren't I?" I said, the words forming almost unbidden on my lips. "I'm not Alex, I'm Sam."

"Bingo," said Sam's voice, but it wasn't really Sam, of course.

An image flashed into my mind. It was Christmas and we were playing, Alex and I, sitting on the second floor landing, rolling the Matchbox cars we'd opened just hours earlier down the stairs. He had just turned five, and I idolized him. He was my big brother, after all.

"Alex!" yelled a voice from the bedroom. It was Daddy. "Have you been playing in my desk again?"

"It wasn't me, Daddy. It was Sam," said Alex instantly, shifting the blame on to me.

I started to cry, not because I'd been in Daddy's desk but because Daddy appeared in the hallway just then, his big black belt in one hand and a bottle of Budweiser in the other, face red with anger.

"Don't lie to me, Alex. I know it was you, Mommy saw you in there earlier."

"It wasn't me," Alex complained. "It was Sam."

"Sam?" he whirled on me, a giant of a man (at least that's how he seemed then) looking to punish someone. "Did you get into my desk?"

I just stared up into his angry eyes, beginning to cry. "No, no, no," I said over and over, "not Sam."

Mother appeared in the hallway, looking annoyed. "Phillip, it's Christmas for God's sake. What's the matter?"

"One of our brats got into my desk again, and if I have to spank both of them to find out which one it was, then I will."

I started sobbing, remembering the feeling of Daddy's belt just a week earlier, the last time I'd gotten into trouble. Alex, however, wasn't crying. "I did it, Daddy," he said stoically. "I got into your desk."

It was a lie. I'd gotten into Daddy's desk, looking for one of my action figures. Why I thought it might be in my father's office I'll never know, but Alex was going to take my punishment for me.

"Come here, you little shit," Father said, reaching for Alex.

"Phillip, he admitted that he did it. Isn't that enough?"

"Shut up," Father yelled at her, his voice slurred. "The little turd is going to get what's coming to him, and if you don't back me up, so will you."

"No!" I yelled, running at Daddy's legs.

What happened next was a blur. Daddy lunged at Alex but tripped over me, smashing me flat into the carpet. Daddy flew over my prone body, crashing into Alex, and they both tumbled down the steps.

"No!" Mommy yelled, reaching out for them, but it was too late.

Daddy landed on Alex at the bottom of the stairs. Daddy was all right, but Alex...Daddy's beer bottle had shattered, and the sharp end was sticking straight into Alex's chest. My brother's lifeless eyes stared up the stairs at me, and the next thing I knew, I had no brother, I'd never had a brother, and my name was Alex. Sam had never existed, would never exist, until my sister was born three years later.

"You…" I stared at Mother. "You replaced him with me, didn't you? Sam…died, so that Alex could live on."

Mother continued to sob, saying nothing.

Father surprised me by speaking. "We did, son. I'm so sorry. Alex was always her favorite, and she couldn't go on living without him. And we'd had him for five years, and you for just three. What else were we supposed to go?"

"Maybe have a goddamned funeral," I screamed, enjoying a certain sense of satisfaction when my father flinched away from me.

"We buried Alex in the woods, and then we moved the next year. From Ohio to this little town, to Carthage. Do you remember when we moved? You were four then, two years before Samantha was born."

"He *is* Alex," Mother sobbed from the floor. "Sam died, not Alex. Alex was always Alex. Samantha was a mistake, I didn't want to get pregnant again, but he made me, and he made me name her Samantha, after Samuel."

"I didn't make you do anything," Father shouted. "You're the one that said you wanted to try again. You!"

"Oh my God," Samantha said, tears rolling down her cheeks. "I was, what? A consolation prize?"

"You were *nothing*!" Mother spat. "You were a mistake that never should have happened. You were a reminder from the past, when what you should have been was an abortion."

I looked from Samantha to Mother and then to Father, who just hung his head. Jordyn stood silently beside Sam, holding her hand.

"It's my fault," I said. "I was in Daddy's desk."

"I'm you," said my imaginary friend Sam. He hadn't spoken to me this much in a long time. *"And you're me. It all makes sense now. Whoever would have thought it?"*

"You were just a little boy," Father said. "It was my fault, it was all my fault. That was before I'd stopped drinking. That damned bottle. I never took another drink after that."

"I didn't know any of this," said Samantha, looking pleadingly into my eyes from across the room. "I swear I didn't. I don't know what I thought when I found that picture, but never this."

"Liar!" yelled my mother, rising from her knees. "You were always jealous of my Alex, you wanted to hurt him, and guess what? Now you have. Go to your room, Samantha. Go to your room!"

"My entire life is a lie," I whispered, staring at my mother, "and none of it is Samantha's fault. Leave her alone."

"You tell her, brother," whispered Sam, in my mind. *"Or better yet, let's tell her together."*

"Alex, honey, you don't understand," Mother said, turning to me. "You are Alex. *My* Alex. That's all that matters. Samuel was just a little shit. He tripped your Daddy and almost killed you, after he'd gotten into your Daddy's desk. You were the only one that mattered. You're the only one that's ever mattered."

"Shut up," I screamed, unaware that I had picked up the knife from the coffee cake. "All of you, just shut up."

"Alex, I really think everyone needs to calm down," said Jordyn, putting her hand on my shoulder.

"Don't touch him," said my mother, shoving Jordyn away from me. "Get your filthy hands off my little boy."

"Mother," I said, shoving the knife deep between her ribs, "if you're not going to shut up, you can just go straight to your room."

She gasped, grasping in vain at the knife. Blood was everywhere, and then she was falling into my arms, whispering over and over that she loved me, that she'd done it all for me, her darling Alexander, the light of her life.

People were screaming around me then. Samantha or Jordyn, or maybe both of them, I don't remember. And my father, finally my father, doing something after all these years, wrenching the knife from my hand, hurling it across the floor to skitter into the Christmas tree, knocking Samantha's white owl from the branches.

As if in slow motion, I watched the ornament as it fell to the floor. It shattered upon impact, little white shards scattering everywhere. I felt something in me shatter as well, but I couldn't understand what it was.

What I did understand, however, was that, finally, after twenty years, Father was doing something again. He held me as I cried, stroking my hair, saying over and over again how sorry he was, and that everything would be okay. But why was he sorry? I could never figure that out. If anything, he really should have apologized to Alex.

I'm Sam, and I'm three years old. I'll be four in February, and I have an imaginary friend named Alex. No one can see him but me. He talks to me sometimes, tells me how things used to be, before I started living in the hospital. Alex is a grown-up and I love him a lot, but I don't understand about half of what he says. But we have fun when we play with our Matchbox cars. Oh, how we have fun!

My big sister Samantha comes to see me twice a week, like clockwork. Daddy shows up once a month or so, and he's always sad. Jordyn, Alex's girlfriend from when he was real, came once, but she left in tears. I think she misses Alex. Me, I miss Mommy. I haven't seen her since before I came to the hospital, but I don't really expect her to visit. After all, I was never Mommy's favorite.

A Stranger with Your Hair

"I saw a stranger with your hair,
tried to make her give it back,
so I could send it off to you,
maybe Federal Express,
'cause I know you'd miss it"

—John Gorka, *I Saw a Stranger with Your Hair*

When I wished upon a falling star, I never in a million years imagined it would wind up quite like this.

My name is Parker McCain, and I haven't always been a good man. I've fallen in love many times during my life, and fallen out just as often. At thirty-eight, I'd finally come to the conclusion that I was never going to find "the one," when I saw that wonderful, awful meteoroid that we all call a falling star burning up in the Earth's atmosphere. I made my wish, and now I have to live with it.

It was the next morning that I saw her. Erica Holly had been my high school sweetheart, and, at eighteen months, the longest relationship I'd ever been in to date. She had the most amazing long, blonde hair that she tied into a ponytail, which was what first attracted me to her in my sophomore year. She was a junior, and as a rule junior girls didn't date sophomore boys. Hell, they rarely even dated junior boys, but for me she made an exception.

The woman walking on the other side of the street had Erica's hair, and, in an instant, I knew it was her. Entranced, I immediately jay-walked across 34th street, cars honking and drivers cursing, but I didn't care. Erica Holly! I hadn't thought about her in years, hardly at all since that night we broke up.

Erica Holly was my first, but she was far from my last. She was a girl of above average looks, but her defining feature was definitely her hair. Long, luxurious, and naturally blonde, I knew I had to have her the very first day I saw her, on the day she transferred to Carthage High School.

It took six months of wooing her before she finally agreed to a date, and it was almost a year and a half later, three weeks before she graduated, when I finally got her into bed. We were both virgins and made love like a baby taking its first steps, but it wasn't until she came (or, more than likely, pretended to come) that I realized just how an-noying her voice was.

We broke up the next day. I'd had many women since, but none with hair even close to as gorgeous as Erica Holly's. And there she was, right in front of me, her hair still as long and blonde and beautiful as it had been back in high school.

"Erica," I called, pushing past window shoppers and early morning commuters. "Hey, Erica, wait up."

"Watch it, buddy," said a man about my age, carrying a massive metal birdcage with a sleeping white owl inside. "I'll be mighty pissed off if I lose my bird."

"Sorry, trying to catch up with an old friend," I said, just for a sec-ond meeting his eyes.

When I turned back toward my quarry, she was gone. I searched everywhere, in the shops that decorated both sides of the street, down alleyways, but she was nowhere to be found. I'd been on my way to the office, to the little advertising agency where I worked, but called in sick instead so I could continue my search. Nothing. If it had actually been

Erica Holly, she had vanished in the teeming metropolis that we call New York City.

Defeated, I finally limped into work around noon. I pushed past Alicia Dominguez, the spicy little Latina secretary with the most perfect breasts I'd ever seen, without even a nod hello.

"Hey, jerk, I thought you were sick," she called after me.

I deserved the moniker and didn't begrudge her use of it. We'd slept together after the Christmas party last year, and I'd never called her. I was, indeed, a jerk, and probably a thousand other words much, much worse.

"I got better," I mumbled over my shoulder, pushing open the door to the large office I shared with Frank Douglass.

"How's it hanging, my brother?" said Frank, using outdated street slang that belied his pot-bellied, gray-haired, middle-aged appearance. "Alicia said you were sick. Hangover?"

"No such luck. Stomach thing," I lied, "but I'm feeling better, so I thought I might as well come into work. The Peterson account won't fix itself, after all."

I worked on the Peterson account until around three, getting very little done. My mind kept wandering back to Erica Holly. I was sure now that the woman I'd seen across 34th Street hadn't been her, after all. I mean, what are the odds? Last I'd heard, she'd stayed in Carthage and married a football jock who had been a few grades ahead of her in high school.

Finally, I gave in to temptation and looked her up online. She wasn't hard to find. She had indeed married the jock, a now-balding car salesman by the name of Todd Masters, and had three children. The oldest was a sixteen-year-old boy named Todd Jr. Her last Facebook entry was last night, something about running to the grocery store, and it said nothing about her being in New York. Mystery solved. Whoever I'd seen wasn't Erica Holly.

I felt unexpectedly sad at that revelation. Was I really expecting to reunite with my old girlfriend from high school? I'd been married and divorced twice since then, and slept with countless women, so why did Erica Holly fascinate me so? But of course it wasn't her, not really. Just the memory of her long, beautiful blonde hair, and the things we had done the one and only time we made love.

"Weekend plans?" asked Frank, and I realized it was almost time to go home. I'd spent most of the day daydreaming about Erica.

"Not really," I said, hoping he wouldn't invite me along to something.

He didn't.

Maybe I really was coming down with something, after all. I copied all the Peterson files onto a thumb drive and tossed it into my briefcase, hoping to get caught up on work over the weekend.

On the walk to the subway, something happened to momentarily make me forget that Erica Holly ever existed. I heard someone call my name, but the streets were so crowded that I could never see who it was. But I recognized the voice, or at least I thought I did.

Haven Malone, my first wife, divorced fifteen years this coming September. I'd fallen in love with her over the phone, before we even met. She had the most gorgeous voice, the kind that could melt butter. She'd been dating my brother then, and I'd nearly destroyed my relationship with him when I stole her away, but it had all been worth it.

"Haven?" I called into the crowd, rewarded only with dirty looks from tired commuters on their way home.

With no children or family to bind us, and less than a year's worth of marriage to tie us together, we hadn't spoken since a few months after the divorce. But I'd never forgotten her voice, because it was that voice more than anything that I'd fallen in love with all those years ago. In my heart I knew it was Haven, but there were too many people on the street to find her.

"Park," I heard her call again, "Where did you go, Park?"

I spun in every direction but couldn't find her. It had to be Haven. No one else had ever called me by that nickname. I pushed through the crowd in the direction I thought I'd heard the voice come from, tripped, and spilled the contents of my briefcase everywhere.

"Do you need help?" asked a female voice.

Haven! No, it wasn't Haven. I looked up into the most beautiful pair of crystal blue eyes I'd ever seen. Dressed in a black miniskirt with dark patterned stockings and wearing a blue blouse, a woman of maybe twenty-five crouched down beside me. She brushed a long strand of dyed-blue hair out of her eyes and repeated the question, while I just stared.

"Uh, yeah," I managed to get out, as she started to help me scoop up the contents of my briefcase. "I'm Parker, Parker McCain."

"Kasie Winters," she said with a nod of her head, before shoving a sheaf of papers marked 'private and confidential' into my briefcase. "So, come here often?"

I saw that she was smiling. "Just when I'm trying to meet pretty girls by making a complete and absolute fool of myself."

"So that was intentional?" she asked, hands on her hips. She must have noticed the look on my face because she started to laugh. "I'm just teasing, Parker, Parker McCain."

I stood up, dusting myself off. I'd never felt so tongue tied in all my life, and try as I might I couldn't rip my eyes from hers. They were the most perfect eyes I'd ever seen.

"So, would you like to get a drink?" I asked, knowing immediately that the line would fail.

"I'm a busy bee today, Parker, Parker McCain," she said, with an apologetic shrug. "I'm already late, for a very important date."

"Not even coffee?" I countered. "There's always time for coffee."

She folded her arms over her small, pert breasts and cocked her head, as if considering. Then her cell phone rang. She held up a finger and took the call.

"I really do have to run," she said after a minute, holding her hand over the phone. "Ships passing in the night, and all that. Have a good weekend, Parker, Parker McCain."

I fumbled in my wallet, pulling out a business card. I quickly jotted down my cell number on the back of the card and handed it to her before she could walk away. She was already talking on the phone again but smiled and raised her eyebrows.

It was everything I could do to tear my gaze away from her retreating back, but somehow I managed, because after a subway ride and a three block walk I found myself home. I was determined to ignore this funk I'd found myself in and get some work done.

It was almost ten o'clock when I realized I couldn't find the thumb drive I'd dropped into my briefcase some five hours ago. I must have lost it on the sidewalk when I'd spilled my briefcase.

Shit! There was some very confidential information on that drive, and if it got out that I'd lost it, I could very well lose my job or even get sued by Peterson Tires, Incorporated. Hopefully, it'd gotten kicked into a storm drain or something, where only the alligators would find it.

The phone rang, startling me. The caller ID said unknown, and I usually ignored those calls, but for some reason I decided to answer it anyway.

"Parker, Parker McCain, is that you?" said a female voice on the other end.

"Kasie?"

"The one and only. You gave me your card, are you surprised that I called?"

"A little," I admitted, "but happily so."

"So, did you drop a flash drive? I stepped on one as I was leaving. Never the sort of girl to leave orphaned flash drives alone on a lonely sidewalk, I picked it up, but when I turned back around you were already gone."

"Kasie Winters, you're a life saver," I gushed into the phone. "Yep, it's mine, all right. You might have just saved my job."

"That's me, the life and job saver."

"So..." I said, stretching out the word, "can I come pick it up?"

Awkward silence, and then, "Parker, Parker McCain, it's a little late, you know, and I don't normally invite strange men to my apartment..."

"But, for me, you'll make an exception?" I said, interrupting her.

She laughed. "No, but I will meet you for that drink. Do you know where McNulty's is? On Walker Street?"

I did, in fact, know where McNulty's was, and I said as much. We made plans to meet in forty-five minutes. Enough with being haunted by women from my past. I was excited to get my thumb drive back, but absolutely thrilled to once again see the girl with the beautiful blue eyes and hair to match.

One cab ride later and I was at the bar. She was already there when I walked in, dressed in a short strapless pink dress and a blue denim jacket that almost but not quite matched her hair and eyes. Her high-heeled shoes matched the dress, while her purse matched the jacket.

Her eyes caught mine from across the bar, and I felt a familiar stirring in my stomach that I did my best to push down. Her smile melted whatever reserve I had, however, and I walked across the room with a spring in my step and a swagger in my hips.

"Thank you so much," I said, as she handed me the thumb drive. I shoved it into my pocket. "You really are a life saver. What can I get you to drink?"

"How about a club soda?" Kasie said demurely.

"A club soda? It's Friday night. Live a little. I promise I won't get you too drunk."

"I don't want to get carded," she said, biting her lip.

Carded? Oh, shit. "Kasie, how old are you?"

She leaned close to me, her lips almost brushing against my ear. "Well, I'll be twenty-one...in a little over a year and a half."

Math was never my strong suite, but it didn't take much calculation to realize that this girl was only nineteen years old. I was twice her age, and easily old enough to be her father. I started to say something, but forgot what as I stared into those perfect blue eyes.

"Would you *want* something to drink?" I heard myself saying, instantly knowing I was headed for trouble. "If you could, I mean."

"Parker, Parker McCain, whatever am I going to do with you?" she said, a half-smile forming on her lips. "If I could, yes, I'd love a drink."

"What would you like?"

"Surprise me. You seem to be good at that."

"One surprise, coming up," I said, rising from the little table near the front of the bar where we'd sat. "Be right back."

The bartender, however, wasn't too keen on helping me impress Kasie. He knew who I'd been sitting with and demanded I produce her ID before he'd sell me the two glasses of white wine I'd ordered. I claimed they were both for me, but he wasn't having any of it. Finally, three folded $20 bills pressed into his hand later, he changed his mind.

"One drink, then she's outta here," he warned me, as he pocketed the twenties. "Sixty bucks ain't worth losing my job over, mister."

I wanted to ask how one drink was any different than twelve since it was just as illegal, and how much money *would* be worth losing his job over, but instead I let it go and took the drinks back to our table.

"I come here a lot with friends," she said, taking a slow sip, "and he has to know I'm not legal. How on Earth did you do that?"

"Magic," I said, grinning.

True to my word, we left McNulty's after one drink. I asked Kasie back to my place, but she said hers was closer. She lived just six blocks from the bar, a tiny two-bedroom apartment that she shared with a couple of roommates. Fortunately, neither roommate was home.

We sat on a second-hand blue couch in the apartment's tiny living room, sipping wine that I'd picked up from a liquor store halfway between McNulty's and her apartment. It was a white Zinfandel, and she seemed to like it very much. I couldn't stop staring into those gorgeous blue eyes.

The apartment was a mess, and, when we couldn't find any clean glasses, she ripped open a package of red Solo cups for the wine. It was the first time I'd ever drank wine from a plastic cup, but the company more than made up for the lack of crystalware.

Kasie was a student at NYU, studying fashion while working a full-time job as a waitress at an Italian restaurant just two subway stops from her apartment. She'd only been in the city a year and lived with her older sister and her sister's boyfriend. To earn extra money she'd taken up posing nude for an art class, which is where she'd been rushing off to when we met earlier today.

"So, Parker, Parker McCain," she whispered into my ear, setting aside her cup of wine, "are we going to talk all night, or are you going to fuck me?"

She didn't have to ask me twice. Once we started kissing, we couldn't keep our hands off each other. She dragged me into the smaller of the two bedrooms, pushed me down on an unmade twin bed, and climbed on top of me, most of our clothing a trail of bread crumbs behind us.

We made love three times that night. It'd been years since I'd been with someone that young—since my college years, in fact—and I was worried that I wouldn't be able to keep up. I'm proud to say that, despite my age and the alcohol I'd consumed, I managed to rise to the occasion more than once.

Unlike most women I'd been with, she made love with her eyes open. I fell in love with those deep sapphire baby blues every time she came, which was probably six or seven times that night. Around four in the morning, exhausted and spent, we finally fell asleep in each other's arms.

Kasie woke me up screaming. I sat up in bed with a start, my heart banging against my ribcage, confused as to where I was. Kasie was already sitting up in bed, rocking back and forth. She was holding her face in her hands, screaming at the top of her lungs. Blood ran through her fingers, staining the white bed sheets.

"What's wrong?" I asked dumbly, grabbing her wrists.

"What did you do to me?" she sobbed.

"I didn't do anything. What happened? Let me see."

I pried her hands away from her face, blood gushing through my fingers. Her beautiful blue eyes had been ripped from her face, leaving only bleeding sockets in their place. I gasped, releasing her hands, and nearly fell off the bed.

"What the fuck?" said another woman's voice as the bedroom door pushed open.

An older version of Kasie stood there, dressed in pink pajamas, her long, blonde hair in tangles and sleep still in her eyes. Her sister. She stared at me, then at Kasie, and started to scream.

"Call 911," I barked, now standing naked beside the bed.

"Who are you? What did you do to her?"

"Elise, is that you?" Kasie asked, between sobs. "Why can't I see? It hurts so much."

"You son of a bitch!" Elise growled, her hands balled up in fists. "What did you do to my sister?"

"I told you, I didn't do anything," I said, but she was on me in an instant.

I easily blocked her punch, but wasn't quick enough for the knee that sank deep into my crotch. I doubled over and fell to the ground, feeling like I was about to throw up.

"Jesus, what happened to Kasie?" said a skinny man of maybe twenty-five, rushing through the door.

"I said, call 911," I managed to croak out, my testicles on fire.

He looked to Elise, who nodded. "Tell them Kasie's been attacked, and the piece of shit who did it is still here."

"Parker?" cried Kasie from the bed, hands once again covering her face. "Did you do this to me?"

"No! It wasn't me, Kasie. I swear to God, it wasn't me."

Elise kicked me in the ribs, sending a tremor of pain through my entire body. I had to get out of here. Ignoring the pain in my ribs as well as my still-aching crotch, I grabbed her ankle and pulled it as hard as I could, sending her falling backwards and into the little wooden dresser that stood beside the entrance to the tiny bedroom.

"Hey!" yelled the boyfriend, eyes wide in alarm.

He rushed to Elise's side, giving me time to pull on the pair of pants I'd taken off and left at the foot of the bed the night before. Elise was holding the back of her head, crying, but the boyfriend abandoned her as soon as I tried to sneak past them.

I punched him hard in the nose, instantly covering his face in blood. He fell backwards into Elise, and I was able to snake past them and into the living room to retrieve the rest of my clothes.

Kasie's screams filled the tiny apartment and I wanted to help her, I truly did, but I knew I had to get out of there. I had her blood on my hands and had assaulted her sister and her sister's boyfriend. Even though I was innocent, the circumstantial evidence was overwhelming.

I ran out the front door, heart still beating rapidly in my chest. A wizened, gray-haired old lady stared at me like I was a criminal, and I suppose now I was. I pushed past her, decided against the elevator, and instead took the stairs to the first floor and out of the apartment. And from there I just kept running.

My cell phone—thank God I'd left it in my pants pocket last night—said it was just past eight in the morning. Kasie knew my name and phone number and could easily give the police enough to track me down, so I probably should have stayed and pled my case to New York City's finest. But my fight or flight instinct had always leaned toward flight, and this time was no different.

By the time I reached Central Park, I was out of breath. My chest ached, and my legs felt like they were on fire. I closed my eyes and bent over at the waist, feeling like I might throw up, but all I could do was think about Kasie's eyes.

Who could do such a thing to another human being, especially someone with such beautiful eyes? And then it hit me. Maybe that was the point. Maybe some serial killer had noticed her perfect blue eyes and decided to take them for their collection.

A shiver traveled down my spine, and I jumped when my cell phone rang. I stared at the caller ID: it was Frank, calling from his personal phone. I gave it three more rings to let my heart settle back to normal before answering.

"Parker?" Frank said, "What the hell is going on?"

"What do you mean?" I asked, going cold. How could he possibly know about Kasie?

"I went by the office this morning, and about a millions cops were there. The whole building was surrounded by police tape."

"So what happened?" I interrupted.

"Alicia Dominguez," Frank said. "She's dead, Parker. The police weren't giving out details, but I did a little snooping. Apparently, someone broke into the office not long after we left and attacked her."

Jesus. Alicia was dead? "Do they know who did it?"

"That I don't know, but I do know she was carved up really badly. Her chest…remember that police officer Mike Hoffman? We did some work for his brother's restaurant last year? Yeah, he was there, and he let it slip that her…her breasts, Parker. They were cut from her chest, and she was left there to bleed out. Charlie from the mailroom found her this morning."

I stared numbly into the park, empty save for a few early morning joggers. First Kasie, and now Alicia. What the fuck was going on? No, correction: first Alicia, and then Kasie. Could the two crimes somehow be related?

"You still there, buddy?" asked Frank.

"I'm here," I managed, though part of me was still back in Kasie's apartment.

"I said they'll probably be calling you, since you and I were more than likely the last two people to see her alive. I'm supposed to go to the police station at noon today to give a statement. You want me to swing by and pick you up?"

"Jesus, no!" I yelled, startling myself.

"Whoa there, buddy. Are you okay?"

"Sorry, Frank," I mumbled into the phone, my mind racing. "I'm just a little freaked out, I guess."

"You and me both, buddy. You and me both."

I hung up, wondering what to do or where to go next. Now that the adrenaline was draining from my system, I found myself nearly numb with indecision. I was connected to both crimes, even if just by association. That wouldn't look good to the police. Hell, it didn't even look good to me.

Something was niggling at my brain, something that would help me begin to start to sort this whole mess out, but I couldn't manage to grab hold of it quite yet and drag it out into the light of the day. Could someone be setting me up? But that didn't make any sense, and seemed damned narcissistic to boot.

On impulse, I used my phone to once again stalk Erica Holly's Facebook profile. The latest status update chilled my blood and almost caused me to drop the phone. It read:

My wife, Erica Holly Masters, has been missing since Thursday evening. She ran to the County Market for groceries but didn't come home. Have you seen her? Todd Jr., Alexis, Clark and I are worried sick about her. If you know anything, please call me at 217-555-3288. The Carthage Sheriff's department says they can't do anything until she's been missing for 72 hours, but I know Erica. She just wouldn't run off and abandon her family. Please pray for us. Thank you.

I stared at the screen, panic rising in my throat. It wasn't just my usual hubris, after all. Someone was stalking my past lovers and, at least in Alicia's case, murdering them.

Either that, or it was all some strange, awful coincidence. I wasn't exactly a praying man, but right then it just didn't matter. I prayed with all my heart for Erica to return to her family safe and sound, and for Kasie to somehow build a new life without her eyes. Sadly, there was no longer anything God or anyone else could do for Alicia Dominguez.

My cell rang, replacing Facebook with a Caller ID screen: the New York City Police Department. Were they calling about Kasie or Alicia? No matter, I wasn't about to answer. In fact, I turned the phone off and tossed it into the first trash can I could find. I'd watched plenty of cop shows. If I really was a suspect in either assault, it wouldn't take much for the police to triangulate my location using my cell phone.

The nice thing about living in New York City was that little electronic shops were everywhere, including all around Central Park. It took me less than five minutes to walk to Bud's Discount Computers and Phones. Another five minutes and one hundred dollars later, I had a cheap "pay as you go" phone with Internet capabilities and $60 worth of phone cards.

Surfing once again to Erica Holly Master's Facebook page, I keyed in the number her husband had posted. Todd Masters answered on the second ring.

"Todd, this is Johnny Nugent," I spoke into the phone, using the alias I'd had on a phony driver's license as a teenager. "I used to work with Erica and was so sorry to read about her on Facebook. Do you have any news?"

Silence, and then: "Erica's dead, Johnny. They found her body about ten minutes ago."

My heart froze in my throat, and my mouth could no longer form words. I finally mumbled something unintelligible into the phone, as the world around me seem to constrict.

"Are you still there?"

"I'm so sorry," I said, finally finding my voice. "What happened?"

"She was scalped," he said in a low, flat voice. "Scalped and left to die at the lake, like…like some goddamned animal, like some…raccoon or something."

Like some goddamned raccoon. I couldn't think, couldn't even breathe. Three women I'd had sex with, all dead or maimed within 24 hours.

"Are you there, Johnny?" Todd said, his voice sounding at once tired but raw with emotion.

"I'm so sorry for your loss," I said, before thumbing the button to end the call.

I immediately searched Facebook for Haven Malone, but couldn't find her. It had been so long since we'd last communicated, she could easily have gotten married and changed her name.

Forgetting about Haven for the moment, my thoughts instead jumped to my second wife. Unlike with Haven, Renee and I had remained on friendly terms. She'd even kept my last name. We were friends on Facebook, and I remembered that she'd messaged me her new phone number after her move to San Francisco several months ago. I signed into Facebook and retrieved the message.

Renee had almost been the one. Whip-smart and sexy as hell, she had a face that could launch a thousand ships. High cheekbones, full lips, and the most perfect smile I'd ever seen, her features met the golden ratio of feminine beauty with a bull's-eye. Our marriage had lasted almost a year and a half, and we might still be together today if she hadn't caught me in bed with her sister.

I sighed, took a deep breath, and clicked on the phone number in the text of her message. She answered on the second ring.

"Hello?" She said tentatively.

"Renee, thank God," I said, relief flooding through my system.

"Parker? Did you get a new phone? I didn't recognize the number."

"Never mind that, are you okay?"

"Of course I'm okay," she said, sounding amused. "Why wouldn't I be okay?"

I started to tell her, then stumbled, unsure of myself. The last twenty-four hours felt like a dream. Nothing made sense anymore. If someone was really targeting my former flames, why would they skip my ex-wife?

"Parker, are you still there?"

"I'm here," I finally said. "I just…had a bad dream about you last night, that's all. I just wanted to make sure you were okay."

"That's sweet of you, Parker, but I'm fine. Better than fine, actually. I'd put off telling you this, for obvious reasons, but I've met someone and we're getting married. You'll be invited to the wedding, of course. Please be happy for me."

My heart sank. I wanted to be happy for her, and I should be happy for her, but all I could think about was that I'd stupidly let her go, in search of my next great love. But instead of saying all of that, I swallowed my regret and said that, yes, I was thrilled for her, how lucky this man that I suddenly hated was, and that of course I'd attend the wedding. We were saying our goodbyes when someone knocked at her door.

"Hold on just a minute," she said, "I'm not quite done with you yet. I need to tell you just one more piece of good news."

I agreed to wait, listening as she walked across what sounded like a wooden floor to answer the door. I heard her unlatch the door, the sound of metal against metal echoing through the telephone, and then she screamed. I'd never know that second piece of good news that she'd wanted to tell me.

"Renee," I shouted again and again into the speaker, ignoring the strange looks I received from passers-by all around me.

"You have such a beautiful face," I heard a voice say on the other end, a voice I recognized. "At least Park always thought so, and really, that's all that matters."

"Leave her alone, you bitch!" I screamed helplessly into the phone, my words drowned out by Renee's screams.

And then, just like that, they stopped. Silence. At least until the phone was picked up once again on the other end.

"I'm almost finished, Park, and then I'll come for you."

"Haven, you fucking psycho bitch!" I shouted into the phone as the world seemed to constrict around me. "Why are you doing this?"

"You still don't know?" she said, her voice every bit as beautiful as I remembered. "Don't worry, we'll be together soon."

The line went dead.

My first wife, Haven Malone, had murdered two women and taken the eyes of one more. She'd probably also just killed Renee, and was coming after me next.

"That's him," said a small Asian man, a police officer by his side. "He won't stop screaming into that phone."

My heart jumped a beat, and I folded the cell phone into my pocket. "I'm sorry, sir. Just an argument. I didn't meant to disturb you."

"I'm NYPD officer Dwight Barratt. Can I see some ID, please?" said the officer, a tall, black man probably in his late twenties.

I felt panicky and it must have shown, because his hand jumped to the gun on his hip. I took a deep breath, counted to ten, and stuck my hand into my pocket.

"Careful," he warned, drawing his revolver. "Nice and slow now."

"I'm just getting my wallet."

The little Asian man's eyes darted from me to Barratt and back again, as he slowly backed away. "I don't want any trouble, I just don't want him screaming outside my store."

I ignored him and produced my wallet, letting it fall open to show my driver's license. I rarely drove in the city, but I did own a car, and I wished to God I was in it right now.

He stared at the license, seemingly satisfied, and I thanked my lucky stars that the cops weren't looking for me yet. I was about to walk away when a cop car pulled up to the curb and two more officers got out of the squad car, and I instantly knew that I had relaxed too soon.

"Officer Tom Phelps. Is everything all right here?" asked the first officer to get out of the car.

"I think we're all good," said Barratt, handing me back my wallet. "Right, Mr. McCain?"

"Right as rain," I said, pocketing the wallet. "I appreciate your vigilance, Officer Barratt."

I watched as the second officer exited the car. It was a woman of maybe thirty, with short brunette hair and a trim, athletic body. She exchanged looks with the other officer, and then looked down at a piece of paper that she held in her hands.

"What's your first name, Mr. McCain?" asked the officer, her badge identifying her as Melanie Austen.

Her hands were beautiful, slender and delicate, and I was instantly ashamed for noticing such a thing despite my current predicament. I turned away, my face turning red.

"Parker, right?" asked Officer Barratt, looking from me to the officers and back again.

I started to run, but they were on me in a second. Before I knew it, I was face planted into the hard cement sidewalk and one of the cops had my arms behind my back. I felt metal clasp around each wrist. Handcuffs. I'd encountered handcuffs before, but never quite like this.

"We have a BOLO for you, Mr. McCain," said the female cop with the beautiful hands, "to bring you in for questioning. I would have been much happier escorting you downtown, but you just had to run, didn't you?"

My mouth hurt and I tasted blood on my tongue. My blood. And it felt like some of my teeth were broken.

"I didn't do anything," I said, knowing how lame it sounded the moment the words left my bleeding lips. "It was Haven Malone. She killed them! She blinded Kasie. She's behind everything."

"You have the right to remain silent and refuse to answer questions. Do you understand?" said Austen, ignoring my protests, as Barratt and Phelps hauled me to my feet. "Anything you say or do may be used against you in a court of law. Do you understand?"

I never responded, but she went on anyway, reading me my full Miranda rights. It was different than the shortened version they use on television, yet somehow even more terrifying. When he was done, Barratt pushed me into the back of the squad car and strapped the seat belt around my chest.

It seemed like I was sitting there forever, but it was probably no longer than ten or fifteen minutes. I stared forlornly out the window as Austen talked to the other two cops, crossing whatever T's and dotting whatever I's were necessary before hauling me off to jail. Before I knew it, she and her partner climbed into the squad car and we began our journey to the police station to meet my interrogators.

I closed my eyes and rested my head against the smelly vinyl upholstery of the bench seat, wanting nothing more than for all of this to be over. I hadn't done anything and so I really had nothing to worry about, right? We'd only been moving a few minutes, however, when I heard someone scream.

"What is that?" Austen yelled, bringing me out of my stupor.

I looked up just in time to catch a glimpse of a beautiful woman with long, flowing blonde hair holding a fiery sword standing in front of the car. And then the car skidded around her, and she disappeared from view.

The police cruiser hit something, careened against another car, and in less than a second the car was flipping in mid-air, turning upside down. The seat belt cut hard into my waist and shoulder but held true, leaving me dangling from the bench seat. My wrists, still handcuffed behind my back, felt like they were on fire.

I heard the screech of metal cutting against metal, louder than even the shouts of the officers and what sounded like a crowd gathering around us.

The front half of the car was torn from the back, metal and plastic shards flying into my face. I closed my eyes, and the next thing I knew someone was unbuckling my seat belt. I winced for the impact I know was coming, but I didn't hit the roof of the upside down police car. Instead, I felt strong hands hauling me out through the hole in the front of the car.

I opened my eyes, blinking against the fiery sun. No, it wasn't the sun, it was that flaming sword I'd seen earlier, and it was held by my ex-wife Renee. I blinked stupidly, ignoring the shouts of people around us and the sound of ambulances in the distance.

"Renee, how did you get here? What's going on?"

But it wasn't Renee, not really. She had Renee's face, but Renee had dark hair, not blonde. And she didn't own any fiery sword, as far as I knew, and certainly didn't have large, feathery wings sprouting from her back.

The woman standing before me was dressed in a chainmail top and wore a long, flowing white skirt with a slit up to the top of her thigh. I stared at the chainmail, which covered the most perfect pair of breasts I'd ever seen.

I'd know those breasts anywhere. They were Alicia's breasts, and the blonde hair belonged to Erica Holly.

Still holding my shoulder, she spun me around with ease.

"Be still," said Haven's voice, and I felt the heat of her sword as it sliced through the chain that held my handcuffs like butter.

I let my arms fall to my side as I turned to face her, this amalgamation of my perfect woman. And then I remembered the wish.

Renee's face smiled, but once again it was Haven's voice that came out of her mouth. "Do you like me, Parker? Am I everything you thought I would be?"

The sun caught her beautiful blue eyes, but it wasn't her eyes, not really. Those eyes belonged to Kasie Winters, the woman I'd so casually bedded the night before.

"I didn't want any of this," I said, feeling like I might choke.

"Oh, but you did," the angel countered. "You wished for it. I heard you. And I answered. You wanted the perfect woman, Parker McCain, made up of all the best parts of the women you'd been with before."

Was any of this real, or was I dreaming? It couldn't be real, could it? The two officers, Sherman and Austen, lay some fifty feet away inside the remains of the front half of the car. Neither were moving, and Austen's hands had been severed at the wrists.

All around us, people were taking photos with their phone. Sirens grew closer, but I knew now that nothing could save me from my desires.

"How many?" I asked, at the same time fearing the answer. "How many different women are you made from?"

"Seventeen," said Haven's voice. "I'm your perfect woman, Parker. Perfect in every way that's important to you."

She twirled in a circle, her white skirt floating around her waist. Her lean, delicate ankles were from a girl I'd bedded in college, and her ass I recognized from my best friend in college's mother, whom I'd slept with during spring break.

Her hands, of course, belonged to NYPD police officer Melanie Austen, or had up until just a few moments ago. The beautiful, young police officer lay bleeding to death simply because I'd noticed the one perfect thing about her.

Seventeen women, maimed or dead, all because I'd loved a perfect part of them but couldn't love them as a whole. I remember my wish now, and I spoke it out loud.

"'Dear God or the universe or whoever's listening,'" I repeated the drunken wish I'd made two nights ago. "'I've fallen in and out of love so many times. Please, bring me the woman who's perfect for me, the best of all of the women I've loved before, who will love me like I love her, who I can give my heart to.'"

"Could you love me, Parker?" the angel asked. "Could you give me your heart?"

"I...I don't know," I said, ashamed that I'd even hesitated.

I wanted to say no. I wanted to push her away, to damn her for what she'd done, but how could I? I'd made the wish. Kasie, Erica, Haven, Renee, Alicia, Melanie Austen…it was all my fault. Those six women and eleven more, most of whose names I couldn't even remember, parts taken from each woman to create this angel who stood before me.

God help me, how could I refuse their sacrifice? How could I refuse *her*?

I looked into Kasie's eyes and smiled, and Renee's face smiled back at me. The angel lowered her sword and moved towards me, touching my cheek with her free hand, with Melanie Austen's hand, caressing my skin.

"Parker," she said, leaning in to brush her lips against mine, "will you be mine? Will you give me your heart?"

Her lips sent electricity through my soul, and in an instant I knew that those lips had once upon a time graced the mouth of Monique Giroux, the French exchange student I'd made out with a couple of times in my senior year of high school.

I realized something else as well. I could no longer deny her, this angel who had come down from the heavens to fulfill my wish.

I pulled her close, returning her kiss, and whispered, "Yes."

In an instant I felt the most incredible, excruciating pain I'd ever known, and then nothing. Nothing at all. She pulled away from me, my still-beating heart grasped in her hand, my blood dripping from between her fingers.

I'd gotten my wish. She was the perfect woman, made up of all the women I'd loved before, and I'd given her my heart. The world grew dark as I watched her shove the organ deep into her own chest, and then…

The Wish

Melissa Carnegie was livid. She'd been going to Curves for almost a year now, three times a week, and yet she was still a good sixty pounds overweight. But that's not what she was livid about. She was livid because Nikki Melon, her former best friend, had been working out for a mere ten months and now was a svelte 119 pounds. Worse yet, she never missed an opportunity to rub Melissa's face in it.

"It's just easier for some of us than it is for others," Nikki had said just a few minutes ago, while playing with her long, red hair. "Don't beat yourself up about it. Although there is quite a lot to beat, now isn't there?" And then she laughed and added a "just kidding," as if that made everything okay.

It didn't make everything okay; it just made it worse. If you were going to be a bitch, at least own up to it.

Melissa had just finished the so-called biceps/triceps machine (so-called because she'd been doing it for a year and didn't seem to be developing either set of muscles) and was about to go on to the recovery board when she saw Christina McAfee, a once-petite blonde who, like her, had gained weight during her pregnancy and never managed to lose it, step into the foyer of the Curves franchise in Rogers, Arkansas.

Chrissy gave her a small half-wave, then gestured toward Nikki and rolled her eyes. That usually meant that Chrissy had some dirt on their shared rival, so, instead of spending time on the recovery board, Melissa made a beeline for her best friend.

"Hey, girl, what's up?" She said, giving her a quick hug.

"Meh. Didn't really feel like exercising today, but thought I'd drop by before lunch." She lowered her voice. "Want to hear a little gossip? Miss skinny britches over there, she's at it again."

Chrissy, Nikki, and Melissa has been friends for years, until Nikki was the only one who'd started losing weight after Melissa had finally managed to drag the other two to Curves. They'd been happy for her, at first, but then the digs started. To top that off, Nikki, who was newly-divorced, had started sleeping with the various dads at the elementary school where their kids all went. Some were single, some married, but they all seemed to want Nikki Melon.

"Who is it this time?" Melissa asked, rolling her eyes.

"I'm not sure," said Chrissy. "Gabrielle Morrison saw her and some guy coming out of one of those sleazy hotels on 8th Street last Friday. They couldn't keep their hands off each other, Gabby said."

It was probably a teacher or a dad at the school their kids all attended. The little slut wouldn't be satisfied until she'd slept with every man who was in any way associated with the Arkansas Academy of Fine Arts Elementary. She'd even put the moves on Melissa's husband once when they were all at a school play earlier this year. Well, she'd caught them talking, and saw Nikki touch Rob's elbow. If that wasn't flirting, what was?

"Something has to be done about her," Melissa said, but it was the same thing she'd been saying for the last couple of months. Truth was, there wasn't really a damned thing either one of them could do.

"But what can we do?" said Chrissy, seemingly echoing her friend's thoughts.

Melissa was about to say as much when she noticed Robin Simmons, the owner of the Curves franchise, struggling with a large cardboard box as she pushed through the front door.

"Hey, ladies, a little help here?" asked Robin, balancing the box in her arms while trying to kick the door closed with her foot.

Melissa grabbed one end of the box, which said Dream Water Pro, while Chrissy closed the door behind them. Together, Melissa and Robin managed to get the box over to the counter despite the fact that it seemed to grow heavier by the second.

Melissa felt out of breath, and her arms ached. That biceps/triceps machine was definitely not doing its job.

"So, what have we got here?" asked Chrissy, staring at the box.

"A new smart water. Supposed to give you energy. Guy was by last week and talked me into it. UPS dropped off a case of twenty-four at my house this morning."

Melissa stared at the logo: a flying white owl in the middle of an orange and yellow infinity symbol. Below that were words that proclaimed the water would "make all your dreams and wishes come true."

"That's some advertising," she said, watching as Robin cut open the box.

"You two are my first customers," said the Curves owner, pulling two brightly colored plastic bottles out of the carton. "On the house."

"I'll take it," said Chrissy, snatching one of the bottles. She twisted off the cap and took a long drink. "Tastes...lemony, maybe? With a hint of grapefruit? I don't know. Not bad. I really worked up a sweat watching you two lug that box around, you know."

Melissa took the other bottle, but dropped it into her bag. "Thanks. I'll try it later," she said, her eyes on the big wall clock near the back of the gym. She had an appointment in an hour, and wanted to run home first to take a quick shower.

"Heavy date?" asked Chrissy, waggling her blonde eyebrows as she followed Melissa's gaze to the clock.

"Ha. I wish," she said, rolling her eyes. She and Rob hadn't had a date night in forever. "No, I have a parent-teacher conference for Megan at one and another for Timothy right after."

"Thanks again," Robin called after her as she made her way to the car, Chrissy behind her making the universal sign for 'call me' with her thumb and pinkie.

Melissa climbed into her blue Kia Sedona minivan, then turned Sirius XM radio to the smooth jazz channel. Sade's *The Sweetest Taboo* poured out from the speakers, and for some reason that made her think of Nikki and her string of affairs. She felt a pang of jealousy, and immediately felt guilty for it.

It wasn't that she wanted to have an affair. She was happily married. Well, happily enough, at least, and she knew Rob would never cheat on her. Still, she envied Nikki's ability to attract men and leave them drooling over her. And, truthfully, she missed the romance that she and Rob had had before the kids were born.

Melissa pulled out of the Curves parking lot, ostensibly heading home to take a shower, but she nevertheless found herself taking the long route, going well out of her way and down to 8th Street, near the section of seedy hotels that Chrissy had mentioned.

And there was Nikki's brand new red sports car, parked outside the Rogers Park 'n Stay. Wow. She just couldn't get enough, could she? Melissa wondered what poor sap she had reeled in this time, and had almost convinced herself to peek in a few windows when she noticed the shiny black SUV with silver trim parked at the very end of the lot.

She stared at the SUV, a GMC Yukon. It couldn't be Rob's, could it? No, he'd never cheat on her. Cars behind her began to honk, and she realized that she was parked in the middle of the road, blocking traffic.

Trembling, she pressed on the gas and accelerated past the hotel, pulling into the little Indian restaurant half a block away. She felt hot tears on her face, and instantly hated herself for jumping to conclusions. There was no way in hell that Rob would cheat on her. Was there? The SUV might not even belong to whoever Nikki was screwing this week.

She parked the minivan and turned off the car, letting herself out the door. Before she knew it, she was walking back to the motel. She knew it wasn't Rob's car—she *knew* it—but she also knew that she would always wonder if she didn't at least check.

Walking down the sidewalk, she passed a Mexican bakery and a little discount electronics shop before finally reaching the motel. The building's courtyard was in the shape of a "U," and so she walked around the far side, as far away from Nikki's car as possible, to stare at the SUV from across the parking lot.

The SUV's vanity license plate read: ROBSTOY. Rob's toy. Nikki's latest conquest was Rob, after all. She felt sick and threw up a little in her mouth as she felt her knees go weak. She leaned against the wall for support, feeling like her life was over.

It was bad enough that Rob was cheating on her, but why did it have to be with Nikki Melon? It had to have been Nikki who went after Rob, she decided, though that certainly didn't excuse the son of a bitch. Rob was a trophy to her, one final slap in the face to her fat former friend.

Melissa desperately wanted to kick in the door of their room and confront her cheating husband and his mistress, punching them both until her knuckles hurt, but she finally decided against it. She had to be smarter than that.

Instead, she stumbled back to her minivan in a daze, intent on retrieving the little camera she always kept in the glove compartment. She'd look in the window and snap a few photos, and then divorce his ass and take him for everything he owned.

Melissa let herself into the minivan, reaching for the water she'd been given at Curves to rinse the taste out of her mouth. She twisted the cap off and gray smoke began spewing from the bottle. What on Earth? Startled, she threw the bottle to the ground, and when the smoke cleared an instant later, she was no longer alone.

A dark-skinned man in a black suit sat in the passenger seat, smiling at her. She threw herself against the driver's side door, blinking her eyes. Nope, he was still there.

"Who are you, and how the hell did you get into my car?" she asked, heart pounding.

"My name is Juzam," he said, with an accent that she couldn't quite place, "and I am a Djinn. You have freed me from my prison, and, in accordance with tradition…"

"A Djinn? You mean, like a Genie? Oh, come on," she interrupted him. "What is this? Did Rob hire you? Or maybe I had an aneurism and am just imagining all this. Probably, with my luck."

She was babbling, but couldn't stop herself. On moment she was alone in her car, and the next this man was sitting next to her. This incredibly handsome man, she thought to herself, truly noticing him for the first time.

"As I was saying, you freed me from my prison, and, in accordance with tradition, you get a wish. However, there are certain conditions."

"Hold on a second," she said, for the moment putting aside the thought of an aneurism and why in the hell he'd been in a water bottle. "You said 'wish.' Don't Genies usually grant three wishes?"

"We used to, yes, but times have changed. Wishes are more expensive than they used to be, and we just don't have the funds. Now, if you'll quit interrupting me and let me finish, I'll explain further."

She folded her arms in front of her chest. If she was having a hallucination, she might as well go with it. "Please continue."

"In the past, we found that people often wasted their wish or wishes because they didn't take the time to truly think about it, and so, after much deliberation, we decided to place a condition on the wish.

You can wish for absolutely anything you want. Fame, fortune, longevity, anything. Whatever you ask for, I will grant. But the condition is this: whatever you wish for, 'o mistress, your best friend will get your wish halved, and your worst enemy will get it doubled."

She stared at him. "What kind of condition is that? That's insane. I can see rewarding my best friend, but why would I want to help my worst enemy?"

"Exactly," he said, smiling. "This is a wish you'll actually have to think through, and thus will not waste."

Thus? Who says thus?

Her first instinct was to wish for $1,000,000, but that meant that while Chrissy would get $500,000, that home-wrecking slut Nikki Melon would get $2,000,000. There was no way in hell that she was going to reward Nikki for sleeping with her husband.

She also thought about wishing that she'd get beaten half to death. That would mean Chrissy got roughed up pretty badly and Nikki was murdered, but, much as she wanted that bitch out of her life, she couldn't stomach the idea of hurting Chrissy or, let's face it, herself.

Damn it, why would Rob cheat on her anyway? She'd done everything for that man. She'd worked her tail off to help him get his Master's degree in business administration, and always made sure he had everything he wanted. Hell, his stupid Yukon was less than a year old, while she was driving a 2009 minivan.

She knew she wasn't perfect. She'd never been able to lose the weight after she'd had Timothy, but she was trying. And she never turned him down for sex, even when she didn't feel like it.

And then she had it.

"Come on," she said to Juzam, opening the car door and sliding out.

"But where are we going?" he said, following her out of the minivan.

"I'll make my wish when we get there," said Melissa, "but I have to see something with my own eyes first."

Just a few minutes later, they were standing in front of Nikki's red sports car, looking through the window of room number 26. Rob and Nikki lay in bed, sleeping, tangled in covers and each other's arms. Her stupid husband hadn't even thought to shut the curtains.

She felt tears pushing at her eyes but managed to hold them back. She told Juzam her wish, and he slowly smiled.

"Are you sure? With something like this, there's no going back."

"Oh, I'm sure," she said, eyes still on her sleeping husband and former best friend. "I want to lose sixty pounds, instantly. That is my wish."

"Then so shall it be," said the Djinn, snapping his fingers.

She watched through the window as Nikki, who just last week had reached her target of 119 pounds, disappeared. Rob just turned and rolled over, oblivious to it all. She had a feeling that Chrissy, wherever she was, was very happy right now, having immediately dropped 30 pounds of excess weight.

Melissa looked at her reflection in the mirror: damn, she looked good. Curves where curves ought to be, and no bulges. By the way Juzam was looking at her, she thought he noticed as well.

"You know," he said, raising his eyebrows, "technically, I have twenty-four hours before I have to be back in that bottle."

"Then go get in the car," she said, winking, as she tossed him the keys. "I'm gonna rock your world when I get you home, but first I need to make a phone call."

"Yes, 'o mistress," said Juzam, giving her a little half bow before turning to walk back to the minivan. "Just don't take too long. I've been cooped up in one bottle or another for centuries, and I'd really like the chance to stretch my legs before I have to go back inside again."

"Just give me a few minutes, and I'm all yours," she said, rolling her eyes.

She took out her cell phone, calling the school to cancel her parent/teacher conference. She never cancelled these things, so they'd get over it. And since it was a Friday, she made arrangements for both Megan and Timothy to spend the night with friends. Juzam had twenty-four hours, and she was going to make the most of it.

Her phone rang, startling her. It was Chrissy, undoubtedly calling to tell her about her unexpected thirty-pound weight loss. She smiled, then thumbed the phone to silent. She'd catch up with Chrissy later.

Melissa slipped the phone back into her purse before walking to the electronics store she'd seen earlier. Inside, she paid cash for a "pay as you go" telephone and a 100-minute phone card, then returned to her vehicle and the waiting Djinn.

He started to say something as she climbed into the minivan, but she silenced him with a finger to his lips. She broke the new phone out of its plastic and dialed 911.

"Hello, police?" she said, holding the phone away from her mouth in an effort to disguise her voice. "I think I just witnessed a murder. I'm outside this little motel on 8th street in Rogers, the Park 'n Stay I think it's called, and this tall man with black hair...I saw him strangle this woman. It was in room 26. She was skinny and had long, red hair. After she was dead, he threw her over his shoulder, dumped her in the back of a black SUV, and zoomed off."

She read Rob's license plate to the dispatcher, and then said, "Oh my God, he's back. He's back at the motel. I've got to go!" With that, she immediately hung up the phone.

"Nice," said the Djinn, smiling.

She wasn't sure whether the Rogers district attorney would be able to convict her soon-to-be ex-husband with no physical evidence of a crime, but he would certainly be arrested. If nothing else, the whole thing would inconvenience him for a long time to come and pretty much insure that she got everything in the divorce.

Melissa smiled back as she turned off the phone, removed the battery, and drove out of the Indian restaurant's parking lot. She'd drop the burner in the next dumpster she saw, and then she'd take Juzam home and get him out of that black business suit. Melissa had a lot of living to do now, and she didn't intend to waste a minute.

Smoke (A Small Things Story)

May 4, 1979

Smoke hung dense in the air, obscuring sight and assaulting the lungs of those hanging back, too afraid or too curious to run away. Flames licked through the windows, and the stench of burning wood and plastic filled Jacob Wang's nostrils.

He couldn't believe it. Ruskin's Pizzeria was going up in smoke, and it was all his fault. It wasn't intentional, of course, and he never could have predicted what happened, but it was still his fault. Worse yet, his sister seemed to be insisting on taking the blame.

"I'm so sorry, Mr. Ruskin," said Lisa Wang. "If I forgot to turn something off, I'll never forgive myself."

Lisa had been waitressing at Ruskin's for almost two years. She'd closed up last night, and was afraid that she'd left the oven on or done something else to cause the fire. Of course, she hadn't done anything of the sort. Jacob wished he could tell her the truth.

The building had old wiring, Mr. Ruskin said, and he suspected that was probably the culprit. He was sure that Lisa had nothing to do with it. He trusted her. The old man put his arm around her shoulder and gave her a gentle hug. Jacob was glad that Lisa had Ruskin in her life, looking out for her in ways that Jacob unfortunately could not.

The crowd was finally starting to disperse now that the Carthage Fire Department had the blaze under control. People enjoyed a good show, even when it came at their neighbor's expense.

Lisa started coughing, so Ruskin took her by the arm and led her across the street and away from the fire, where Jacob followed. They watched for another ten minutes as the firefighters worked to put out the fire, finally extinguishing it altogether. The restaurant was ruined. The south wall had caved in, and the entire area was covered in soot.

He hoped that something could be salvaged from the mess, but it didn't look very promising.

"Fred," said one of the firefighters, a tall, carrot-haired man named Frank, who had crossed the street to talk to them, "we need to get Artie down here to confirm it, but I'm sorry to say that your fire looks like arson."

"Arson!" Lisa said. "Who would do such a thing?"

Jacob wished that Mr. Ruskin's niece, Jenny McGee, and her boyfriend, Shawn Spencer were here, but they were both finishing up their first year of college at Western Illinois University in Macomb. Macomb was less than thirty miles from Carthage, but Jacob couldn't travel that far on his own. Heck, he wasn't even supposed to know about Shawn's magic.

Besides that, every time Shawn used the talisman, he risked attracting the attention of those searching for it. That had already happened three times that Jacob knew about, and he didn't want to put them in danger a fourth time. No, this was definitely something he'd have to handle himself. The fire proved that. Trying to ask Lisa for help hadn't worked out so well, and he couldn't risk anyone else getting hurt.

"It looks like it was started in the bathroom," said Frank, "with a bunch of menus, of all things. Not sure what they used for an accelerant, though."

"Frank, are you sure?"

"Well, like I said, Artie will need to investigate, but I'm pretty sure, yeah. Did you have insurance?"

"Of course I had insurance, Frank," Ruskin said. "Are you trying to insinuate something?"

At well over six feet in height and built like a grizzly bear, Ruskin struck an intimidating figure, even at 55 years old. Frank backed away, hands held out in front of him.

"Jesus, Fred, not at all. You loved that restaurant, and there's no way in hell you'd burn it down. But if it was arson, you'll have a devil of a time getting insurance to cover it, at least until we prove it wasn't you."

"Sorry, Frank," Ruskin said, "I'm just not in a good place right now."

"I understand, believe me. But we'll get to the bottom of this. Artie is good. If I'm right and it was arson, he'll know what to do next."

"Oh, Fred," said Candy Ruskin, running past Jacob to throw herself into her husband's arms. "I'm so sorry."

"It'll be okay," Ruskin said. "We'll rebuild it. We have to."

Lisa walked away from the Ruskins to stare at the ruined building, and Jacob followed her, as he always seemed to be doing. They were, after all, twins. He reached out to take her hand, but she shivered and pulled away.

Jacob missed holding his sister's hand. It had been ten years since Jacob died, and he missed a lot of things. He sighed as he thought about Moss Ridge Cemetery, the place where he was buried, and vanished.

"I think I might've left the stove on," said Maribel, an elderly ghost wearing a gray prairie skirt, to her husband Walt. "Maybe we'd better go back and check."

"Nonsense," said Walt, dressed in black slacks and a collared shirt. "I don't want to be late for Bingo again, do you?"

"I suppose not, dear."

Jacob smiled at the couple, but they didn't smile back. They didn't even see him, really. They were in their own little world, and had been for at least the last ten years, when, at the ripe old age of ten, Jacob had joined them in the cemetery.

It was strange. Many of the ghosts, like Walt and Maribel, didn't even seem to realize they were dead and just repeated conversations from their life over and over, while a handful were like Jacob and remembered all too well that they were dead. More still were asleep underground, where they'd been buried. Even counting those, there weren't enough ghosts here to account for the number of headstones. Some seemed to have moved on, though whether to heaven or somewhere else Jacob hadn't a clue.

Even Margaret, the wisest ghost he'd ever met, didn't seem to know what happened when a ghost went missing. It was a little scary, if he were to admit it, and he had no plan to find out where they went when they moved on anytime soon. He needed to watch out for Lisa and his big sister Maya, not to mention their parents. Just because he was dead didn't mean he couldn't be a good brother and son to his family.

"How are you doing this morning, Jacob?" said Margaret's voice from behind him, startling Jacob. He whirled around to face the ghost.

"Don't do that," he said. "I almost had a heart attack. Well, if I had a heart."

Margaret smiled. "Oh, you do have a heart, insomuch as anyone does, and yours is three times larger than most."

"Yeah, tell that to my sister. Or your husband. His restaurant burned down this morning, and it's all my fault."

"He'll rebuild it," she said, "and make it better. Lisa will be okay as well. She has a long and happy life ahead of her, as does Maya."

Unlike the rest of the spirits, Margaret Ruskin seemed to be somehow tied into the future. He didn't understand it, and she'd avoided his questions the few times he'd quizzed her about her knowledge. She let very little slip about incidents yet to unfold, but whatever she did share was always unerringly accurate.

"I still feel bad. I was being selfish. It took me all night to move some menus into the bathroom. I had a bottle of Elmer's Glue I'd found in the store room, and I wanted to use some of the words in the menu to glue a message on to the mirror. It was working, too, until *he* showed up. It was a silly idea."

"Ill-advised, perhaps, but not silly."

Huey and Marvin showed up just then, playing hide-and-seek.

"Have you seen Robbie?" Huey asked Jacob, as Marvin ducked his head through a tree.

Like Jacob, Huey, Marvin, and Robbie had all been between ten and twelve years old when they died. They had mentally stayed that age, however, while Jacob seemed to progress mentally, if not physically, as the years moved on. No one had any idea why, not even Margaret, though Jacob suspected that it might have something to do with his twin sister Lisa.

Huey had died from the flu in the early 1920's, Marvin drowned in the Carthage Lake in 1933, and Robbie was murdered by his father in 1952. The three were great friends, and they spent the afterlife playing hide-and-seek, tag, and other children's games. Jacob played with them for a while, for a few months after his death, but quickly grew tired of the monotony. After all, there were only so many good hiding spots in a cemetery.

"Sorry, guys," Jacob finally said, shaking his head. "Maybe try over by that big oak tree."

"Thanks, pal," said Huey, as he and Marvin dashed off to the south side of the graveyard.

"Do you ever miss playing with them?" asked Margaret.

"A little," he admitted, "but not so much. I'd rather hang out with you."

Margaret smiled, and Jacob would have felt himself flush had he been alive. He had a huge crush on Margaret, and he knew that she knew, but even so they both pretended to be oblivious to that fact. It was probably for the best, anyway. He had the ectomorphic body of a child, while she would always be devoted to her widower. The afterlife was complicated.

He was grateful not to be stuck in time like his ghostly brethren, but was sick to death (pun intended) of looking like a child when he felt like anything but. Maybe if he didn't look like a little kid he might have a chance with Margaret, but it wasn't something he could change.

"I'm gonna go check on Maya," he finally said, willing himself to Carthage Memorial Hospital, where his big sister worked.

He vanished from the cemetery and reappeared half a second later in the hospital, next to Maya, who was pushing an elderly man in a wheelchair through the hospital.

"Did you feel that?" Maya asked her patient, pausing to scan the hallway.

"Feel what?" he responded, looking up at her with rheumy eyes. "I didn't feel anything."

"Just a breeze or something, I guess," she said, looking down both ends of the hallway one last time before once again pushing her patient toward radiology.

Jacob followed Maya to the radiology room, where she handed her patient off to an attractive nurse whose name tag identified her as Vanessa Wages, RN. She followed Wages and the patient into the room, made sure he was settled, and then set off for the nurse's station.

It was like this much of the time when he visited Maya at work. She went from room to room, checking on patients, taking them for x-rays, wheeling them to physical therapy, and dispensing medicine to them. Jacob remembered that Maya had always wanted to be a nurse and was proud of her for following her dreams, but, boy, did the job seem boring.

Lisa had gone to nursing school for a while but dropped out, instead taking on full-time hours at Ruskin's. Jacob wondered for a moment what she'd do now that the restaurant was destroyed, but then shoved it out of his mind.

It was apparently time for Maya's break, as she wound through the halls of the hospital and eventually sat down at a table by herself in the cafeteria. Jacob hovered nearby, watching her take sips from a can of RC Cola through a straw as she read a library copy of a hardback novel called *The Stand* by Stephen King.

Maya had gotten married a year or so ago, to Noah Delacroix, a man she'd dated on and off throughout high school and nursing school. Jacob learned these things by osmosis, by eavesdropping on his family, but it still made him sad that he'd missed so much of his siblings' lives. He wished not for the first time that he'd just let that damned astronaut helmet go.

Ten Years Ago

Jacob and Lisa were standing in the back of Daniel's Treasures, an old thrift store on the east side of the town square that occupied the middle of Carthage, looking through shelves filled with bins holding used toys. Lisa had found yet another Barbie that she wanted, while Jacob held a *Man from U.n.c.l.e* action figure in his hand. It was Illya Kuryakin, the same one he'd lost at the Carthage Lake last year, only missing his gun. It would be nice to finally have a replacement.

He and his sister had each received a brand-new, crisp ten dollar bill from Grandmother Haya a month ago, for their tenth birthday. Lisa had already spent most of hers, but Jacob still had eight dollars left. Illya was just a quarter, so he would still have plenty left over for ice cream at Tastee Freez after.

"Are you sure you want that?" Jacob asked, indicating the Barbie. "Her hair is pretty ratty, you know."

"I can comb it out, and she'll be just fine. What do you care?"

"Just looking out for my little sister," he said, grinning. He was, after all, five minutes older than her.

She stuck her tongue out at him. "What about your dolls? That guy is stupid. I don't even like that show."

"It's not a doll, it's an action figure. And you're stupid."

"Not as stupid as you are!"

"At least I don't play with Barbies!"

It went back and forth like that for a few minutes, before both of them tired of the needling and went back to digging through toys.

"It's probably about time to go," Lisa finally said, staring down at her Minnie Mouse wristwatch. "Mommy said ten minutes, and it's been fifteen. She and Maya are probably done at Royalty's by now."

Royalty's was a clothing store, and Jacob didn't want any part of it. Clothes were boring. Thankfully, Maya had talked Mom into letting the twins take a detour through the thrift shop while they shopped for Maya's prom dress.

"Just a few more minutes," he muttered, pulling a blond-haired G.I. Joe out of one of the bins. It was dressed in an astronaut suit and even had the helmet. Another twenty-five cents well spent.

"Come on, Jacob!"

"You go on. I'll catch up in a minute."

"But Mommy said we need to stick together," said Lisa, stomping her foot.

Jacob sighed. "Okay, maybe we can come back later."

They made their way to the register at the front, where a tall, lanky man with dark hair sat on a wooden stool. His nametag identified him simply as "Dan."

"You two ready to check out?" he asked. "It's about time to close up shop."

Lisa paid for her Barbie, then waited by the counter as Jacob dug out a one dollar bill from the Cowboy-style wallet he carried and handed it over to Dan. The clerk punched some numbers into the register and handed him back 46 cents. Jacob hated tax. It made things too confusing, and you never knew how much money you could spend without calculating the tax first, something he was loathe to do.

"Thank you, sir," Jacob said, as he walked with Lisa out of the store.

As it turned out, they could have spent another twenty minutes in Daniel's Treasures. When they arrived at Royalty's, Maya was still trying on dresses. She was on her fifth dress by then, and still wasn't satisfied.

"Told you so," Jacob said to his twin, who thumbed her nose at him in response.

After what seemed like an eternity, Maya was finally done. She'd decided on a long, pink monstrosity that made her look like an elongated piece of chewed-up bubble gum. Of course, Lisa loved the dress. Girls.

"So, what did you two find?" Mommy asked Jacob and Lisa, as they were walking to the car.

Lisa pulled her Barbie out from the paper bag Dan from the thrift store had given her, proudly displaying it for all to see. Maya and their mother oohed and aahed over the doll, while Jacob just rolled his eyes.

"How about you, Jacob?" Maya finally asked.

Jacob proudly pulled Illya Kuryakin out from his bag, followed by the astronaut, holding both up in the afternoon light.

"Isn't that like the one you lost at the lake?" Maya asked, surprising him that she remembered.

"Sure is," Jacob said, beaming. It had been almost a year since that day at the lake, and it was nice to finally have a replacement for Illya.

"This other one is nice, too," said Mommy, her Japanese accent adding a lilt to her words. "Who is he supposed to be?"

"A G.I. Joe astronaut," Jacob said, waving the figure at his mother. "See? He even has his—"

His words trailed off. The helmet! Where was the astronaut's helmet? He immediately tore into the bag, but the helmet wasn't there. He started back toward Royalty's, but remembered he hadn't removed the action figures since Dan had stuffed them in the bag.

"What's wrong, Jacob?" Maya asked, frowning.

"His helmet," Jacob said, feeling a panic deep in his stomach. "He had his helmet, that's why I bought him, but now it's gone. It's gone!"

"Don't worry, Jacob," Mommy said, laying her hand on his shoulder. "We'll find you another helmet."

"No," he yelled, shrugging away, "he needs his helmet! I must have dropped it in the store."

He turned to look at Daniel's Treasures only to see that someone, presumably Dan, had flipped the "Open" sign to "Sorry, we're closed." He remembered the clerk saying that he was about to close the store. Now he'd never find the helmet!

Maya saw the sign, too, for she said, "It's no big deal, little brother. We'll come back tomorrow, first thing, and I'll help you look for it. I'll drive you myself, if it's okay with Mom."

Mommy nodded. "That's just fine. Now, it is getting late. We'd better get to Tastee Freez before it closes, too, and before your father gets home from work."

"It'll be gone by then," Jacob said, his heart racing. "It'll get lost."

Jacob pulled away from his family, running toward Daniel's Treasures. He started banging on the door, tears in his eyes, ignoring his mother yelling for him to come back, to get in the car this instant, young man. Lisa was sticking her tongue out at him, holding something up in the air for him to see, but he couldn't quite make out what it was.

He yanked the handle and the door flew open. The store might've been closed, and the lights were off, but no one had bothered to lock the door.

Jacob barreled into the store, instantly creeped out by the shadows that danced across the floor and aisles. He smelled something sharp and acidic, but ignored it, intent on finding the astronaut's lost helmet. It wasn't near the entrance, nor the cash register. He retraced his path down the aisle toward the toys, as the store grew darker around him.

And then things got a whole lot brighter. An orange glow filled the store, and Jacob realized it was getting hotter. Abandoning the astronaut helmet, he turned back toward the front of the store only to be met by a wall of flame. The store was on fire!

"Mommy," he yelled out, "help! Maya, help!"

"Oh Jesus Christ," said a voice from deeper into the store. "Who's in here?"

A man appeared, holding a handful of newspapers. Smoke filled the air around him, and Jacob couldn't make out the man's face. He backed away, stumbling against a shelf filled with toy trucks and bulldozers, knocking some of the toys to the floor.

"Leave me alone," Jacob whispered, trying to see through the smoke. "Please, don't hurt me."

The man dropped the can and reached through the smoke for Jacob. He loomed closer, and the boy saw that he was wearing a black ski mask. His fingers closed around Jacob's arm...

...And that's the last thing Jacob Wang remembered about that day. He knew that he had died in the fire, and later found out from listening to snippets of conversation between Maya and his mother that the owner, Dan, had perished there as well. However, he never learned who the man in the ski mask was, or why he'd torched the store. There was only so much information available in the cemetery, after all, and it had taken him nearly three years before he'd even learned how to leave the grounds, much less travel around town.

Once he realized Dan was also dead, he'd searched the graveyard and found the man's plot, but Dan's ghost was nowhere to be found. He had put the mystery of his own death out of his head until about a week ago, when the arsonist showed up at the cemetery. Or, rather, the ghost of the arsonist showed up. Apparently, he had also died in the fire, or maybe sometime after, since he'd never heard Maya, Lisa, or his mother speak of a third body found in the remains of Daniel's Treasures.

Jacob had been talking to Huey when a glowing orange light showed up on the periphery of his vision. He spun on his heels to see the shape of a ghost bathed in flames staring at him, its hands clenched in fiery fists.

"You!" the ghost yelled, pointing at him.

Jacob stared for a moment, uncomprehending, and then remembered the hand reaching through the darkness of the burning store, grasping his arm. It was the same man.

The ghost ran at Jacob and Jacob instinctively sped away, ducking behind trees and phasing through tombstones, running the perimeter of the graveyard until he finally remembered that he could leave the confines of the area. In an instant he appeared beside Lisa in her little apartment, where she was watching *The Twilight Zone* reruns on late night television.

It only took the ghost two more encounters to learn to follow Jacob, but, thankfully, it didn't follow him that night. Scared and confused, Jacob stayed with Lisa until an hour later, two *Zones* worth, when she finally padded off to bed.

Maya closed her book and drained the last of her RC Cola, bringing Jacob back to the present. Apparently, break time was over. He watched as his big sister rose from the little table in the cafeteria, disposed of her trash, and disappeared down the halls of Carthage Memorial Hospital.

Jacob willed himself to his father, who was busy filling a prescription at McHugh Drug Store on the square, where he worked as a pharmacist. Blood pressure medicine for Henry Spencer, Shawn's father. Time marched on, and everyone got older—everyone, that is, except for Jacob and the gang of ghosts at Moss Ridge cemetery.

He moved to the next person on his rounds, his mother, and found her sitting at the large oak table in the dining room, weeping. He was by her side in an instant, wanting to console her, to find out what was wrong, frustrated that he couldn't. Much like Maya and Lisa, his parents could sometimes feel his presence, but they never seemed to realize that it was him.

She had a scrapbook open, the one that was devoted solely to Jacob, and it was turned to the *Hancock Journal-Pilot* newspaper article about his death. The paper was dated May 7th, 1969, but the fire had happened on May the 4th, three days earlier. The paper only came out on Wednesdays, so it had to wait three extra days before reporting the news.

Maybe the fire at Ruskin's Pizzeria had prompted her to take out the old scrapbook, because she usually only drug it out of storage on his birthday and the date he died. A thought struck him and he whirled to look at the Marine Bank giveaway calendar that always hung on the wall beside the entryway that led to the kitchen. Today was Friday, May the 4th, 1979, ten years to the day of his death. He knew the date was coming up, but hadn't been aware it was here already. The fire at the restaurant where Lisa worked must have brought it all back full circle for his mother.

"Oh, Mom, I'm so, so sorry," he whispered into her ear, knowing that she couldn't hear him. "I never wanted to leave you, but I'm still here. I love you, Mommy."

He placed a phantom hand on her cheek, and, by sheer coincidence or divine intervention, she placed her own hand over his, and for a moment they touched, even if she'd never know it.

"Oh, Jacob," she said, startling him.

"Yes, Mommy, I'm here! I'm always here."

"I miss you so much, my son," she said, talking over him, pulling away to bury her head in her hands. "I love you, Jacob. Please watch over your twin, and keep her out of trouble. She needs you now more than ever."

"I will, Mom," he said, disappointed that she hadn't felt him, after all. "I always do."

He vanished, reappearing in Lisa's apartment almost instantaneously. Lisa had company, a red-haired young woman dressed in a blue blouse and floral print skirt. It was Ruskin's niece, Jenny McGee! Jacob now knew the weekend was approaching, so maybe she was home for that, or had come back once she heard about the restaurant. Shawn couldn't be too far behind.

The two women were holding hands, and Jacob could see that Lisa had been crying. Her mascara was running, framing her eyes in black.

"Of all days for this to happen," said Lisa, somewhere between a laugh and a sob. "Watching the restaurant burn down just brought it all back. My brother. My fucking twin! Gone, all because of me."

Because of her? His death wasn't her fault, not even slightly. What was she talking about? It was him that ran blindly into a closed store for a stupid toy helmet, not her.

"It's okay," said Jenny, squeezing Lisa's hand. "Fred will rebuild. The insurance stuff will get worked out. This is nothing more than a coincidence. Bad timing, that's all. And you had no way of knowing the store would catch fire. It wasn't your fault, not really."

"I know," Lisa finally said, "but that doesn't make it hurt any less."

Jacob remembered now that he, Lisa, and Shawn had all been in the same class growing up, along with Jenny's brother Tanner, with Jenny a year behind them. Jacob had been in fourth grade when he died. It's amazing the things that ghosts forget, though he'd thought himself mostly immune to the paranormal amnesia that seemed to affect most of his friends at Moss Ridge.

But what was this about his death being her fault? The last thing that he remembered was her watching him run helter-skelter into the building, her tongue stuck out, holding something up in the air for him to see. What was it she was showing him? He couldn't remember, wasn't sure he even recognized it in the first place.

Jacob turned to stare at the poster on the wall, to the left of the little couch where the girls sat. It was for a science fiction movie called *Star Wars*, and showed various characters from the movie. In the middle, it said, "May the force be with you." Anytime he came to Lisa's apartment, he always wondered exactly what the movie was about. He'd missed out on a lot since his death. After all, there was no cable television or movie theaters in the afterlife.

"You!" screamed a voice behind him, causing him to jump. "You did this! You burned me alive!"

Jacob turned on his heels. It was the fiery ghost from the cemetery, still dressed in the black ski mask from ten years ago.

"What are you talking about?" he said, fighting the urge to run. "You set the store on fire, not me. You burned *me* alive!"

The flaming phantom stared at him, uncomprehending. It began to shake its head violently back and forth, hands covering its ears. "No, no, no! Stop lying!

"I'm not lying," he said, positioning himself between the still-oblivious women and the ghost. "You burned the store down, and you killed me and the owner."

The ghost recoiled at Jacob's words, jutting out his hand in front of him. A wall of fire appeared, moving quickly through Jacob and toward the girls.

"Jesus, what is that?" shrieked Jenny, grabbing Lisa and rolling to the floor just as the blast of flame hit the couch they'd been sitting on.

The furniture burst into flame, engulfing the couch in an instant, flames licking at the curtains behind it Jacob ran at the ghost, tried to tackle it, but of course just passed right through, tumbling halfway through the wall that separated the living room from Lisa's bedroom in the small apartment.

Lisa was up and running through the living room and into the kitchen, returning with a small red fire extinguisher. She ran past Jenny, who stood staring at the flames, and opened the nozzle, spraying the couch and curtains with fluffy clouds of carbon dioxide, putting the fire out in an instant.

Jacob wanted to stay to make sure the girls were all right, but knew he couldn't risk another fire. "Catch me if you can," he yelled at the ghost of the arsonist, as he disappeared and reappeared in the cemetery.

The ghost appeared beside him, but Jacob disappeared again, reappearing at the high school Lisa, Jenny, and Shawn had all graduated from a couple of years ago. It went on like that for a while, Jacob leading the fire spirit on a chase throughout the small Midwestern town of Carthage, Illinois, until finally, thankfully, the ghost either lost the trail or gave up.

Jacob looked around. He stood in a laundromat, and what used to be Daniel's Treasures, the place where he had lost his life. Ironically, it was the one place that the ghost didn't seem to want to visit. He collapsed to the floor, spent, drained of energy for the moment. Why was this happening to him, and why now, after all this time?

He sat on the floor like that for a while, ignoring the laundromat's customers as they walked from washer to dryer carrying basketfuls of clothing, boxes of detergent, and handfuls of change to feed the machines. He had to figure out a way to lose this spirit, lest he put his family and friends in anymore danger. Margaret couldn't help, and none of the other spirits in Moss Ridge seemed to even acknowledge the problem.

He was going to have to go with his original plan, after all, the one that had led to the fire at Ruskin's Pizzeria. He needed to finally make contact with Lisa, and, through her, with Shawn. That magical nickel that he kept hidden beneath a loose floorboard in his room at his parents' house in Carthage had gotten Shawn out of almost as many jams as it had gotten him into. Surely, the boy could use it to help out an old friend, even if that old friend was long dead and buried.

Satisfied that the spirit wouldn't be after him again for a while, he concentrated on Lisa and willed himself back to his twin sister's apartment. What he found was a very different scene than the one he'd left ten minutes earlier.

Lisa and Jenny were still there, standing in the living room opposite the blackened couch, but Fred Ruskin and Shawn Spencer had joined them. Shawn had a dim, blue glow around him, which probably meant that he had the nickel. That glow had almost blinded him when, a couple of years ago, right after Ruskin's Pizzeria had opened, Shawn encountered his time-traveling son from the future, who had brought back his version of the nickel with him.

"Two fires in the same day can't be a coincidence," said Ruskin, starting at the couch, "especially not with the way you said this one started."

"It just came at us out of nowhere," Lisa said, her voice shaking. "If Jenny hadn't pulled me out of the way, I'd be as charred as my poor thrift store couch and that *Star Wars* poster. I got that from an old *Dynamite* magazine, you know. I'll miss it more than I will the couch. It's all just so strange." She squeezed Jenny's hand, and the red-haired girl returned the gesture.

"Definitely strange," agreed Shawn, kneeling beside the couch, "and definitely supernatural."

Jacob stood between Shawn and the burned furniture, yelling and jumping up and down, to no avail. He'd hoped that the talisman might somehow enable his old friend to see him, but apparently not. He concentrated, using one of the tricks he'd learned over the years, and caused the temperature in the room to drop a few degrees.

"Wow, it's getting cold in here," said Jenny, hugging herself. "That's kind of weird."

Ruskin shrugged, and went back to studying the couch. Shawn looked around the room for a few seconds, but still didn't see Jacob. This was frustrating.

Remembering what he tried to do with the menus in the pizzeria this morning, Jacob moved to the coffee table that sat between the burned couch and the little color television that stood against the opposite wall, staring at a small stack of magazines on top.

Concentrating harder than he ever had before, reaching out a ghostly hand, he managed to push the top magazine—a *TV Guide*—closer and closer to the edge of the coffee table. Finally, it teetered and fell off the wood veneer coffee table, landing on Jenny's foot.

Jenny bent over, picked up the issue of *TV Guide*, and sat it back on top of the stack of magazines. This wasn't working, and it was making Jacob angry. He punched a fist uselessly through the wall, kicked at the destroyed couch, and screamed at the top of his lungs.

Shawn stood stock still. "Did you hear something?"

No one else had, but, then again, no one else had the nickel. Jacob screamed even louder, getting angrier now, and finally kicked the coffee table. His foot flew through the wood but sent the magazines scattering off the table, causing Jenny and Lisa to jump back.

"Something's here," said Shawn, immediately thrusting his hand into his pocket to retrieve the old Buffalo head nickel.

Jacob stopped his tantrum, and instead waved his arms in front of Shawn's face. No response, but Shawn's blue glow grew brighter. He watched as Shawn grasped the nickel tightly in the palm of his hand, his eyes growing darker and darker until they were almost pitch black.

"Can you see me?" asked Jacob, hoping with everything in him that this was working.

Shawn stared right through him, blinked, and then their eyes met. "Jacob, is that you?"

"Jacob?" asked Lisa, eyes wide.

"Shh!" Shawn admonished her, holding up a hand.

"It's me, old friend," said Jacob, ghostly tears running down his cheeks. Finally, someone who wasn't Margaret Ruskin could see him. "I'm in trouble, and you've got to help me."

"What's going on?" asked Shawn.

Lisa misinterpreted the question, and said, "How should I know, Shawn? You tell us!"

In response, Shawn reached out and took her hand. Lisa startled for a second, and then relaxed as her pupils also faded to black. Her other hand shot up and grabbed her mouth as she laid eyes on her dead twin brother.

"Oh my God, Jacob," she said between her fingers. "This can't be real. Is this real? Jacob, is that you? You look just like you did when you…when you…"

"It's me, Lisa," he said, wanting more than anything to hug her. He reached a trembling hand toward his sister, but then let it fall to his side. He knew this was all he could have, and it was enough. "I love you."

"I'm so sorry, Jacob," she whispered, eyes filling with tears. "I miss you so much. So, so much. I love you, brother!"

"So why have you come back?" Shawn said, taking control of the conversation.

That was a good thing. Jacob didn't know how long he had before the arsonist once again tracked him down.

"I'm in trouble," he repeated, "and so are you. It's my fault Mr. Ruskin's restaurant burned down, and your old couch, that's on me, too."

Jenny gently pried Lisa's hand from her mouth, grasping it in her own. Her eyes, too, took on a darkness that mirrored Shawn's, and Jacob could tell that she could see him now as well. Taking the hint, Ruskin laid a massive hand on Shawn's shoulder, joining the makeshift séance.

"But how? And why?"

"The guy that started the fire that killed me," Jacob said. "He's dead, too, now. I think he died in the fire. I was at Mr. Ruskin's restaurant trying to leave a message for Lisa, and he found me and started the fire. And then earlier, I was here with you and Jenny, and he showed up and tried to fry me again. He got your couch instead."

Lisa stared at him. "There were only two bodies in the fire, Jacob. You and the guy that owned the store, Daniel Jennings. No one knows how the fire started, but it wasn't arson."

"It was arson. Lisa, I saw it with my own two eyes. I ran into the store looking for that stupid astronaut helmet I'd dropped and there was a man in there wearing a ski mask. He had a bunch of crushed up newspapers in his hand, and there were flames all around us. He dropped the newspapers and grabbed me, and the next thing I know I'm wandering around Moss Ridge cemetery, confused and lost, not to mention a ghost."

Lisa started crying harder, and Jenny hugged her. "You need to tell him," she whispered to Lisa. "After all these years, your chance is finally here."

"Tell me what?" asked Jacob, confused.

"I'm so sorry, Jacob. If I could take it all back, I would, in an instant. I was such a little bitch."

"What are you talking about?"

"I'll be right back," she said, disengaging from Shawn and Jenny and retreating to her bedroom.

She returned a few seconds later, head hanging low, holding something in her hand. Jenny was holding hands with Shawn, so she placed one trembling hand on Jenny's shoulder and then opened her other hand to reveal the long-lost astronaut helmet.

"You found it?" Jacob asked, startled. "But how?"

"I had it all along," she whispered, not meeting his eyes. "You were making fun of my Barbie, remember? I swiped it while you were getting money out of your wallet to pay for your dolls. Your action figures, I mean. It's my fault that you're dead, Jacob. It's all my fault, and I'm so sorry."

Jacob stared at her for a second, and then began to laugh. He couldn't find the damned thing because it wasn't in the store to begin with. It all made sense now, and it was priceless. After ten long years of wondering what happened to that silly helmet, it all made sense.

"So you don't hate me?" she asked, for the first time her once-again dark eyes finding his own.

"Why would I hate you? I was being a brat, Lisa, and you were just playing a prank, like we always did to each other. You had no way of knowing that someone was going to burn down the store, or even that I was going to run back in to begin with. It's not your fault."

She was crying hard now, hiccoughing into her sleeve. "So you forgive me?" She let the helmet fall from her fingers, were it bounced against the blue Berber carpet that covered the apartment floor.

"There's nothing to forgive, Lisa, but, sure, I forgive you. Death isn't so bad, especially now that I've figured out how to talk to my favorite twin sister."

"I've been depressed ever since it happened, Jacob. I've tried to commit suicide twice," she said, eyes still locked with her brother's. "On our eleventh birthday, and once again when I was fourteen. I went to nursing school for a while, but then dropped out. I've been so useless without you. I felt so guilty, and I missed you so much."

This time he did reach out to her, touching her cheek with his fingers. Her hand closed over his own and, for an instant, he could almost feel her touch. He sighed and pulled away.

"Don't be sad, little sister. A good friend of mine says you'll live a long and happy life. She's yet to be wrong, so I'm glad you didn't manage to kill yourself."

"A friend?" she asked, eyes growing wide.

Jacob glanced at Fred Ruskin, and decided not to bring up Margaret. He knew that she and Ruskin had briefly communicated a few years ago, when the former sheriff was nearly killed during a battle in the cemetery, but Jacob didn't want to say anything else without talking to Margaret first. Instead, he just said, "Yes, even ghosts have friends," smiled, and left it at that.

"So, how can we help you?" Shawn asked. "I mean, with this ghost that's been chasing you."

As if on cue, the fiery spirit reappeared, standing beside Jacob. It reached for his arm, but of course went right through him. "You!" it yelled, stumbling at him. "You did this! You burned me alive!"

Those were the exact same words it had said to him earlier in the apartment. It was like the ghost was a vinyl record player and was skipping, playing the same groove over and over.

Lisa screamed and leaped backward, pulling Jenny with her, breaking the connection. Both their eyes returned to normal. Shawn raised his hand just as the ghost reared back to shoot a massive ball of fire at Jacob. Blue energy shot from Shawn's fist to engulf the fireball, snuffing it out.

"Meet me at the dam on the lake in two hours!" shouted Jacob, before vanishing and leading the arsonist on another wild goose through town.

Jacob flickered to the yard in front of the Spencer Heights apartment building on Randolph Street, and then to the rock in the middle of the Carthage square where Abraham Lincoln once stood. After that, he teleported behind the Old Carthage Jail, to the hospital, to Moss Ridge cemetery, to his father's side at McHugh's Pharmacy, and back to the laundromat that used to be Daniel's Treasures before finally losing the spirit. This was getting harder or the spirit was getting better at keeping up. Whatever the case, he was exhausted. He crumbled to the floor, fighting the urge to sleep, thinking he would give just about anything right now for an alarm clock.

Jacob appeared beside the dam at Carthage Lake, near the spot where, a few years ago, Jenny McGee's brother Tanner had drowned. He scanned the area, found Lisa, Shawn, Jenny, and Mr. Ruskin waiting for him.

"There he is!" yelled Shawn, pointing at Jacob.

Jacob floated over to them as they all linked hands so they could see him.

"I was so worried," Lisa said, her face tense. "Where were you?"

It'd happened again, hadn't it? Of course it had. "What time is it?"

"Almost two in the afternoon. You disappeared from your sister's apartment almost four hours ago," said Jenny.

"It isn't always easy for us to keep time," he said. "Sorry about that."

"It's okay," said Shawn. "I had a little time to go through the microfiche at the library before we headed here, and—"

"You!" screamed the ghost made of fire, appearing just behind Jacob, interrupting Shawn. "You did this! You burned me—"

"No, Daniel Jennings," interrupted Shawn, "he didn't."

The ghost turned to Shawn, his tirade seemingly forgotten for the moment. "You…what did you say?"

"Your name is Daniel Jennings. You owned Daniel's Treasures," said Shawn, "and you burned it down."

Jacob stared at Shawn. "Wait a minute. The arsonist killed me and Dan. How can the arsonist *be* Dan?"

"Why don't you tell him," Shawn said, looking at the flaming ghost.

His flames muted a little, growing dimmer, and the man beneath the fire became easier to see. Jacob had to admit, it did look like the clerk he remembered from that fateful day ten years ago. He focused on the man's shirt, finding a name tag. It read, simply, "Dan."

"But why would you do that?" Jacob asked.

"I don't…oh God, I think it's true. You didn't burn me to death, I burned you to death." The ghost fell to his knees, shaking his head. "All this time, I thought it was you."

"It's okay," Jacob said quietly, walking over to the fallen spirit. "Tell me what you remember."

"Daniel's Treasures had been my dream. I was so hopeful when I opened the store, but a year and a half later I was two months behind on my rent, my wife was getting ready to leave me, and I was losing my shirt. I was at my wit's end, and I didn't know what to do."

"So you burned down your store," Fred Ruskin prompted him, and the spirit nodded. "For the insurance money."

"I think I did. I must have. I remember closing the store and spreading newspapers everywhere, and lighting the fire. And then I heard a voice."

"That voice was me," said Jacob, remembering. "You came out of the flame, and you had that mask on. You grabbed my arm and I thought you were trying to hurt me, but I think maybe you were trying to save me instead."

The ghost, nearly flame-free now, pulled off the ski mask. It was indeed Daniel Jennings, better known to Jacob as Dan, the clerk who'd sold him the action figures.

"I was walking out the back door into the alley when I heard you. I almost had a heart attack. I'd forgotten to lock the front door! It was bad enough I was burning down my own store, I couldn't let anyone else get hurt in the process."

"So instead we both died," Jacob said.

"We both died," agreed Dan, nodding.

"I remember it all now," said Jacob. "You grabbed me, pulled me toward the back of the store, all the while I was kicking and screaming. We stumbled into one of the shelves that was on fire, and the wall collapsed and..."

"And it crushed us," Dan finished for him. "I'm so sorry, kid."

"Sorry? You're sorry?" yelled Lisa, up until now silent. "You murdered my twin brother."

"Things happen," Jacob said, shrugging. "If he hadn't burned down his store, we'd both be alive. If his wife hadn't left him, he probably wouldn't have burned down the store. If I hadn't run back in the store, we wouldn't even be talking. It's like a line of dominos, all in a row."

"And if I hadn't pulled that stupid prank with your helmet," said Lisa, the anger draining from her face, "you'd still be alive."

Dan turned to Lisa. "I'm sorry. I'm so sorry."

"Tell it to him."

"I'm sorry," he said, turning back to Jacob. "If I could take it all back, if I could go back in time and change any of this..."

"But you can't, and I forgive you."

"Thank you," said the ghost, the flames entirely gone now. "That makes it better, somehow." He smiled, and then faded from view.

"Where did he go?" Lisa asked, still connected to Shawn by way of Jenny.

"Back to the cemetery, maybe," Jacob answered, "or maybe somewhere else. Does it really matter?"

"I guess not," said Lisa, a half-smile on her lips. Jacob thought he saw acceptance there, as well. "So what now?"

"I don't know, sis," Jacob said. "Back to the cemetery for me, I guess. But I'll be around, watching over you and Maya. And maybe when Shawn's in town, we can even visit from time to time."

"You got it, buddy," said Shawn, tears in his eyes.

"And you, Mr. Ruskin. I have it on good authority that you'll rebuild the restaurant and make it even better than ever."

Ruskin smiled. "Thank you, son. And please know your sister will always have a job with me, for as long as she wants it."

"I love you, Jacob," said Lisa, staring at him. "What're you—"

"He's...changing," Jenny said.

Jacob looked down at himself, and realized it was true. Gone was the body of a child, replaced by the form of the man his twenty years on Earth would have reflected had he still been alive. His features now mirrored Lisa's, truly twins again. Even ghosts could grow, it seemed, especially ghosts inexorably tied to their twin sister. And if he could grow and change, who knew what else he might be able to do?

He said his goodbyes, thought of Margaret Ruskin, and reappeared in the cemetery. Life after death was finally getting interesting.

The Kitten Tree

I often wondered if Joey saying it somehow made it happen, or if it would have happened anyway. I suppose I'll never know. What I do know was that I'd had Cherry since I was a kid, and a more faithful, gentle companion I never could have imagined. She didn't deserve what happened any more than we did.

Cherry had been a present for my eleventh birthday. I'd always wanted a cat, but was never allowed to have one because my stepfather didn't like animals. My mother took me to the animal shelter and let me pick out whatever animal I wanted, and I picked the tiny, spunky, pure-white long haired kitten that wouldn't stop mewling at me.

She was nearly 23 years old when she passed away, ironically enough on Joey's eleventh birthday. One week she seemed just fine, and then the next her whole body seemed to give out. She stopped eating, stopped drinking, and picked out a spot under Joey's bed and just lay there, waiting to die.

I didn't let her die under Joey's bed, of course. I coaxed her out and put her in her little cat house, along with a small bowl of water and some food, but she ignored all of it and managed to crawl back to Joey's room the moment I turned my back.

"Charlie, we should take her to the vet and have her put down," Lisa told me. "We can't let her die in our son's room, of all places, and certainly not on his birthday."

"Don't you think I know that?" I snapped, instantly regretting it.

Lisa loved Cherry, and I knew that. Hell, she'd lived with the cat for twelve years, just as I'd lived with her old German shepherd, Jack. A newly-married couple with a dog and a cat, not to mention, a year later, a newborn baby boy, but somehow we'd made it all work. Cherry and Jack had even learned to get along, albeit always in a temporary truce sort of way.

In the end, I ended up taking Cherry to the backyard. I wrapped her in a blanket and sat on the back porch holding her and talking to her for almost three hours before she finally let go. All the vet could do was pump her full of chemicals until she died, and at least this way she'd go knowing she was loved.

It was a Friday so Joey was at school, and I had promised to wait to bury Cherry until he was home. Cherry loved Joey and Joey absolutely adored Cherry, and was just as upset as I was at the cat's passing, so it seemed right that my son be there for the interment.

Because I worked from home as a graphic illustrator, it was always up to me to pick up Joey from school. I normally cherished that twenty minute ride to and from the Arkansas Academy of Fine Arts Elementary, but today was different.

Joey decided he wanted to bury Cherry under the cherry tree that we had planted in the backyard around the time Joey was born. We were being cute, planting a cherry tree. Did that have anything to do with what happened? I know it sounds insane, but I have to think that it more than likely did. Maybe it was a combination of things. I'll probably never know, and I'm not even sure it matters anymore.

"Wouldn't it be funny," Joey asked thoughtfully, "if now kittens grew instead of cherries?"

That was a funny thought, I agreed, and also a bit of a macabre one, though I didn't say that part out loud. Instead, I just hugged Joey and then got back to digging.

When we were done, I gently lowered the cat into the hole and Joey and I each said a few words about Cherry before I covered her with the dark red Arkansas soil. It reminded me of another funeral I'd attended, over half a lifetime ago. I pushed away the thought, not wanting to dwell on the past.

That night, we celebrated Joey's birthday with as much excitement as we could muster. Everyone was in a bad mood, including the birthday boy himself, but Lisa and I did all we could to lift our son's spirits.

"Blow out the candles, Joey," said Lisa, as we all sat around the dining room table, "and make a wish."

The cake was vanilla with green frosting and shaped like a creeper from the Minecraft video game, which was Joey's current obsession. His gifts reflected the theme as well, including a giant stuffed Creeper and various Minecraft-related action figures.

Joey closed his eyes, his forehead bunching up. I was pretty sure I knew what he was wishing for, and, in a moment of blind intuition, I almost stopped him. Instead I just watched as my son opened his eyes and then blew out all 11 of the green candles with one big breath.

We clapped and cheered, and once again sang happy birthday to him. Later, as the night was winding down, Lisa asked Joey what he wished for.

"C'mon, Mommy, you know I can't tell you that," he said, rolling his eyes. The boy had clearly learned sarcasm from the master. "If I do, it won't come true."

"Was it about Cherry?"

The boy looked as though he might start crying again. "I miss her. Why'd she have to die?"

I started to respond with some nonsense about the cycle of life, and everything having a season, but instead just pulled my son into an embrace and let him cry it out. Before he was done, I realized I was also crying.

"I don't know, Joey," I said, sniffling, "but I miss her, too. I'll tell you what. In a few weeks or months, however long it takes for you to feel okay with it, we'll go to the shelter and get a new kitten. It won't be Cherry, but I have a feeling you'll love him or her anyway. What do you think about that?"

"I guess so," he said, his lip trembling. "Maybe in a year or two."

It turns out that we didn't have to wait a year or two, or even a week, though the way we got the new kitten wasn't at all how I had envisioned. It was just six days later when Joey came running into my home office, shouting excitedly, holding something in his arms.

"Can we keep her, Daddy? Please? Can we keep her?"

Bleary-eyed from staring at my computer screen all day, I looked up in confusion to see a small, white kitten in Joey's arms. The kitten had long hair and green eyes, just like Cherry.

"Where did you get that?" I asked, turning away from my work.

"I found her in the back yard. Can we keep her? Please?"

"I don't know, Joey, she might belong to someone. Are you sure you're even ready for another cat? I'm not sure if I am."

"I am, Daddy. Please?"

I talked to Lisa and, in the end, we finally agreed that he could keep the kitten. What else could we do? I did, however, have one caveat. We would put up signs around the neighborhood in case someone had lost her. If no one claimed the kitten, then and only then would we consider her ours.

After a week, no one had called or shown up at the door, and so I took down the signs and officially declared her part of the Coleridge family. I still missed Cherry, but Joey seemed to have found a ready replacement in this cute little fluffy kitten. I'll admit this bothered me a little, but he was happy and so I tried to be happy for him.

Everything was great, at first. Joey wanted to name the kitten Cherry II, but, after I objected, he eventually settled on "Strawberry." Strawberry was playful and energetic, and spent each night sleeping at the foot of Joey's bed. She seemed wary of Jack, but mostly ignored the old German shepherd. He, however, seemed deathly afraid of Strawberry, and would cross over chairs and couches just to avoid her. He would even forego eating (something he never did) if the kitten was anywhere near his food bowl.

"What do you think's gotten into Jack?" Lisa asked me that night as we sat around the dining table.

"He's never really been around a kitten before," I said, between bites of my wife's amazing lasagna. "He'll get used to her, I'm sure."

Jack was one of the most easygoing dogs I'd ever met, and it had taken him less than a day to get used to Cherry. That had been over a dozen years ago, of course, and by now Jack was certainly set in his ways, but I'd never seen him react this way to anyone or anything.

"Maybe we should get rid of him?" Joey said about the dog he'd known all his life. "If he doesn't like Strawberry, I don't want him around."

"Joey!" I yelled. "What an awful thing to say. Jack is part of our family, and you don't just get rid of family. Besides, he'll get used to her. It just takes a little time."

Lisa started to say something, but before she could get a word out Joey ran crying from the room. She followed him, leaving me alone with my thoughts and the lasagna. Not 30 seconds later I heard her scream. My heart racing, I ran into Joey's bedroom.

"That cat," she whispered, holding her left cheek, "it jumped on me from the dresser and clawed my face." Blood trickled between her fingers, dripping down her chin to stain her blouse.

Joey sat on the bed, stroking Strawberry's long, white fur. He was no longer crying and didn't even look upset. In fact, our son was smiling.

Seeing the blood trickle down Lisa's face immediately brought back a memory that I hadn't thought about in years. I was huddled in the corner of the living room, trying not to cry, as my step-father beat the holy shit out of my mother. Her crime? Being five minutes late with supper. He broke her arm that night, and gave me a black eye and a bloody nose when I finally worked up the courage to interfere.

That wasn't the first time he beat her, but it did end up being one of the last. He died just three months later, his alcoholism finally catching up with him when, in a drunken stupor, he accidentally blew his own head off while cleaning his pistol in the garage. I cried the night he died, not because he was dead but because I wanted to be the one to kill him and that opportunity had been stolen from me by his incessant drinking and carelessness.

Staring at Lisa's bloody face now, I could almost see my mother after one of my step-father's beatings. I shook my head, leaning against the wall to steady myself. Something was niggling at my memory, but I pushed it away, not wanting to deal with it now.

Ignoring Joey and Strawberry for the moment, I took Lisa into the bathroom, washed her cheek, and applied Neosporin. The scratches weren't as bad as the blood at first indicated, but one was long and fairly deep. Neither of us thought she'd need stitches. Instead, I applied a bandage, and then together we went back into Joey's room.

He had fallen asleep with the kitten lying on top of his chest. I started to walk over to him, to wake him, but Lisa touched my arm and shook her head. Better to let him sleep, her eyes seemed to say, and talk about it in the morning. After a moment's hesitation I agreed, and we trundled off to bed.

Within second of my head hitting the pillow I was asleep, and before long I was dreaming. I was in the little yellow house where I grew up, on the outskirts of Carthage, a small town in Western Illinois, right across the Mississippi River from Iowa. It was summer, and the air conditioner was broken. My step-dad had been working on the AC all day, in between drinking bottles of Pabst Blue Ribbon, and was in a bad mood.

It was our fault, he said, for running the damn thing all day and all night while he was out working to make Hancock County a safe place to live. My step-father, you see, was a police officer, which in the end is why he never got punished for abusing us. The police protect their own, even when one of their own is a sociopath. Everything he ever did, including breaking my mother's arm, was swept under the rug or explained away as an unfortunate accident.

He had become my step-father five years previously, after my real father, Richard, died from cancer. The two had been partners on the police force, and he'd started coming around more and more often after my father's death. He seemed to feel that he was entitled to the family that his partner had left behind, and after a while it seemed that my mother just gave in and married him.

Harry has been kind at first, from what little I remember about the beginning of their marriage, but had quickly grown mean. He seemed to resent me for reasons I still don't understand, and always accused my mother of loving my father more than she did him.

In real life, his power seemed limitless; in the dream, it *was* limitless. He was chasing us through the house now, though it wasn't our house, not anymore. This house was bigger, and had rooms I'd never seen before. My mother and I ducked inside a small room off the dining room, then took another door that inexplicably led to my third grade classroom. Harry was behind us, screaming, telling us if we stopped running he'd make it quick and not let us suffer too much. But we didn't stop running.

We ran out of the classroom and were back in the house again, but, this being a dream, the house was different. We were in our living room, but it was so big that it was almost a cavern. Three open tunnels led out of the room, and somehow I knew that the one directly in front of me led to Lisa and Joey. I started to take that tunnel but then Cherry was there, standing in front of me, moving to get in my way every time

I tried to take a step. She meowed plaintively at me, as if warning me not to take that tunnel.

My mother started to go around the cat, but I yanked her arm, pulling her in the opposite direction. And then we were in the garage, not the garage that currently attaches to the ranch-style house I live in now, but the little garage that was attached to our house then.

He had gotten in front of us, somehow, and was waiting for us, his mouth having grown fangs and his hands claws red with blood.

"Bitch," he screamed, slashing my mother's cheek. She recoiled, slamming into the old Ford Harry kept parked in the garage. "I'm gonna kill you and your little shit, like I should have done a long time ago."

I tried to move toward them, but was paralyzed. My feet felt like they were encased in lead. I watched in slow motion as my step-father removed his police service revolver from his belt, having instantaneously changed into his uniform, and brought it up to point at my mother's face.

"Please, Harry," she said, her cheek bleeding where he had struck her. "If you want to kill me, fine, go ahead, but leave Charlie alone."

"Oh, I'm just getting started," he said, grinning.

And then Lisa was there, shaking me, yelling something, something I couldn't quite understand. I tried to pull from her grasp but she held me tight, shouting in my ear so loud that it drowned out everything else around me.

"Charlie, wake up," she said again, shaking my shoulders. "You're dreaming."

I opened my eyes to see my wife kneeling above me, her long, blonde hair falling down around her face, her features a mixture of confusion and fear. My heart was beating wildly against my ribcage, and I almost bolted from the bed. Instead I took a deep breath, centered myself, and pressed my hand to her undamaged cheek.

"Nightmare," I finally said, as my heart rate began to slow. "I'm sorry I woke you."

"Oh, babe," she said, leaning down to kiss me, "don't apologize. What was the dream about?"

"Harry," I said, and watched her wince.

Lisa knew all about my step-father, how he had abused us, and how relieved I'd been when he accidentally killed himself. My mother passed away my junior year in college and so Lisa had never really gotten to know her, but she'd heard enough stories about dear old Harry to fill a book.

"I'm so sorry," Lisa said, stroking my cheek. "Do you want to talk about it?"

"I don't remember much," I lied, coming more awake now. "Just that it was about him. I want to go back to sleep, if I can."

She lay down in my arms, her head pressed tight against my chest, and within minutes she'd fallen back asleep. I always envied her that, her ability to fall asleep almost instantaneously. Me, I lay there wide awake, remembering the dream, one I've had many times before but somehow never remembered until now.

It had all happened in real life, at least the part about the air conditioner and the garage. I remembered with cold clarity my step-father slapping my mother, the chunky white gold ring shaped like an owl that he always wore ripping into her cheek. I remembered him pulling the gun on her and shoving it into her face. I also remembered what happened after, something I hadn't thought about since that night. My step-father hadn't been cleaning his gun that night, and he hadn't shot himself.

I tried to push the memory away, finally succeeding, and at last fell back asleep. I dreamt no more that night, perhaps because my subconscious mind knew of the real-life nightmare yet to come and wanted to give me a moment of mercy before my whole world came crashing down around my feet.

Things got even worse the next morning, when Lisa woke up with a fever. Her forehead was hot to the touch, and her damaged cheek even hotter. When I changed the bandage, I realized that not only weren't the scratches healing, they were festering. I applied more Neosporin and tried to get her to go to one of the rent-a-doc clinics, but she insisted she'd be better after taking some Tylenol.

It was a Saturday, so at least she didn't have to go to work. I let her fall back asleep, and then put on my slippers to take Jack out. Except there was no Jack. He usually slept in his dog bed by the dresser and didn't get up until one of us took him out, but he wasn't there. I didn't think much of it at first, assuming maybe Strawberry has spooked him and he'd gone off to hunker down in some other part of the house.

Putting off Jack's walk for the moment, I decided to talk with Joey about what happened last night. I steeled myself and opened the door to his room, but he wasn't there. I looked at my watch. It was just past seven. Joey never got up early on a Saturday.

Feeling panic, I raced into the living room but didn't find him there, either. I looked through the window into the backyard and both mysteries were solved. Jack was sunning himself on the cement porch, while Joey sat in the grass with his back to the dog. My heart, which I didn't even realize was beating overtime, settled into a regular beat. But what were they doing outside this early?

"Joey, what's up?" I asked him, as I pushed through the door. He just sat there, ignoring me, talking quietly under his breath.

I looked at Jack and my breath caught in my throat as I realized he wasn't moving. I knelt beside the old German shepherd, touching his shoulder, and my hand came back covered in blood. I rolled him on to his back, gasping at what I saw. His throat had been flayed open, resulting in a sort of bloody smile beneath his chin.

"He was bothering the cats," said Joey, his back still toward me. His voice sounded dull. "Now he won't bother anyone ever again."

Cats, plural? What was he talking about? I pushed myself to my feet and walked numbly toward Joey, my slippers tracking a trail of blood. This wasn't happening. Joey would never hurt a fly, let alone kill the dog he'd known and loved his entire life. There had to be another explanation. Anything but this.

"Joey, come on, let's go inside."

He ignored me, so I said his name again, louder this time. No answer. I felt anger flare inside me. I bent over and placed my hand on his shoulder, shaking him.

He turned around, surprise in his eyes. He held Strawberry in his lap, as well as two other, near-identical kittens in each hand. The only difference between the three was that the newcomers were smaller. Other than that, they all looked identical, which is to say they were dead-ringers for Cherry.

A carving knife from the kitchen, covered in blood, lay beside him in the grass. The knife he'd used to murder Jack. I didn't want to believe it, but the evidence was damning. The anger drained out of my body, immediately replaced by dread.

"Why, Joey?" I asked.

"I told you, he was bothering the cats. They didn't like him, and neither did I."

"Joey, where did those kittens come from?"

"I found them out here, Daddy. Please, can I keep them? This one," he held up the kitten in his right hand, "is Stinky, and the other one is Sweet Cheeks."

I stared at my son and the three kittens that were climbing all over him. Where had the two new ones come from, and why did those names sound so familiar? I shook my head, forcing myself to forget about what he'd called them for the moment.

"Joey. You killed Jack," I said, almost not believing the words were coming from my own mouth.

"He deserved it."

"My God, Joey…"

"Look, Daddy, can I keep the cats or not?"

"No, you can't keep the fucking cats!"

"I don't care, I'm keeping them. If you don't like it, you can…you can just stuff it, mister!"

I reeled back as if slapped, not knowing what to say or how to react. I'd never heard such defiance in his voice, nor had he ever said anything like that to me before.

"Joey, you need to go to your room now. Now!"

"No."

"Excuse me, young man? What did you say to me?" I locked eyes with my son and within them I saw someone else.

"I said NO," he screamed at the top of his lungs, balling his little hands into fists.

All three cats immediately raised their hackles and began to hiss. The one he'd called Sweet Cheeks swatted at me, narrowly missing my hand. Strawberry began to growl, a low, throaty hum, and I could almost swear her eyes turned red as she glared at me.

She scuttled off Joey's lap and sat back on her haunches, her eyes never leaving me, ready to pounce. I backed away from the kitten before risking a glance at Joey. He was standing now, still holding Stinky and Sweet Cheeks, staring at me, his mouth turned down at the corners. And then he said something I'll never forget:

"I'm gonna fuck you up, you little shit."

I instinctively grabbed Joey's arm and yanked him toward me, hard. He yelped in pain and dropped Stinky, who landed on her feet and scampered away.

The moment I laid my hands on him, I regretted it. No matter what he'd done, he was still my son. I'd never so much as spanked Joey, no matter how angry I'd been. I'd gone through enough of that as a kid and swore I'd never treat my own son that way, and now I'd broken that promise.

"Daddy?" he said, looking up at me. The old Joey was back. "What happened to Jack?"

"Joey," I said, my hands on his shoulders, "are you okay? I'm so sorry I did—ouch!"

One of the kittens sank its fangs into my bare foot, immediately drawing blood. Letting go of Joey, I kicked the kitten away from me, watching as it and my slipper tumbled into the grass.

"Leave her alone, dumbass!" shouted Joey, spitting and baring his teeth at me like a rabid dog. He was alien to me again.

My back flared with pain as another kitten buried its claws deep into my skin. I reached around behind me, ripped the cat off of my back, and threw it to the ground. It quickly got to its feet, poised to spring again, this time joined by Strawberry.

I backed away from the kittens, my mind reeling. The one I'd thrown into the grass ran up and swatted at me, and then there was another one, and another, and another still. Where were they coming from? There were six kittens now, all seemingly intent on ripping me to shreds.

Kicking at them, I lost my other slipper but managed to keep the kittens at bay as I retreated toward the porch. Kick, back up, and then kick again, and all the while Joey stared at me with malevolent eyes that seemed to bore deep into my soul. He had the knife in his hand now, and I felt a chill raise the hairs on my arms.

"Oh my God, Jack!"

I whipped my head around to see Lisa standing in the doorway, staring at her dead dog. She was barefoot and still wearing the long, oversized Fozzy concert t-shirt she'd slept in last night. Her left cheek was swollen even worse than it had been ten minutes ago, and now she was crying, her eyes open wide in shock.

"Lisa, get back in the house. Now!"

"What happened to my dog?"

"I killed him, Mommy," Joey said proudly. "He was making the cats nervous. Bad dog! Bad!"

"I don't understand. This can't be happening!"

And then the kittens were abandoning me to run at her, leaping on to her legs, clawing and biting, scaling her body. She screamed, backing up, shaking her arms and legs to get them off.

I did the only thing I could think to do. I ran to her, yanking kittens off of her, and throwing them to the ground. One slammed so hard against the brick exterior of the house that it exploded in a ball of fur, bones, and teeth.

I stared at the mess as it slid down the wall, astonished because there was no blood and very little else there. What once had been a kitten was now just bits of fur, bones, and a few teeth. I blinked at the remains of the kitten, confused, forgetting that I had another kitten in my hand. It bit through the web of flesh between my thumb and forefinger, causing an arc of blood to spray into my eyes. Half-blind, I stumbled against Lisa, knocking her into the patio door, as I flung the kitten somewhere behind me.

"You killed Fudge Packer!" screamed Joey. "Leave my kittens alone!"

I wiped the blood from my eyes, and the first thing I saw was our little cherry tree. I started across the yard. The tree looked dead, or close to it, and instead of cherries the tree sported long, black sacs of…something. And the sacs were wriggling. I stumbled forward mindlessly, forgetting for the moment about Lisa and Joey, and watched as a small, white paw poked through one of the sacs.

A searing pain burned into my thigh, and I turned around to see Joey next to me, the knife in his hand, fresh blood dripping from the blade. All of the kittens were behind him, like a little army, ready to strike.

"Leave the kitten tree alone, Daddy," he said, his voice once again monotone. "If you don't, I'll kill you and that slut wife of yours."

"Please, Joey," I heard Lisa's shaking voice say somewhere behind me, "just stop."

"I'll be finished when I'm finished, Mommy, and not a moment sooner."

I recognized that phrase, and it was then that I realized why those words sounded so familiar. Sweet Cheeks had been one of the things he called my mother, while he'd reserved names like fudge packer and little shit for me. My son was channeling my step-father.

"Hello, Harry," I said, and in the instant that he met my eyes I knew that it was true. "I thought I killed your sorry ass in the garage a long time ago, but I guess I was wrong."

I remembered it all now, what had happened all those years ago in the garage. I remembered how I'd rushed at Harry as he pointed the gun at my mother, pushing him into the wall. How the gun had fallen from his hand to clatter to the cement below. I remembered picking up the pistol and shooting him between the eyes, and, afterward, before she called the police, my mother making up the story about him cleaning his gun.

Joey went still, closing his eyes. When he opened them, I saw that my step-father had fully taken control of my son. "I can't die, you little piece of shit," he said, in my son's voice. "You've been carrying me around with you all these years. I can't die, but you can."

I jumped as a hand touched my shoulder, but it was Lisa. She stood beside me, mouth hanging open as she stared at our son.

"I don't understand," she said, sagging against me.

Joey stepped forward and, before I could stop him, slid the carving knife between her ribs. She gasped, clutched her stomach, and crumpled to the ground, moaning in pain.

Before I knew what I was doing, I heard myself scream something unintelligible and slapped my son as hard as I could across the face. He sprawled backward, surprised. The knife flew from his hand and he skidded through the grass, knocking over the kittens that had formed a phalanx behind him.

I knew what I had to do now. I recovered the knife from the ground and raced to the tree, hacking and cutting at the black, writhing sacs that hung from the branches. The moment I cut into the cocoons they stopped moving, and bits of fur and bones from Cherry's corpse spilled from the holes I had made.

Then I began digging at the base, stabbing deep into the earth, searching for Cherry's body. Somehow the dead cat had corrupted the tree, and I knew that if I could separate the two that this madness would stop. Only that's not what happened.

I ripped Cherry's decaying body from its grave and flung it as far as I could from the tree, but the kittens, now on their feet and advancing toward me, didn't disappear. Joey was standing again, and I could tell by his eyes that it was still my step-dad controlling his body.

"It's too late, shit-for-brains," Harry said, through Joey's mouth. "You killed me once, so I'm gonna take you and your whole fucking family, and there's not one goddamned thing you can do about it."

A rush of movement in the periphery of my vision caught my eye, but when I turned my head there was nothing there. And then it happened again, a streak of white, followed by the dash of something black and brown. I tracked the movement, but couldn't see anything.

Joey began to walk toward me, Strawberry and the remaining cats moving in lockstep beside him. Behind them, Lisa lay still in the grass. I couldn't tell whether or not she was still breathing, but I prayed with all my heart that she could hold on just a little bit longer. Help had finally arrived, but it was up to me to help the help.

"You're a coward," I told Harry, looking straight into my son's eyes. "You were a coward back then, and you're still a coward."

He stopped advancing, his smile turning into a frown. "What are you talking about?"

"First you steal your partner's grieving widow, and then you beat her and a defenseless little boy. You're weak. *You're* the piece of shit. You hid behind your badge and your gun back then, and this time you're hiding behind another defenseless little boy. You're pathetic."

"I am not weak!" he shouted, but looked confused. "Your mother was a whore, and you were—"

"Yeah, yeah," I interrupted him, doing my best to sound brave, "it was everyone else's fault, not yours. I get it now. Classic inferiority complex. Life kicks you, and you kick your wife and step-son. You're not a real man. You never could measure up to my father, and you proved it time and time again."

"You're lying!" he yelled, shaking so hard that I thought he might fall apart. "I was strong, it was the rest of you who were weak. And your father was nothing. Nothing! I was stronger than him, and I'm stronger than you'll ever be."

I saw the flash of movement around me again, and knew it was now or never. I let the knife tumble from my bloody fingers to land in the grass at my feet.

"Yeah? Well, prove it. Take me on man to man, without hiding behind a helpless little boy. Come on, big man, show me how it's done!"

I still don't know to this day if I actually saw everything that was about to happen, or if I just sensed it. Harry howled with rage and leapt from my son's body, leaving it to crumple to the ground beside the suddenly-lifeless bits of fur and teeth that had been kittens just seconds earlier.

The spirit of Harry Queen rushed through the air, but before he could reach me those streaks of light that I had recognized threw themselves in his path. I fell on my ass, stunned, as I watched Cherry and Jack rip my step-father's ghost into tiny, little pieces.

He was no match for their fury, for the love and protectiveness they felt for Joey, Lisa, and me, and he was gone in a matter of seconds, his evil, corrupted essence floating away on the wind, back to the nothingness whence it had come.

I felt something leave me as well, a weight on my soul that I hadn't even known was there until it was gone. Harry had finally left me, just as he'd left this earthly plane of existence all those years ago.

Cherry was sitting in my lap now, purring, making biscuits on my stomach, as Jack licked my face, slobbering all over me. Tears ran down my cheeks as I hugged my fur family and my saviors, engulfed in their loyalty and love. I ruffled Cherry's head and kissed Jack on the nose, and then everything went dark.

One of the neighbors had heard the shouting from our backyard and called the police, and they and the paramedics that followed arrived just in time to save Lisa's life. Joey didn't remember much of anything after Cherry's death, and even his finding Strawberry seemed to have been erased from his mind. He didn't remember killing Jack, which was a bigger blessing than I ever could have hoped for. Of course, it hadn't really been him who had done the killing.

Joey and I were in the hospital for two days, Lisa for a week, but eventually we all recovered from the damage that the home invasion had caused. That had been my idea, and the police bought it readily enough, even though nothing had been stolen. They never did catch the burglars, but criminals didn't always come to justice. It was certainly easier to believe than what really happened.

I burned the kitten tree three weeks later. I pulled it out by the roots using a rented backhoe, and then took it out into the woods where I placed it on a pyre and torched it. I knew I didn't have to, that

Harry was gone for good this time, but it was still cathartic. Sometimes from destruction comes rebuilding, and it couldn't start soon enough for us.

Through the smoke of the burning wood, I could swear I saw Jack and Cherry racing into the sky, joyfully going toward whatever reward awaits faithful, loving animal friends after they die. Lisa says she didn't see anything, but I know Joey did, because he squeezed my hand at the exact moment when our beloved four-legged family disappeared from view.

A Chance Meeting in the Park

"My mind is like a heavy hand,
Always making more of what really happened,
A critical imagination always working overtime"

—Katie Herzig, *Free My Mind*

Harvey fed the pigeons every day, without fail. The sun shone down through the trees as if in accompaniment to the warm gentle breezes of summer, but Harvey didn't notice what a beautiful day it was. All Harvey noticed were the pigeons.

A large, stone dolphin statue spat water into the sky, some of it splashing out of the fountain onto the grass surrounding it. None of that mattered to Harvey. He continued to feed the birds, the world around him a fog. At least until she came into view.

The woman in the red dress sat on the park bench across from Harvey, reading *Entertainment Weekly* magazine. She crossed her legs, and Harvey could almost hear the rustle of her silk stockings. Her tight, red dress clung to her like a hungry pigeon to popcorn, and her long, delicate black hair brushed across her face in the wind. Cool, blue eyes gazed out, taking in her surroundings. She couldn't be a day over thirty. Her skin was a light, creamy peach, unblemished by the ravages of the world.

He'd seen her in the park every day for the past six or seven months, but had yet to work up the courage to say hello. She occupied a great deal of his thoughts as of late, but he didn't even know her name. All he knew was that she showed up at precisely 11:37 each morning and sat reading on that bench for twenty-three minutes before going back to wherever she came from. And that's when Harvey had taken a sudden interest in pigeons.

Harvey was forty-one. He'd been married once, for nearly seven years, but his wife had left him a decade earlier. He was boring, she said. She wanted adventure, and Harvey couldn't give her that. Good old Harvey, she'd called him. Good old Harvey was just fine for sitting around the house, going to church on Sundays, and taking in a movie now and then, but precious little else. She'd wanted something more, and so she left. He hadn't heard from her since.

He tried dating for a while, even joined an Internet dating service, but nothing ever really worked out. And the longer he didn't date, the harder it was to get up the nerve to ask someone out. It was a vicious cycle that he didn't know how to break, and so he concentrated on work instead.

He'd been at Miller and Sons Accounting firm for nearly twenty years, almost half his life, and what did he have to show for it? Not a whole heck of a lot, other than a decent bank account and a house paid off fifteen years ahead of schedule. And why not? He had nothing else to spend his paycheck on.

He should be happy, he told himself. He had a comfortable home and a full belly, which was more than a lot of people had in this day and age, but in his heart he knew that he'd trade it all just for a chance with the beautiful, young woman in the red dress sitting on the bench across from him.

Harvey could feel his cheeks flush as he realized she was staring back at him. Quickly turning away, he bumped into the bag of seed, knocking it over, sending it tumbling off the bench and onto his feet.

Two of the birds began to fight over the seed, and the bigger pigeon pecked Harvey's shoe.

The woman in red giggled before turning back to her magazine, which only made Harvey's face grow redder. He brushed the seed off his shoes, finally resorting to taking them off and shaking out the seeds when the pigeons wouldn't leave him alone.

He could imagine how she saw him: old, out of shape, short, brown hair turning to grey, his lusterless blue eyes paling in comparison to her own. Why, she probably wouldn't have noticed him at all were it not for that hungry pigeon.

If he somehow worked up the courage to ask her out, he'd get turned down flat. He imagined it would go something like this...

"It's awfully nice weather we're having today, isn't it?" Harvey said, shuffling his feet. He felt more nervous than he had in years.

"I guess it is. Did you need something, mister?" The woman in red asked, looking annoyed.

She set aside her magazine and pulled a paperback novel from her purse. She started at him, waiting for his answer.

"Well, I've seen you here almost every day for the last six months or so, and I was wondering..." he trailed off, faltering.

"I'm on my lunch break, and I haven't got long. I have to be back to the office in about fifteen minutes, and I really want to get a start on this new book. Did you need something?"

"Would you like to go out sometime?" he asked in a rush, the words coming out between ragged breaths.

"With you? I don't think so," the woman replied, laughing, and then turned her attention to the paperback.

And that's where the fantasy ended. At that point, she'd laugh again, rise to her feet, and walk out of his life forever.

If there was even a chance she'd say yes, he might do it. Might actually ask her out. But there wasn't a point to doing something that would only cause heartache, was there?

His thoughts were interrupted by her movements. She folded the magazine into her purse, stretching languidly across the green metal park bench. Reaching into her purse, she pulled a shiny-covered paperback book out. Something with a white owl on the cover.

Harvey's mouth dropped. It was the same book in his daydream. He couldn't be psychic, could he? He didn't believe in that sort of thing. She must have had the book out before, and his subconscious had picked up on it and used it in his fantasy. That had to be it.

He was spending far more time than he should thinking about this woman. He'd have to get back to the office soon himself, and why ponder over what you can't have? Besides, even if she did agree to go out with him, he'd probably find some way to bungle it.

His thoughts seemed to lose focus, as he fantasized about how his dream date might go...

"I'm glad you agreed to go out with me, Hannah," said Harvey. "I've been going to this restaurant for years, and they serve the best pasta I've ever had."

He and his ex-wife Pamela used to come here once a week, every Friday night. Old habits are hard to break, and so he'd continued the tradition without her.

"I've never been here before, but I'll try anything once," Hannah said, studying the menu.

"Well, would you like to order now?"

"What do you suggest?"

"The linguini in red clam sauce is really great," said Harvey.

"Great. I'll have that, then."

"Would you like some wine? The red wine is delicious."

"Sure, I'd like that," She said, smiling at Harvey.

Harvey waved to the waiter and they placed their orders. A few minutes later, the waiter brought a bottle of Duhart-Milan, a vintage 2010 Bordeaux from France. It was expensive, but he wanted this date to be one that Hannah would remember.

Maybe this night was going somewhere, after all. If only he wasn't so damned nervous. He tried to steady his shaking hands as he began to fill her glass, but the wine sloshed over the edge as Harvey's attention wavered to her smile.

"Oops!" he yelled, loudly enough to draw the attention of half the room, "let me get that." Reaching for a napkin, he managed to knock the full glass of red wine into her lap.

She screamed, leaping to her feet. "My new silk dress, it's ruined! Dammit, I knew I shouldn't have come!"

Yes, he'd bungle it for sure. There was no doubt in his mind. He hadn't been on a date in longer than he could remember. Why, he'd probably forgotten how. If it wasn't the wine, he'd say or do something else wrong.

The rest of the world lost to her novel, the woman in red's eyes danced through the pages as Harvey's gaze once again fell upon her. She shifted in the bench, as if sensing her admirer's gaze. Her black leather purse tumbled on its side and out slipped a matching wallet, gold-embossed with initials HM. In one swift motion she recovered the wallet and stuffed it back into her purse, before once again burying herself in the book's prose.

If life had been a cartoon, Harvey's eyes would have popped out of his head. HM? Her name was Hannah in his fantasy. He shook himself. His imagination really was working overtime today. He must have seen the wallet somehow, or just had a lucky guess. Besides, even if he was blessed with a premonition of some sort, what did it matter? The premonition was bad. His fantasies ended up with him wearing a liberal amount of egg on his face. What good was that?

And the "H" could stand for many different names: Helen, Hayley, Hazel, Heather, Holly, Hillary…Why, it could be anything.

She placed the book face down on the bench, then rose to her feet. Stretching, her form pushed fully against the confines of her dress. Her black pumps showed off her well-developed calf muscles, as she smiled into the distance. Taking a deep breath, she found the bench again and went back to her book.

Harvey's eyes caressed her body longingly. She was the most beautiful woman he'd ever seen, even more so than his ex-wife. Almost imperceptibly, his surroundings once again seemed to fall away and his mind was elsewhere.

"Hannah Montrose, will you marry me?"

"Harvey . . ." She looked away from his eyes, her words faltering.

They'd been dating for two years. He'd asked her out, and she'd actually accepted. Amazingly, she had even seemed to enjoy herself. They'd continued to date off and on, never committing, but growing closer.

"Hannah, I love you."

"You know, that's the first time you've ever said that."

"Well, I do. I've loved you since I first saw you, and I'm asking you to be my wife." He started to cry, swept away by the emotions he felt inside.

"Why did you take so long to tell me?" She found his eyes, reaching out to touch his cheek. "I knew you cared for me. Dating anyone this long has to mean something. But you've only kissed me a handful of times. You've never come into my house. You've never made love to me."

"Hannah!" Harvey blurted, looking away. "I've wanted to, Lord knows I've wanted to. I've just been so scared. I didn't want to scare you off. I didn't want to lose you like I lost Pam."

"I'm not her. I'm me, dammit! Never once have you held me, never once have you taken me away for the weekend. Two years, Harvey! I kept waiting for you to do something—anything!—but you wouldn't."

"I was scared!" His tears fell freely now. "You're so beautiful. I wanted you so much, but I was afraid I'd lose you. That day I met you in the park, I was terrified to ask you out. I managed to do that, some-how, but I've been scared ever since. It took me so long to find you, I didn't want to lose you."

"Harvey…" Tears came to her eyes. "Harvey, if you'd only said something sooner. All this time…I've loved you, I've wanted you to love me. You wouldn't even commit to dating exclusively."

"I haven't dated anyone," he said stiffly. "I've never even looked at another woman since I met you. I haven't wanted to."

"Then why didn't you say something, Harvey?"

"If you don't want to marry me right now, we can wait. We'll take it slow, as slow as you want."

"Harvey, there's someone else. I didn't want to wait. He asked me to marry him. Yes, Harvey, he actually asked. And I accepted! That's why I asked you to meet me here today. To tell you."

He felt as though his heart had been ripped from his chest. "It's Gary, from your office. Isn't it? I knew he had his eye on you."

The world seemed to snap back in place, and Harvey was on the park bench again, pigeons all around him. The fountain was pumping water into the air, creating little rainbows in the sun. Hannah—no, he reminded himself, the woman in red—was still reading. His thoughts were his own again.

"Hannah!" shouted a thirty-something man in a black business suit, about thirty feet from the center of the park. He wore mirrored sunglasses and his blonde hair waved in the wind as he walked briskly towards the woman in red.

Hannah? His thoughts raced, his heart pounding. That was her name, then, and somewhere deep inside of him he knew her last name was Montrose. The world around him seemed to come into focus, defining, gaining a crystal clear edge. The fog he'd lived inside of for so long was gone, replaced by a sharp awareness. He felt his muscles act of their own accord, and he rose from the bench.

"Hey, Gary," she answered, with a voice so sweet it sent chills through Harvey's soul. "Welcome back. How was the business trip?"

Harvey stepped away from the bench, thoughts and images racing through his mind. Thoughts of his wife pleading with him, of a childhood spent bullied and alone, years at a dead end job. Chances not so much lost as never taken in the first place. Opportunities sidestepped in favor of fear. And in an instant, he made a decision.

He knew what he had to do.

"Hannah?" asked Gary, nearly upon them. "I was wondering, if you're not busy—"

"Actually, she is," interrupted Harvey, putting himself between the woman in red and her advancing officemate. "Hannah, could we...talk?"

"Harvey?" she asked, finding his eyes. She smiled.

Going Over

The roar of the crowd always got Tommy Buckley's blood pumping, but he'd never before heard a crowd quite like this. This was Wrestlepalooza, baby, an event he'd dreamed of being involved in all his life, and not only was he involved, he was in the effing main event! He was competing for the National Wrestling Federation's top prize, the world heavyweight championship, against his boyhood idol, "Gentleman" Craig Thornton.

Tommy was standing in the gorilla position, (named after wrestler and announcer "Gorilla" Monsoon) poking his head out the curtains near the entrance to the locker rooms, watching the current match between popular tag team champions "Smooth Jazz" (comprised of twin brothers Chris and Nicky Courage) and their equally-popular opponents, "Cowboy" Bob Dodge and Robert Fernandez. The crowd roared as Dodge hoisted Nicky Courage onto the turnbuckle for his trademark superplex, and cheered even louder as Nicky countered the move and nearly pinned his opponent with a sunset flip.

A babyface versus babyface match in wrestling was rare, even more so for a tag team bout, because, unless it was done perfectly, the fans never knew who to root for. This match, however, was being executed exactly as it should be, and he was proud to be part of the card. Still, though, the previous three matches had also been face versus face, which he thought was a little strange.

"We have the battle royal after this, and then you're up in the title match," said a raspy voice from behind him, interrupting his thoughts. "You ready, Tommy?"

It was Gene Tyler, the very first NWF champion, who'd become a road agent when he hung up his trunks after he broke his leg in a match in 1969. He walked with a cane now, and had for as long as Tommy had known him. Tyler purchased the NWF in the late 1970's, and had served as the company's promoter and head match maker ever since.

"Ready as I'm gonna be, Mr. Tyler," said Tommy, turning to meet the old man's eyes. "I really appreciate this opportunity."

"You've earned it, kid," Tyler said. "And call me Gene. All my friends do."

Gene Tyler considered him a friend? Tommy felt sure he was blushing, and so he looked away from the tall, balding man with the salt-and-pepper hair and deep brown eyes.

"Thank you…Gene," he finally said. "I won't let you down."

Tommy had been in a bad car wreck earlier in the year, one that he'd miraculously escaped from unharmed. He'd been the Television Champ then, having beaten longtime title holder and top heel "Playboy" Eddie Page for the strap just a few weeks earlier. As his car careened off the road he remembered thinking that if he were badly hurt and had to be out of action for too long, he'd probably have to surrender the title.

Thankfully, that didn't happen. He'd eventually dropped the title to his best friend and sometimes road trip partner, the popular, high-flying Native American wrestler John White-Owl. However, that was only booked because he was in line for a bigger push and they needed to get the TV strap off of him before it happened. He just never dreamed that he'd be main eventing Wrestlepalooza so early in his career.

"Believe it, kid," said Tyler, in his trademark raspy voice. "We always knew you were destined for great things. I make the matches, but it's your talent that got you here. Never forget that."

Tommy was about to answer when the bell sounded, ending the tag-team title match. The bout had gone to a one-hour draw. "Cowboy" Bob Dodge and Robert Fernandez traded high-fives and embraces with the Courage Brothers, celebrating in the ring as the 100,000+ crowd celebrated with them.

"Ready for the big match, *ese?*" asked Carlos Murphy, joining Tommy at the gorilla position as Gene Tyler headed to the back.

Carlos was in the battle royal, which was on next.

"Ready as I'm gonna be," Tommy said, hugging Murphy. "Thanks, man. And good luck!"

Other wrestlers soon joined them, including eight-time former world champion Jason Andrews, his half-brother Rex Randolph, Ric Spencer, and the legendary masked wrestler, The Unknown Grappler. They were all participants in the royal, and the winner would get a world title shot at the next pay-per-view.

Tommy could almost feel the electricity in the air. The battle royal was the co-main event on the card, second only to his own championship match with Thornton.

The hairs on his arms stood up as Tori Garcia, the ring announcer, announced each entrant to the ring. Jason Andrews was first, of course, followed by Ric Spencer, Justin Crews, Ted Rhoads, "Jumping" Jim Gonzales, and then Carlos Murphy. One by one the royal's competitors entered the ring, to the thundering cheer of the crowd.

Tommy watched the match unfold, shaking his head. Andrews had just eliminated Rhoads, and Rhoads saluted him as he headed to the back. The noise from the crowd was deafening as they applauded their two heroes. Something wasn't right, but he couldn't quite put his finger on it. It was a great battle royal, but something was missing.

He shook his head again, noticing the butterflies in his stomach. It was probably just a case of the jitters. After all, it wasn't every day that you main-evented Wrestlepalooza.

"What'd you think, kid?" asked Rhoads, entering the gorilla position from the arena. "We worked on that spot for a week."

"Awesome!" Tommy said, with an enthusiasm he didn't quite feel.

Rhoads didn't seem to notice. "Thanks, brother. Are you ready for your match?"

"As ready as I'm gonna be."

"It's about time they put the strap on someone from the next generation," Rhoads said, walking past an approaching Gene Tyler. "You're gonna do great."

Put the strap on *him*?

And then he remembered. Gene had told him last week that he was going over. He was being booked to win the NWF heavyweight championship of the world. Yeah, baby! The world freaking title!

"Feels good, doesn't it, kid?" asked Tyler, slapping him on the shoulder. "You'll make a great world champ."

Ric Spencer walked through the curtain just then, followed by Rex Randolph, both of them having been eliminated by Carlos Murphy. They were grinning like fools.

"I think the buy rate for this Wrestlepalooza is gonna go through the roof," Spencer said, his arm around Randolph's shoulder. "Whadya think, Buckley?"

"I sure hope so," Tommy said, already thinking ahead to his own match.

The battle royal was down to just two grapplers now, Jason Andrews and Carlos Murphy. Andrews threw Murphy into the ropes, then caught him with a wicked-looking lariat on the rebound. The crowd gasped as Andrews yanked Murphy to his feet, hoisted him into the air, and prepared to dump him over the ropes.

Murphy, however, grabbed the top rope and maneuvered his legs around Andrews head, catching him in a head scissors, pulling the former eight-time world champion up and over the ropes and to the floor.

The bell sounded and Murphy stood tall in the ring, the sole-survivor and winner of the 30-man match. The cheers from the crowd reverberated through the arena like thunder, as Murphy soaked in the adoration of the fans.

Tommy's match against Craig Thornton was up next. He felt butterflies fluttering around inside his stomach again, and then his entrance music was playing and he was walking to the ring, high-fiving and hugging fans on the way.

The entrance seemed to go on forever, and Tommy enjoyed every second of it. Finally, though, he reached the ring and vaulted over the top rope to the cheers of the fans. He felt on top of the world. Tonight was his night, what he'd been dreaming of since he was a little boy. All of his dreams were about to come true.

Tommy watched as the champion entered the ring. "Gentlemen" Craig Thornton was wearing a beautiful blue and silver robe, in stark contrast to Tommy's own plain black trunks and lucky red boots. The crowd applauded as Thornton removed the world heavyweight championship belt from around his waist and handed it to referee Brian Hildebrand.

The two fan-favorites shook hands, and then the bell rang. The match went textbook perfect, with no missed or blown spots at all. Thornton dominated the first fifteen minutes of the match, scoring a two-and-a-half count after catching Tommy in his trademarked top-rope German suplex. They took turns dominating for the next twenty minutes, but after that it was all Tommy Buckley.

At the 45-minute mark, after taking the crowd through a series of peaks and valleys, Tommy finally locked in his signature submission maneuver, the Anaconda Leg-lock. Thornton writhed in pretend pain, playing his part to perfection. Hildebrand asked if he wanted to give up, and he shook his head dramatically back and forth, signaling that he wasn't done yet.

Someone at ringside caught Tommy's eye. It was his grandfather, Thomas Buckley, after whom he was named. He held up a white cardboard sign, upon which was written in blue magic marker, "Go get 'em, Tommy!"

That was something he used to say to Tommy when he was a little boy competing in Little League baseball. The old man had been there for all of his games, until…

Until what? He couldn't remember. The Anaconda Leg-lock still locked on Thornton, he paused to look around the arena. Probably one out of every five fans held a sign, and every one of those signs said the same thing:

"Go get 'em, Tommy!"

Stranger still, there were no signs for Thornton. Craig Thornton was just as popular as he was, if not more so, and had been the world champion and face of the company until 2004. So why weren't there any signs for him?

Until 2004? No, that wasn't right. He was the current National Wrestling Federation heavyweight champion, and had been since the late nineties. But something had happened in 2004. Why couldn't he remember what it was?

"We're losing the crowd, Tommy," whispered the referee in his ear, as he pretended to check on Thornton. "Come on, snap out of it and let's throw this thing into gear."

The roar of the crowd grew even louder, every single fan chanting his name. Tom-me! Tom-me! Tom-me! He leaned back to make it look like he was tightening his grip on the leg lock, and suddenly Thornton was slapping the canvas, tapping for all he was worth.

The referee signaled for the bell. The match was over, and Tommy was the new world champion. He released the hold and climbed to his feet, tears streaming down his cheeks. He couldn't believe it. Being the NWF heavyweight champion of the world had been his dream since he was a little boy, watching wrestling on television every Saturday afternoon, and now his dream had finally come true.

He helped Thornton to his feet and embraced the Englishman, who then grabbed his arm and thrust it into the air. He felt Hildebrand, the referee, fastening the belt around his waist as the crowd applauded wildly. Carlos Murphy ran to the ring, followed by Jason Andrews and "Cowboy" Bob Dodge. Before long, the ring was overflowing with wrestlers, hugging him, slapping him on the back, and congratulating him on his victory.

"You did great, Tommy!" said Andrews, having to yell to be heard over the crowd.

"Awesome match, brother," said Eddie Guerrero, slapping him on the shoulder. "You had the crowd eating out of the palm of your hand."

"Bruiser" Brody, wearing his familiar fur-covered boots and standing tall beside Guerrero, said nothing, but gave Tommy a big thumbs-up. Lou Thesz was behind him, followed by The Ultimate Warrior, The Junkyard Dog, and Frank Gotch. They all added their voices to the celebration, congratulating him on winning the title.

"The American Dream" Dusty Rhodes was next, wearing black trunks with his initials sewn onto the material. He sported white knee-pads and his trademarked Cowboy ring boots with blue stars, and was smiling so big that he could have lit up Madison Square Garden.

"You are the man of the hour, Tommy, the tower of power, too sweet to be sour...if you weel," said Rhodes, with a lisp.

Tommy heard music begin to play over the speakers, and smiled to himself. "Rowdy" Roddy Piper was walking down the ramp, carrying a set of bagpipes and dressed in his signature kilt and "Hot Rod" t-shirt. He reached the ring, climbed inside, and hugged Tommy.

"Hell of a match, kid," he said as he released the embrace. "Hell of a match."

"Thanks, Roddy," whispered Tommy, beginning to understand.

Andre the Giant, all 7'4" of him, was the last wrestler to arrive. He was dressed in a custom made suit that probably would have held three regular-sized men. The eighth wonder of the world took a moment to wave to the fans before stepping over the top rope and into the ring.

"Nice job, boss," he said, in his deep French accent, clapping Tommy on the shoulder.

And there was his grandfather, Thomas Buckley, moving past Andre and pushing through the throng of wrestlers surrounding him. Tommy embraced the old man, and then whispered something in his ear. The old man looked surprised, but then slowly nodded.

"Could never hide anything from you, boy," he said, with a wink. "For what it's worth, though, I'm still proud as peaches, Tommy."

"Thanks Grandpa," said Tommy, touching the old man's shoulder before turning to walk to the other side of the ring.

He leaned over the ropes, looked down at announcers Gordon Solie and "Gorilla" Monsoon, and asked them for the microphone. They both looked confused. After all, this wasn't part of the script. Solie, however, always the consummate professional, did as Tommy asked and passed him the microphone.

"Gene, get your ass down to the ring," he yelled into the microphone, and the fans stopped cheering. All eyes were on him, including those of his fellow wrestlers and his grandfather. "You have exactly one minute, or I'm breaking kayfabe into so many pieces not even you will be able to put it all back together again."

Kayfabe was the tradition of wrestlers not revealing to outsiders that professional wrestling was, indeed, scripted. It wasn't as big a deal as it was years ago, and most people knew anyway, but it was still considered bad form to blatantly flaunt it.

It was a good threat, though, and one he knew would get Gene Tyler to the ring.

He looked down at the shiny gold belt strapped around his waist and sighed. Tommy Buckley, National Wrestling Federation heavy-weight champion of the world. It had a nice ring to it, even if it wasn't real. But he was okay with that. He'd lived out his dream. He'd had a 5-star match with his idol and taken the win, all while his grandfather had been there cheering him on. What more could a small-town kid from Illinois ask for?

"You needed something, Tommy?" said Gene Tyler into his own microphone, as the sea of wrestlers parted before him.

"You know what I need."

Tyler shrugged his muscular shoulders, nodding his head. "Okay, so what gave it away? Was it your grandfather? Or maybe the signs? I had a feeling the signs were too much."

He dropped the microphone and stepped closer to Tyler. "Both of those things," Tommy admitted, "but I was starting to put it together even before then. So I died in that car crash, right?"

Tyler turned off his microphone and looked away. "I'm sorry to say that you did, Tommy. They held a tournament for your TV title, named it 'The Tommy Buckley Memorial TV Championship Tournament.' I think you would've been proud."

"John White-Owl won the tournament, right?" Even now, the memories of his friend beating him for the title were fading.

Another nod from Tyler confirmed it for him. "The boys don't know, kid," said Tyler, indicating the other wrestlers in the ring, all of whom had stopped moving and were just standing there with blank expressions on their faces. "Neither do most of the fans. Please don't spoil it for them."

"I won't," he said quietly, for the first time pausing to mourn the life he'd lost. "The fans, too? They're all dead?"

"The fans, the announcers, the referee, every last one of them. So tell me, Tommy, how did you figure it out?"

He thought back to the tag-team match, to the battle royal, and to every other bout on the card. The fans cheered for everyone. There were no bad guys, no heels. Face versus face matches were incredibly rare, and certainly no one would ever build a card that consisted entirely of faces. He told Tyler as much, who frowned.

"But that's all we have to work with," Tyler said.

"Where's Nick Bockwinkel? Where's Rick Rude, or Curt Hennig? Where are…"

Tyler silenced Tommy with the shake of his head. "We don't talk about them here."

"But why? Bockwinkel, Rude, Hennig, not to mention Gino Hernandez and Chris Adams, Randy Savage, Owen Hart, Freddie Blassie, and the Big Bossman…I could go on and on. So many great heels over the years. Where are they?"

"Baby faces go to heaven, Tommy, and that's where you are. Heaven. Tomorrow you'll forget all about this and we'll do it all over again, and you'll win the world title again, though maybe this time I'll cut back a little on the signs."

Tommy was getting angry now. The old man wasn't answering his question. "If this is heaven, where the hell are the heels?"

"Exactly," said Tyler, who began to fade from view. "Heels go to hell. Where else would they go?"

But it's all a work, he tried to say, *it's all pretend,* but the words wouldn't come out of his mouth. Heels weren't necessarily bad guys in real life, just as the baby faces weren't always good guys outside of the ring. In order for the baby faces to be the good guys, there had to be bad guys. Didn't God or whoever was in charge here know that?

Tyler was gone now, and Tommy's newly-won title belt disappeared from his waist. The wrestlers all around him, the fans, his grandfather, and, finally, even the ring itself started to fade, as did Tommy, eventually, and then everything ceased to exist.

The roar of the crowd always got Tommy Buckley's blood pumping, but he'd never heard a crowd quite like this before. This was Wrestlepalooza, baby, an event he'd dreamed of being involved in all his life, and not only was he involved, he was in the effing main event! He was wrestling for the National Wrestling Federation's top prize, the world heavyweight championship, against his boyhood idol, "Gentleman" Craig Thornton.

He'd been waiting for this moment his whole life, and he intended to make the most of it.

Beside Myself

Brandon Sims was in the break room when he heard the explosion. It wasn't fair, he thought, moments before he died. He wasn't a scientist. Hell, he wasn't even a real employee. He was just a Kelly temp working a week-long gig in the mailroom.

All of that went through Brandon's head in the two seconds it took for him to be obliterated out of existence. Right before he died, he noticed that the room around him had changed. The black table and chairs that normally occupied the east side of the room were now gone, replaced by a long, plush tan-colored couch. Brandon looked into a mirror above the couch that used to not be there and saw himself screaming. He closed his eyes, and that was all he knew.

From the Dallas Times Herald,
August 5, 2027

Waxahachie Collider Accident
By Acacia Hale

Waxahachie—The High Luminosity Large Hadron Collider in Waxahachie failed earlier today, resulting in an explosion that leveled the entire complex and several surrounding buildings in a two square mile radius. At least 1,300 people are presumed dead or missing.

The installation, an upgrade of the original Superconducting Super Collider, was turned on at noon central time, and the explosion happened almost instantly, according to witnesses in the surrounding Ellis County. Scientists had hoped to duplicate the big bang in miniature form.

"It was a hell of a thing," said Avery Lincoln, 47, a local business owner. "Most awful noise you ever heard, like metal against metal, shattered all the windows in my restaurant. And then it was over just as quick as it began, with only that awful crater left. A real tragedy."

The Ellis County Sheriff's department in conjunction with state police quickly cordoned off the area. Investigators from the Fort Hood army base are expected shortly.

August 7, 2027

Riley Sims was dressed in the only black suit he owned, standing graveside for his little brother's funeral. He still couldn't quite accept it. One moment Brandon was alive, and the next he wasn't.

He was the one who'd suggested that Brandon, fresh out of college with a BFA in art history, join Kelly Services to make some extra money while trying to trying to find a more permanent job. It was his fault that his brother was dead.

"So many of Brandon's friends came," said Corrine, Riley's mother, as she took his hand. "I'm not sure if he would have been happy or embarrassed."

Riley chuckled. Brandon was a gregarious person, but got embarrassed easily. He suspected it would have been a little of both and said as much.

Corrine squeezed his hand for a second before letting it go. "It seems like we were just here, doesn't it?"

Riley's father had died of emphysema a year and a half ago, just a month before Pfizer announced a new miracle drug that had a 95% cure rate for the deadly disease. He was buried here in Restland, Dallas' premier cemetery, beneath a tree just a few yards from where Brandon had been interred.

"It sure does, Mom," Riley said, staring down at his brother's grave.

The service had ended almost an hour ago and everyone had gone, leaving Riley and his mother to grieve in private. To lose a father and a brother in less than two years was almost unbearable, especially the way they'd lost Brandon. With the emphysema, they'd at least known what was coming. But who would have expected the explosion that had rocked Waxahachie two days ago?

Brandon's body had been unrecoverable, of course, and so the casket was empty, which made the whole thing seem even more unreal. He still kept half-expecting his brother to show up at the cemetery, laughing, explaining it was all some crazy prank.

"Dear lord," Corrine said, gasping.

Riley turned to look at her, and her face had gone pale. "What is it, Mom? What's wrong?"

She raised a trembling hand, pointed across the cemetery to a copse of trees. Riley followed her hand, but didn't understand what was wrong. There was a bald man wearing a blue polo shirt and brown khakis staring back at them. He looked apprehensive, almost scared.

There was something familiar about the man.

He went weak in the knees as it hit him. Riley's father had somehow returned from the dead, looking like he had years before the emphysema ravaged his body, to mourn at his son's funeral.

From the Dallas Times Herald, August 8, 2027

Science Experiment Gone Wrong?
By Acacia Hale

Dallas—Through-out north Texas, seemingly identical duplicates of people are coming forward, claiming to be the original. Reports are also coming in from parts of Arkansas and Oklahoma of similar incidents. The Texas National Guard began rounding these "duplicates" up and taking them to high school gyms across Texas upon order of Texas Governor Rex Morgan, before the President of the United States Cory Booker ordered the guard to stand down.

"We don't yet know what's going on here," said the president in an address early this morning, "but these people appear to be United States citizens, and as such should be afforded the same benefits as any other citizen of our great nation."

Booker went on to declare a state of emergency in Texas, Arkansas, and Oklahoma, indicating the U.S. government would foot the bill for emergency housing of these duplicates.

Physics Professor Dr. Ava Collins at the University of Texas in Dallas has come forth, claiming that the High Luminosity Large Hadron Collider accident in Waxahachie three days ago is responsible for the duplicates.

"The accident somehow created identical copies of seemingly-random individuals within an approximately 500 mile radius of the collider installation," Collins said in a statement released this morning.

Famed CERN physicist Fabiola Gianotti, however, had other ideas. In an interview from Switzerland that aired on CNN yesterday, she said, "These people are no mere duplicates. There are subtle, and sometimes not-so-subtle, differences. The accident clearly opened up a window to another reality, and transported these poor souls into ours."

August 8, 2027

Riley, his mother, and his so-called "father" had stayed up talking into the wee hours of the morning. Thank goodness he was off today, because there's no way he could have dragged himself into work. As it was, he spent the night on his mother's couch and didn't wake up until almost eleven. Sitting in the living room in his boxers and an old *Katie Herzig* concert t-shirt, he inhaled a bowl of Chunky Monkey Cheerios while trying to make sense of everything he'd heard the night before.

According to the man professing to be Walter Sims, he'd never had emphysema and had, in fact, quit smoking before he hit thirty. His version of Corrine, however, had died two years ago, after a long battle with gallbladder cancer. He also claimed never to have had a son named Riley, and instead to have fathered Brandon and a daughter named Hayley.

Brandon was still alive in his world, he explained, but he had come to the cemetery after reading about Brandon's death, hoping to figure out whether he was insane or really had stepped into a universe similar to but not quite his own. He was just as shocked, he said, to see Corrine alive as she had been to see him.

Bullshit. None of this made any sense. It had to be some kind of scam designed to bilk him and his mother out of whatever small insurance settlement they'd get from Brandon's death. He just couldn't quite figure out the angle.

Walter's Texas driver's license certainly looked valid, but Riley knew those could be faked easily enough. In fact, he had all but convinced himself that everything the man said was a lie when he happened upon a CNN interview with actress Chloë Grace Moretz while channel-surfing.

The thing was, there were two of her.

"I was in Dallas to promote my new movie, *Kick-Ass Reborn*," said the one on the right, dressed in a tan skirt with a red blouse, "and I excused myself and stepped into an empty room to take a call from my husband. Halfway through the phone call, we got cut off and it wouldn't connect when I tried to call him back. I gave up and went back into the lobby, and it was deserted."

"So, what did you do then?" asked the interviewer, an older man with salt-and-pepper hair that Riley had seen before but whose name he could never remember.

"So the first thing that she does," said the other Chloë, the one wearing a long, blue dress, "is bum a phone off a janitor and call home, trying to reach her husband."

"And she answers," said the Chloë in the tan skirt, nodding her head at her doppelgänger. "Talk about a freak out moment."

"And, as you probably already know, I'm not married," said the Chloë he was starting to think of as Chloë Alpha, "but somehow we still lived in the same place and had the same phone number."

"So where do you go from here?" asked the interviewer, turning to Chloë Beta.

"Get Universal Pictures to sign off on *Kick-Ass Reborn*?" the actress answered with a half-smile. "Hell, at this point, I'll be her stunt double."

Chloë Alpha reached out to take Chloë Beta's hand. "She's been staying with me," she said, "and is welcome to continue to do so as long as it takes to figure out a way to get her back to her universe."

Her universe? What in the hell was going on?

"I hate to ask this," said the interviewer, his brow creased with concern, "but what if it's permanent? What if Chloë and everyone else can't get home?"

"I'll cross that bridge when I come to it," said Chloë Beta, her voice shaking. "But I'm not ready to give up on Dan and my little girl just yet."

Chloë Alpha stared at the interviewer, then turned to her twin. "We'll get through this, Chloë," she said to Chloë Beta, pulling the now-weeping woman into her arms. "I promise."

Riley stared at the screen as the program went to commercial. If there were two Chloë Grace Moretzes, and if the same thing had happened to other people as well, did that mean Walter's story was true?

"Riley," said his mother, coming in from the kitchen, "I just opened the newspaper. You really need to see this."

From the Dallas Times Herald, August 12, 2027

What Do You Do When You Don't Exist?
by Acacia Hale

Addison—What would you do if you woke up one morning and you no longer existed? Sarah Marie Parker, 27, allegedly from Addison, Texas, is now facing that reality.

She and thousands of other people seem to have simply appeared in north Texas and parts of Arkansas and Oklahoma in the wake of the High Luminosity Large Hadron Collider failure in Waxahachie last Thursday. Unlike most of those people, however, Sarah doesn't have a counterpart. She is without a valid driver's license, social security card, credit rating, bank account, or even a birth certificate, and the three hundred dollars she happened to be carrying in her wallet has been deemed not legal tender. Sarah is, in effect, homeless and broke.

"One minute I was in Tom Thumb, picking up a birthday cake for someone in the office," said Parker, who allegedly worked as a sales analyst for Dr. Pepper in her own reality, "and the next, I'm apparently in a Safeway. But the price tag on the cake still says Tom Thumb. I'm clueless at this point, and I go to check out, and the cake won't ring up."

Tom Wilkins, 56, the manager of the Safeway, called the police after Parker allegedly "made a scene" at the cashier and refused to leave the store. Parker was taken into custody, however charges were not filed.

"I didn't know what to do or where to go," Parker said, after contacting the newspaper to tell her story. "It was the most frightening thing I've ever experienced in my life."

Thanks to President Cory Booker's swift approval of the State of Texas Person Displacement Act, passed by both houses in a joint emergency session and signed into law on Monday, Parker has been living rent-free in a Holiday Inn in downtown Dallas since Monday. She is also being fed three daily meals free of charge and, like every other displaced person in Texas, has been given a $500 a week stipend for clothing and other necessities and access to psychological counseling.

"Thank God for your president," said Parker. "But still, what do I do with my life? Most of these other people, they have duplicates here, or at least family of their duplicates. There are just a handful of us that don't. We don't have jobs, families, or money. We simply don't exist."

What did Parker mean by "your president?" Where she comes from, apparently, Chelsea Clinton followed in her parent's footsteps and is the president of the United States of America.

August 15, 2027

It had been only ten days since his brother's funeral, but life as Riley knew it had changed drastically since then. Walter Sims really seemed to be his father, at least his father from another universe. He and Riley's mother had taken up where they had left off when Riley's real father died, and Walter was now living with her, having apparently already given up on getting back to his own children.

Yes, Brandon was still alive in Walter's universe, at least as far as the old man knew. According to Walter, the Waxahachie complex had been shut down in the early 1990's, before Riley was even born, so Brandon wasn't working as a temp employee there that day. He had a permanent job, in fact, at a store called Wal-Mart. Riley had googled "Wal-Mart," but couldn't find anything. Walter said it was a lot like Target and K-Mart, only bigger and more widespread.

The whole thing boggled Riley's mind. The government still wasn't saying much, but scientists all over the news channels and the Internet claimed that the explosion in Waxahachie had ripped open a hole between this reality and another, similar one, and sucked through random people in the process. Wormholes. Alternate realities. Wal-Mart. Life was turning into a sci-fi novel.

And yet, the loss of his brother notwithstanding, Riley was happier than he had been in years. Not only did he have his father back—in as much as he could—he'd met someone two nights ago at the end of his shift at Red Robin, where he'd been bartending for the last couple of years.

Her name was December, and she had deep green eyes, long black hair, and was drop-dead gorgeous. She was about his age, and he'd met her in the parking lot of the restaurant. She'd walked straight into him as he was leaving, spilling the contents of her purse all over the sidewalk. After he'd helped her gather up everything, and they'd both apologized multiple times for the collision, she'd blushed and given him her cell phone number.

They'd gone out last night, and it was the best first date he'd ever had. He'd taken her to Fred's, a new upscale chain Italian restaurant started by the guy who owned Ruskin's Pizzeria, where they had killed a bottle of wine and dined on lasagna and Fettuccine Alfredo.

She had kissed him goodnight when he dropped her off at her apartment complex in Addison at half past ten, and her lips had tasted so sweet that it was all he could do to get back in the car and drive home. He'd stammered like an idiot and asked if he could see her again, and she had laughed and said of course, how about Thursday?

Thursday was just four days away, but he wasn't sure he could wait that long. It was almost as if she could read his mind, for it was at that moment that December texted him.

December: How r u?

Riley: Better now. I was just thinking about you.

December: O, really? Funny, cuz I was thinking about u 2

Riley: What were you thinking about?

December: Our date, silly! What else?

Riley: I could think of a few things... ;)

They went on like that for a while, flirting and joking back and forth, until December finally said she had to get back to work. They'd firmed up their plans for Thursday, which now included dinner at her favorite Thai place as well as seeing *The Avengers vs The X-Men* at the new, fully immersive "4-D" theater in Plano.

Riley sighed and slipped his cell phone into his pocket. He had to work tonight, which was never fun, but at least he was off Thursday. He hadn't dated anyone since his last girlfriend broke up with him nine months ago, and he had a good feeling about December. After all, he was born on December the 4th. If that wasn't a sign, what was?

From Time.com, August 16, 2027

A Few Key Differences between the Realities
By Elizabeth K. Young

Twelve days ago, the High Luminosity Large Hadron Collider in Waxahachie failed, resulting in an explosion that obliterated not only the entire complex but also several other buildings in a two square mile radius. 1,127 people have since been confirmed dead, while 185 still remain unaccounted for

What seemed the fodder of science fiction less than two weeks ago is very much reality today, as more people come forward claiming to be from an alternate universe very similar to our own.

One such refugee from that other universe, history professor Edward L. Montgomery, 56, sat down to talk with me earlier today about some of the key differences in his reality and our own.

"In my reality, the Waxahachie super collider project was cancelled in 1993 due to budget problems. This was after $2 billion dollars had already been spent on the installation, mind you," said Professor Montgomery, who taught American History at the other reality's University of Texas at Arlington. "A chemical company named Magnablend took over the main building in 2012 after they lost their original site in a fire."

"That isn't the only difference between our realities, of course. In my universe, World War II ended on May 8th, 1945, but here the war lasted until June 5th of 1949. Another example is John Lennon. Here, he's still alive, while in my reality he was murdered in 1980 by someone named Mark David Chapman."

The professor went on to say that in his reality, George W. Bush was elected president in 2000, while of course in ours Al Gore won the office. Less than a year later, in Montgomery's reality, the World Trade Center was destroyed by a group of terrorists know as al-Qaeda, while our version of the twin towers remains standing. Professor Montgomery, one of the estimated 5-10% of people who don't have a counterpart in this reality, plans to author a book detailing the historic differences between his home and our own.

Something that hits a little closer to home for those of us on staff at the *Times Herald*: in Montgomery's reality, this newspaper shut down in 1993, leaving the *Dallas Morning News* as the sole surviving newspaper in Dallas. In our reality, of course, the *Morning News* shut down in 2017, leaving the *Dallas Times Herald* as the survivor of the Dallas newspaper wars.

August 17, 2027

No one sent letters anymore. Almost everyone sent email, so when an actual paper letter showed up, it was usually bad news. Riley had just pulled into the driveway of his mother's house and stepped out of his car when the three-times-weekly automated mail delivery bot showed up and deposited mail into the mail box. He spoke the access code to open the secured box, then reached in and pulled out the mail.

He stared down at the K-Mart circular and the letter from Stanfield insurance that he now held in his hand. Stanfield Insurance was handling the claims from the Collider accident, and would be responsible for reimbursing Riley and his mother for Brandon's burial expenses.

The coffin was empty, of course. Brandon's body had been incinerated, along with everyone else in the building at the time. Random bone fragments and some teeth were recovered from the site, but that was pretty much it. Riley shuddered at the thought of his brother going out like that.

Riley almost opened the envelope, but instead took it inside. He handed it and the K-Mart circular to Corrine Sims, who immediately opened the envelope, took out the letter, and began to read.

"They think he might still be alive," she said, letting both the letter and the circular slip from her fingers. "Do you think it could be true?"

Ignoring the question, Riley bent over to retrieve the letter and began to read:

Dear Mrs. Sims,

We are sorry to inform you that we cannot pay the life insurance policy claim for your son Brandon Harold Sims at this time, due to the accident at the High Luminosity Large Hadron Collider in Waxahachie, Texas still being under investigation.

Because people from another, near-identical universe were allegedly transported to our world as a direct result of the accident, there is every reason to hope that the same thing might have happened to Brandon and some of the others caught in the explosion.

We will contact you again when our research is complete.

Sincerely,
Herman Slott
Claims adjustor
Stanfield Insurance

"This is such bullshit, Mom," Riley said, crumpling the letter into his fist. He looked at her, expecting anger, but instead she was smiling.

"What's bullshit?" asked Walter, coming into the room from the kitchen. "What's going on?"

"They think Brandon might still be alive," said Corrine, turning to look at Walter, "trapped in your universe, just like you're trapped here."

"He's *not*," Riley said. "They found remains, Mom. Remains. Bones and teeth. Everything else was incinerated. Brandon is dead."

"They don't know whose remains they found," she countered. "My baby might not be gone, after all."

From the Dallas Observer, August 18, 2027

Alternate Animals
By Katy Cooper

We are not alone. Aside from the estimated 18,000 humans that appeared in North Texas and parts of Arkansas and Oklahoma following the High Luminosity Large Hadron Collider failure in Waxahachie on August 5, a handful of animal species have also apparently crossed over into our universe.

At the Dallas Zoo, three bonobos, two orangutans, a chimpanzee, a rhesus macaque, and a gorilla have all met their counterparts, while a second gorilla who apparently has no counterpart in our universe has also appeared. This gorilla, named Arthur, is unusually adept at sign language, and was able to communicate with scientists at the zoo.

"Arthur is amazing," said Dr. Laurie Kitteridge, 37, who leads the gorilla research department at the zoo. "He recognizes and can use over 1,500 signs, and seems to possess a keen sense of self-awareness."

When asked what he thinks happened, Arthur replied with: "Arthur there, Arthur here. Friends still friends, but new friends smell funny. Arthur miss friends. Arthur miss home."

In addition to the primates, four elephants have joined the four elephants already in residence at the zoo. The four newcomers are identical to their counterparts, save one is missing his left tusk. After their initial confusion, the new elephants seemed to calm down and integrate themselves into the herd.

"It's clear that whatever happened, only beings that are truly self-aware were affected," said Kitteridge. "We already know that most animals are to a degree sentient, in that they think and have goals, but only a handful are like humans in the sense that they are self-aware and can pass the mirror test. Primates and elephants certainly fit the bill, and I think Arthur is a prime example."

Developed in the 1970s, the mirror test is an experiment where the experimenters discretely mark an animal's face with dye or a colored dot. When presented with a view of themselves in the mirror, a self-aware animal will usually try to remove the spot or turn to get a better view, proving that the animal is aware that the image in the mirror is his or her own. Non-self-aware animals will assume they are looking at a different animal.

In addition to the elephants and primates, many farmers have reported a larger-than-average amount of crows in the affected area. While there is no proof yet, Kittredge and others believe that the extra crows are also from the other Earth. Crows, part of the Corvid family along with magpies and ravens, have long been thought to be self-aware, giving credence to Kittredge's theory.

August 19, 2027

Riley glanced at his watch. It was just a few minutes 'til six, which meant he was exactly on time. He had purposefully driven slowly so as not to be early, which was very unlike him. December already meant a lot to him, and he didn't want to screw things up.

He pulled up to the gate that separated the expensive downtown Dallas Kirby Place apartments from the rest of the world, surprised to see her waiting there for him. He'd been hoping that she might invite him in, but he took the fact that she'd been anxious enough for their date to wait by the gate as a good sign.

December was dressed in a short red dress that clung to her curves, and wore black stiletto heels that accentuated her long legs. She smiled and gave him a little half-wave as he pulled up beside the gate, and the sight of her took his breath away.

Riley put the car into park and let himself out of his three-year-old Kia Lightning, walking around to open the passenger door for her.

"Cute *and* polite," she said, slipping into the electric car. "I think I'm officially smitten."

"Join the club," said Riley, smiling. "I've been looking forward to this all week."

He put the car into gear and pulled away from the gate, drove past a Holiday Inn Hotel and Suites, and pulled on to Central Expressway. Charlie's House of Thai was just a couple exits down the road, and, even with the heavy Dallas traffic, it only took them a few minutes to arrive.

"So, how are things going with your parents?" December asked, after they'd been seated and had ordered.

He'd told her about Brandon's death and Walter's subsequent appearance, and that he still didn't quite trust the man. They'd talked a lot these past few days, both via text and in late night phone calls that often lasted hours.

"Okay, more or less," he responded. "It just seems…weird, I guess. The way that Mom almost seems to have forgotten that he's not *her* husband, not really. He's moved into the house, and I think they're sleeping together."

"That must be difficult for you."

"It is, and it isn't. I mean, I want her to be happy. I really do. It just seems too convenient, I guess. What does she really know about him?"

December shrugged. "What do you ever know about anyone?"

"True, I guess. His version of my mother passed away from gallbladder cancer two years ago, so I guess maybe they need each other."

"He said she *died?*" A hint of anger flashed across her face, but vanished almost immediately. "Well, that's just awful. The poor man."

"Are you okay?" He asked, reaching out to touch her hand.

The waiter showed up with their food before she had the chance to respond. Pad See Ewe for her, and Evil Jungle Prince for him, both with chicken and both five stars on the spicy scale.

"This is really good," Riley said, in between bites, "I can't believe I've never been here before.

"Anyway, we got a letter a couple of days ago from Stanfield Insurance. They're not paying out on Brandon's claim, because they say he might still be alive in Walter's universe. I don't care about the money, but it's got Mom's hopes up, despite all the evidence that he's dead."

"But are really sure, Riley? I mean, if people can be teleported to this universe—to *our* universe—who's to say the reverse couldn't happen as well?"

"Well, aside from the remains they found, that universe didn't have a collider. From everything I've read about it, there would have had to have been one there as well for the transfer to be a two-way street. It's like a vacuum opened up on this side, sucking those people through. At least, that's what the scientists are saying."

"Scientists also didn't think that powering that thing up would create such a vacuum. If they were wrong about that, maybe they're wrong about this, too."

Riley chewed a mouthful of brown rice, considering what she just said. What about the bones and teeth, he wanted to say, but before he had the chance she continued talking.

"I'm not saying that did happen, but maybe your mother's just not ready to let go yet. Hope can be a wonderful thing, even if it's sometimes misguided."

"In that case," he said, smiling, "I hope that you'll invite me in after the movie, and I hope that hope isn't misguided."

✳ ✳ ✳

It turned out that hope wasn't misguided, after all, though it wasn't her place where they'd wound up. Riley lay in bed inside his little apartment in Addison, thinking about December as she lay sleeping, cuddled next to him. He hadn't expected things to go this far this fast, but he didn't regret it, not for a minute. Two dates in, and he knew he was falling for her.

Dinner at the little Thai restaurant had been delicious, and *The Avengers vs The X-Men* was amazing. December seemed every bit as much a nerd as he was, and caught all of the Easter eggs in the movie. He didn't even have to persuade her to stay for the after-credits teaser, which made him positively giddy.

It was late by the time the movie ended but he'd nevertheless asked her if she wanted to come back to his place for a drink, and to his surprise she said yes. They'd shared a bottle of white wine and then made out on the couch, and almost before he knew what was happening they were naked and making love. They'd eventually progressed to his bed and, after a second, slower lovemaking session, passed out from exhaustion and alcohol.

"What are you grinning about?" she asked, voice groggy.

She was leaning on her elbow, smiling at him. He turned and kissed her soft red lips, feeling his stomach flip as their mouths met. Yes, he was head over heels for sure.

It was like they were made for each other. Hell, even her name was perfect. Riley was, after all, born on December 4th. He felt a connection to her that he had never felt to another woman in his life, and they hadn't even known each other a week. It was exciting, but also a little scary.

"I was just thinking about you," Riley finally said, after their kiss ended. "Thought you were asleep."

"I was, but I had a funny dream. Something about that old *Night at the Museum* movie Robin Williams did right before he killed himself...Riley, why are you looking at me that way? Oh, shit!"

"Robin Williams is still alive," he said, "at least here, he is."

"I'm so sorry, Riley. I just…I knew I should tell you, I just didn't know how." She was sitting up now, the bed's top sheet pulled close around her naked breasts, eyes downcast.

"You're from the other side," Riley said, "and you don't live in that apartment, either. You're staying in the Holiday Inn across the street. That's why you met me at the gate last night."

"Guilty as charged."

"But why? I don't care where you're from. I know this is nuts, we hardly know each other, but…I'm falling pretty hard for you. I know it's a cliché, but I've never felt this way about anyone before."

"I love you too, Riley. I mean, how could I not? But you might change your mind about me," she said, biting her lip, "when you realize who I really am, and why I did what I did."

"So tell me. I'm upset, I won't deny that, but I can't think of anything you could tell me that would change my mind about you."

"Remember that you said that," said December, reaching out to take Riley's hand. "First thing's first. December isn't my real name, it's just a nickname I came up with when I was a little girl, when there was another girl with my name in the same class in kindergarten. I liked it and it stuck."

"So what's your real name?"

"First, let me tell you why I did what I did," she said, her eyes wet with tears, "and hopefully you won't hate me."

From the Dallas Times Herald, August 20, 2027

Alternate Reality Murder in Farmer's Branch

By Acacia Hale

Farmer's Branch – Farmer's Branch Police this morning arrested Michael David Donavon, 35, on suspicion of murdering his double,

Michael David Donavon, also 35. Police were alerted by neighbors, who called 911 when they heard shots coming from Donavon's residence on the 2200 block of McArthur Street in Farmer's Branch.

Donavon was found face down in the garage, having been shot twice in the chest. He was pronounced dead by paramedics at 7:52 this morning.

The other Michael Donavon was found standing over the body, gun in hand, screaming, "I'm the real Mike Donavon, you son of a bitch, and you're not," over and over. When police confronted him, he surrendered his weapon and allowed himself to be apprehended without incident.

Police have yet to determine who is the legal (or primary) Michael David Donavon, as the perpetrator was in possession of both his own and his victim's IDs at the time of the apprehension. Michael Donavon's wife, Melanie Hughes Donavon, 31, was not present in the home at the time of the incident. The couple had no children.

This is thought to be the first alternate-reality related capital crime committed since the High Luminosity Large Hadron Collider in Waxahachie accident 15 days ago.

August 21, 2027

When Riley called and asked if he could bring his new girlfriend for dinner Saturday night, of course his mother said yes. She even seemed excited, and when he said to please make sure that Walter was there, she was positively ecstatic. He almost felt bad for the way things were going to go down.

He, December, and his mother sat in the living room of the house he'd grown up in, while Walter worked on dinner in the kitchen. This Walter was so unlike his real father in that way. He didn't remember his father ever helping out with household chores, much less cooking dinner. When he wasn't working, he was usually puttering around in the garage or tinkering with his car. This Walter was definitely different, in more ways than one.

Riley turned his attention for a moment to the television, which was muted. His Mom had in on MSFOX, the news channel, and they were covering the same thing they'd been covering for the last two weeks—the duplicates. Chloë Grace Moretz Alpha and Beta were being interviewed again, along with Aaron Taylor-Johnson. From what he could gather, this reality's Universal Studios had apparently decided to produce *Kick-Ass Reborn*, after all.

"It's so nice that you could come, December," Corrine Simms said, sitting beside them on the long yellow couch that occupied most of the south side of the room. "I've heard a lot about you."

"I've heard a lot about you as well, Mrs. Simms," said the woman who's name wasn't really December, "Riley speaks very highly of you."

They'd been here less than five minutes, and already Riley was tired of the chit-chat. He just wanted to get this done. He still had misgivings about what they were about to do, but if everything that December told him was true, they really had no choice.

He thought back to when he was a boy, maybe seven or eight years old. Brandon must have been three or four. They were in Florida, at Disneyworld, for a family vacation. They'd spent all day at the park and were exhausted, but he had been so excited that sleep eluded him as completely as it had overtaken his little brother. He'd lain awake for what seemed like hours when he heard his parents arguing.

"I saw how you looked at that woman at the park today," his mother said, in a loud whisper. "Your tongue practically fell out of your mouth."

"Corrine," his father whispered in reply, "I don't even know who you're talking about."

"You do too know who I'm talking about. That blonde in the black miniskirt, by the teacup ride."

Riley had his eyes closed, pretending to be asleep, but he imagined his mother with her arms crossed, staring daggers at his father. He felt his heart begin to race. It always made him anxious whenever they argued, and they'd been arguing a lot lately.

"I know you don't trust me right now, and I don't blame you. I had an affair, it was wrong, and I'm sorry. It was a stupid, meaningless fling, and it never should have happened. But I didn't even notice this blonde you're talking about. Corrine, I love you, and I swear to you that it'll never happen again."

As far as Riley knew, it never had. He'd never told anyone about the overheard conversation until two nights ago, when he shared that secret with the woman now sitting beside him on the couch. His father had been a good man who made one very bad mistake. The Walter in the kitchen, however, had taken that a step further.

"Mission control to Riley," he heard a voice say. "Come in, Riley, come in."

He looked up to see his mother staring at him. That bit about mission control had started when Riley was just a little boy, fascinated by the space program.

"Sorry, Mom," he said, "I was daydreaming. What'd you say?"

He would never find out, for at that moment Walter walked in from the kitchen wearing a white "kiss the cook" apron that belonged to Riley's mother and carrying a tray containing a pitcher of iced tea and four glasses.

"Dinner will be ready in about fifteen minutes, but in the mean time I thought we might have some iced tea and…" Walter stopped mid-sentence as his eyes fell on December. The tray tumbled from his fingers and the glassware shattered on the wooden floor, sending tea, glass shards, and ice cubes flying everywhere.

"Walter!" shouted Corrine, jumping up from the couch. "Are you all right? What happened?"

"I happened, Mrs. Simms," December said, also rising from the couch with Riley quickly following suit. "Hi, Daddy."

Corrine looked from December to Walter, and then back again. "Daddy? December, what are you talking about?"

"My name isn't really December, Mrs. Simms. It's Hayley. December is a nickname. I'm from the other universe, just like he is. Walter is my father." She reached for Riley's hand, and his fingers intertwined with hers.

Riley's mother found his face, searching his eyes for the truth. He nodded once and then turned away, wishing he could spare her the pain of learning about Walter.

"But how?" Walter asked, face ashen as he stared at Hayley. "You were nowhere near Waxahachie. How did you get here? How?"

"I was driving from Chicago to see Brandon, Dad. I was in Northwest Arkansas when it happened. I'd stopped at a convenience store called Kum 'n Go to grab a Coke. When I left, the building had turned into a Target Express."

"Baby, I'm so glad to see you," he walked toward her, arms out, but she backed away.

"You're a real son of a bitch, Dad. Mom died from gallbladder cancer? That's priceless."

"How…how did she die?" asked Corrine.

"She isn't dead! She's alive and well and lives in Iowa, with her husband Steve. They've been married almost ten years now. This bastard left her when I was just a little girl, but only after screwing everything that moved. I have two half-sisters from two different women. Did he tell you that? Daddy is quite the player."

"Now, Hayley, that isn't fair," Walter said, clenching and unclenching his fists. "There's more to the story than that."

"Fair? Want to talk about fair? Was lying to Riley's mother fair? Was pretending to be a better man than you are fair?" Her fingers tightened around Riley's. "You abandoned us, Dad. Was that *fair*?"

"Why did you lie to me?" asked Corrine, turning away from Hayley to face Walter.

"I didn't lie, Corinne," he said. "Well, okay, I guess I did about one little thing, but I just wanted to start over. Is that so bad?"

"One little thing?" Riley said, speaking for the first time since Walter entered the room. "You told us that Hayley's mother was dead. That isn't a little thing. My real father wasn't perfect, but he was nothing like you."

"And what about you," Walter countered, turning to face Riley. "Hayley is your girlfriend, huh? She's more like your sister, or…or…"

"I'm him," said Hayley, gripping Riley's hand even tighter, "or who I would have been, if I'd been born male. We're each other's other half."

"That's disgusting!"

"Hayley is everything I always wanted in a woman," Riley said, "and I know how crazy that sounds, but it's true. People always say that you have to love yourself before you can love someone else, after all, and—"

"My Walter cheated on me, once," Corrine interrupted, finally speaking again, "and I forgave him. You never knew this, Riley. It happened when you were little. It took us a long time to work through it, but to his credit it never happened again.

"But you…Walter…whoever you are, you ran out on your own kids, not to mention your wife?

"I'm not that same man, Corrine. I'm not…"

They'd never find out what he was about to say he wasn't, for at that moment Walter Simms blinked out of existence. Corrine gasped and took a step toward Riley. "Where did he go?"

"Oh, fuck," said Riley, turning his attention to the television.

A "breaking news" banner danced across the bottom of the 3D flat screen. Riley grabbed the remote from the coffee table and unmuted MSFOX.

"...she just vanished," said a blonde reporter, holding a microphone in front of her face.

"She just vanished?" asked a male voice off camera.

The reporter adjusted her earpiece, looked around, and screamed. "Marty?" she asked, voice trembling, "did you see that?

"No, I had the camera on you," replied another male voice, this one testy. "Gimme a second."

The camera panned the landscape. Two identical teenage girls were walking across the scene when one of them suddenly disappeared. The other walked on for a few more seconds, oblivious, until she finally noticed her companion's sudden disappearance. She looked left and right, searching in vain for her twin.

They were standing in front of the remains of the High Luminosity Large Hadron Collider in Waxahachie, where they'd been reporting from on and off since the day of the accident.

"Melissa, are you still there? What's happening?" asked the first male voice. And then: "Oh no. In the last minute or two, we've apparently gotten dozens of reports from the Waxahachie area of the duplicates suddenly vanishing."

Riley turned his eyes to Hayley, and she stared at him, fear in her eyes. They still held hands, and her fingers squeezed his tighter.

"Riley, I don't want to go back."

"You're not going anywhere," he promised pulling her close to him, enfolding her in his arms.

"Apparently, those closest to the epicenter are disappearing first," intoned the voice from the television. "We've just received a report from Oklahoma of a Duplicate vanishing, and now one from Arkansas. Are they going back to their own reality? We have no way of knowing."

"What should we do?" asked Corrine, fluttering her arms helplessly in the air.

"Don't let me go," cried Hayley, holding him tight. "I love you, Riley. I don't want to go back."

"I love you, too, Hayley," he whispered into her ear, squeezing her tighter, and then he felt his arms collapse in on themselves.

He squeezed his eyes shut, not wanting, not daring to open them, dreading what he'd see when he did. But he couldn't keep them closed forever. He opened his eyes to find that he and his mother were alone in the living room. Hayley was gone, following her father to the alternate universe that gave birth to both of them.

His life would never be the same again.

✳ ✳ ✳

From the Dallas Morning News, August 5, 2029

An Alternate Universe Anniversary
by Jack Fletcher

Waxahachie—It has been two years since approximately 2,850 people disappeared from our universe, only to reappear two weeks and two days later, claiming to have briefly lived in an alternate universe. At first thought to be a massive hoax, their story was quickly backed up by the money, electronics, and even bacteria that they brought back with them.

A year and a half ago, The United States government, under an executive order from President Chelsea Clinton that was later backed by both branches of congress, purchased the original building where the Superconducting Super Collider in Waxahachie had been housed. Scientists at the newly-revamped facility are currently working to recreate the experiment (with better safeguards) that brought 2,850 souls from our universe into the alternate universe that (in a nod to DC Comics) President Clinton has named Earth 2.

All four "Earth 2 babies" that were conceived on the other side are healthy and are doing fine. The mothers, who continue to remain anonymous, are also healthy and have suffered no post-partum side effects from the births.

"This is an unprecedented opportunity to establish communication and commerce with an essentially alien universe," President Clinton said in an address to commemorate the event this morning. "If we can open up a doorway to the other universe—a safe, dependable doorway—the opportunities are limitless. Safety is our first concern, of course, and so the doorway may take years if not decades to open, but we are confident that if it can be done, it will be done."

August 6, 2029

Brandon Simms sat in the living room of his sister's three-bedroom ranch-style house, the house paid for by the U.S. government, reading the newspaper. It was the same old same old, but maybe they'd actually make it work someday. For his sister's sake, he sure hoped so.

"Did you read this?" he asked, folding the newspaper and dropping it to the coffee table. 'If it can be done, it will be done.' Well, duh. It's the same thing they've been saying since you got back."

"I read it," said Hayley. "Typical political speak. But at least there's hope."

"I guess so," Brandon said, "I'd like to meet this brother I never had, and the alternate universe version of Mom."

"And December would love to finally meet her Daddy," Hayley said, holding her fifteen-month old daughter in her lap. "Wouldn't you, Decey?"

The dark-haired toddler ignored her mother, instead devoting her attention to a stuffed tiger. She shoved the tiger's paw in her mouth, chewed it for a moment, and then spit it out.

"Do you want to meet your daddy, Decey?" prompted Brandon.

"Daddy?" she finally asked, letting go of the tiger and letting it tumble to the floor.

"Yes, Daddy," whispered Hayley, hoping against hope that she would someday again be with the father of her child. "Your sweet, wonderful daddy." She couldn't imagine herself with anyone else.

There was a knock, and Hayley held her breath as Brandon got up to answer the door. It was Monday, which meant it was time for December's weekly blood draw. She turned to watch the door open, and glimpsed the ever-present guards outside as they moved aside to admit the nurse.

Hayley hugged her daughter and realized she had Riley's eyes, which were, of course, also her own. In a way, she guessed, they were both already with him, after all.

The toddler started to flicker, like she'd been doing every few days for the last six months. She stopped, thankfully, just before the nurse came in to take her blood. She wondered whether anyone had seen her on the other side yet. If anyone did, she hoped it would be Riley.

Troll

Jonathan J. Chambray's fifth book, the second in his *Farmhouse Murders* trilogy, had cracked the New York Time's top ten list just in time for Labor Day, and because of that he'd been able to add an extra zero to his latest contract extension. He knew he should be in a good mood, but couldn't get past his latest Amazon review.

He stared at the words on the screen again:

This book is just more of the same half-baked tripe from a writer who, at one time, had a small amount of potential but who is now nothing more than a has-been who never was. I don't know why I even bother anymore. 1-Star.

That was the entirety of the review from "Thomas Roll," the critic who had panned all of Chambray's books since the beginning of his career seven years ago. After the second review, he'd realized that, when you just used the reviewer's first initial, T. Roll spelled out "Troll." Amazon, Barnes and Noble, Goodreads, and just about every other book site on the Internet—the troll had hit them all.

Kira told him to just let it go, to ignore the troll's reviews and instead to concentrate on the thousands of good reviews his books had garnered, but for whatever reason he just couldn't take his wife's advice. Every time he read one of the troll's reviews, he saw red. Who hides behind such a goofy screen name, anyway?

For the second time this morning, Chambray typed in a reply to the troll's review but then erased it. Accept every review with grace, they said, and never, ever reply to the bad ones. He'd managed to hold his tongue for seven years, but, with every bad review the troll left, it was getting harder. He doubted the guy had really even read any of his books, which made it that much worse.

The phone rang, startling him. It was almost ten at night. He looked at the Caller ID. It was Rich Wayne, the detective he'd hired. He answered the phone.

"Mr. Chambray?" said a voice with a thick Boston accent.

"Speaking."

"I'm sorry for calling so late."

"It's all right. Do you have any news?"

"Not yet. I was just—"

"What do you mean, 'not yet'?" Chambray asked, cutting him off. "You've been on this for almost two weeks. How hard can it be to track this asshole down?"

"None of this is as easy as you think, Mr. Chambray. All we have is his ID on a handful of websites, and even then there's no guarantee that it's actually the same person."

"It is. I know it is."

"You're probably right," Wayne said, "but there's no proof, and even if there was, he hasn't done anything illegal. And it's practically impossible to hack into Amazon or Barnes and Noble to get his address. I just need to keep poking around."

Chambray terminated the call, fuming. He was paying the detective $300 per day and had absolutely nothing to show for the money. Who was this troll to call him out, to criticize his work? Was it, perhaps, a failed writer, or maybe one of his former students to whom he'd given a bad mark from his days teaching creative writing at the University of San Diego? He needed to get past this, to move on like Kira said, but he just couldn't.

The thing was, the troll didn't leave bad reviews for anyone but him. He could almost have blown it off if it wasn't for that. Koontz, King, Preston and Child, Meltzer, Isles, Spencer, even Grisham, for God's sake—all four and five star reviews, glowing with praise. Chambray was the only author for whom he left one star, scathing reviews. The fact that he left good reviews for the other authors made the bad ones he left for Chambray look even more believable.

He began typing, and, once he was done, stared at the screen:

How can anyone take the word of a reviewer too cowardly to use his real name? If you have any real critique to offer, please contact me via my website and we will discuss it. I seriously doubt, however, that I'll ever hear from you.

His finger hovered over the send button. He was finally going to do it, going to send the message and let the chips fall where they may. Just as he was about to press the key, the hairs on the back of his neck stood up and he felt the presence of someone behind him. He swung around his office chair to stare into the eyes of his wife of 15 years, and she didn't look happy.

"Really, Jon?" Kira asked, hands on her hips. "How many times have we been over this? Nothing good can ever come from responding to trolls."

He sighed. She was right, of course. She was always right when it came to things like this. He closed the Google Chrome tab containing the review and let his comment disappear along with it.

"Wise decision," said Kira, leaning over to brush her lips against his. She took his hand and pulled him to his feet. "Now, come on to bed."

He smiled, doing his best to put the troll out of his mind, and followed her into the bedroom.

Chambray lay awake in in his California king-sized bed, his wife's long, black hair pooled on her pillow as she slept next to him. The clock on his nightstand said it was just after two, but it felt as if he'd been lying there for days.

He and Kira made love earlier, and it had been good, but, no matter what he said or did, he couldn't stop thinking about the troll. He knew it was ludicrous to hate someone he'd never even met, but hate him he did, and with a white hot passion.

If he ever met the man, he knew he'd have to kill him.

He extracted himself from the bed, careful not to wake Kira, and walked naked through the house to his office. He avoided turning on the light, instead just moved the mouse so the screensaver would deactivate. The monitor provided all the light he'd need.

Chambray lowered himself to the brown leather chair that sat before his desk, the material feeling cold to his ass cheeks, and navigated the Google Chrome browser he'd left open back to the troll's review for *Death by Tractor*, the second book in his *Farmhouse Murders* trilogy.

He stared once again at the hateful words that filled his screen:

This book is just more of the same half-baked tripe from a writer who, at one time, had a small amount of potential but who is now nothing more than a has-been who never was. I don't know why I even bother anymore. 1-Star.

Just who in the hell did this guy think he was? He quickly typed a reply:

Listen, motherfucker, leave me the hell alone, or I'll rip your fucking throat out. I'm a wealthy man, and I will use every resource at my disposal to fucking break you into a million little fucking pieces!

He thought writing that would make him feel better, but it only served to increase his anxiety. How would he look, threatening some anonymous reviewer? He backspaced over the entire message and started again, going with a different tact.

A good writer is always striving to improve his craft and thus thrives on criticism, and you, sir, have long been my harshest critic. I'd love the chance to win you over. Contact me via my website and give me your mailing address and I'll send you the unpublished third book in the Farmhouse Murders *trilogy. When it comes out on Amazon, you can be the first to review it!*

Chambray looked over what he'd just written. It was genius. One does, after all, capture more flies with honey than one ever would with vinegar. If the man responded—and he knew that was a huge "if"— he'd ask the detective to pay him a little visit.

Holding his breath, he hit the send button, watching as his message was posted for all the world to see. There was no turning back now.

Chambray knew there was a chance that others would read the response and write him through his website, claiming to be Thomas Roll in order to claim the book that he hadn't actually even finished yet, but he also knew that only the original poster would receive an email from Amazon letting him know that his review now had a comment. With any luck, no one but the troll would actually read the reply. Whatever happened, he would delete his message within twenty four hours.

Satisfied with himself, relieved that he'd finally figured out a way to respond to the troll without looking like a total ass, he left his office and padded back to bed.

Chambray usually received a few dozen messages each day through his website, most asking for autographs, and some asking him to read their books. He didn't normally respond to any of them, instead leaving such correspondence to Laura, his virtual assistant, who worked out of her home somewhere in Arkansas.

This morning, however, he found himself eagerly scanning through the messages from the site, hoping to find a message from the troll. No such luck. Frustrated, he was about to give up when a new message came through. It was from tomroll42@gmail.com! His heart thumping in his chest, Chambray opened the message. It was just one line, and read:

Are you sure you want to do this?

The arrogant little prick was goading him. Of course he wanted to do this! He quickly wrote out a response:

I have your email address now, you little shithead! I'm going to track you down, rip your head off, and shit down your fucking neck!

He stared at the screen, but didn't click send. Instead, he took a deep breath and bit back his anger, backspaced over the entire response, and instead wrote:

Yes, I want to send you the book. Please give me your address and I'll mail it first thing in the morning.

That was much better. He clicked send, and then immediately called Rich Wayne. The detective answered on the first ring, but said he couldn't trace Gmail addresses.

"What do you mean, you can't trace it?"

"Exactly that," said Wayne. "Google's security is too good. I can try to guess his password, or I can email him pretending to be someone else and get him to reveal himself, but—"

"Those are all things I can do myself," Chambray said, "so why am I paying you to do it for me? You're fired. Send me a bill for your time up until this point."

"But Mr. Chambray, don't you think—"

Chambray turned off the phone, sat it aside, and checked his email once again. The troll had already responded. He clicked on the message:

Okay, if you say so. But don't say I didn't warn you, because I did.

The message was followed by an address in Carthage, Illinois. He'd heard of Carthage—that hack Shawn Spencer had set his novel *Small Things* there—but didn't really know anything about the town other than that it was a flyspeck and was close to where Illinois, Iowa, and Missouri all met.

Chambray picked up the phone to dial the detective, thought better of it, and then sat the phone back down. Screw Rich Wayne. The detective had done nothing but pad his own bank account. He'd handle this himself, like he should have all along.

He awoke with a start, opened his eyes, and wondered for a moment where he was. He was surrounded by white brick walls on all sides. A wooden dresser stood in front of him, atop which sat a small television, and beside the dresser stood an uncomfortable-looking green chair. A window-unit air conditioner was embedded into the wall to his left.

Chambray closed his eyes for a moment, stretched, and opened them again. He lay in a king-sized bed, dressed only in his boxers. He remembered where he was now. Carthage, population just below 3,000.

The flight from San Diego to Quincy, Illinois on American Airlines included two layovers—one in Phoenix, Arizona, and the other in St. Louis, Missouri—and had taken nearly ten hours and cost him almost $600. Chambray was exhausted by the time he arrived at the small Quincy airport, and it had only gotten worse from there. He remembered driving the 45 minutes from Quincy to Carthage in a haze before collapsing into bed about 30 seconds after a young woman in a St. Louis Cardinals ball cap had shown him to his motel room.

He'd rented a cheap room at the Prairie Winds Motel. The room wasn't bad, really. A little sparse, but the bed was comfortable enough. Someone on Yelp had rated the motel two stars, but he wasn't here for a vacation. He was here to finally meet his troll and knock some sense into him. Besides, the little town didn't have a lot of choices when it came to last-minute lodging.

Chambray thought of Kira and winced. He'd lied to her and told her that room on a discussion panel had opened up at an important literary convention in Chicago, and that his publisher had begged him to take the spot. He hated lying to her, but she just wouldn't understand. That has been two days ago, on a Thursday, and he'd booked his flight and left the next morning.

He looked at his watch. Shit. It was nearly ten. He needed to get up, get moving, and get this thing done. He reached over to the nightstand and picked up a map of Carthage, something he only vaguely remembered taking last night from the cramped motel lobby. When his GPS couldn't find the address "Thomas Roll" had given him—1 Bridge Road—he just assumed that the technology had bypassed this little village, but he couldn't find the address on the map, either.

If that son of a bitch had lied to him…but, no, he didn't think that he had. Perhaps the address was in a new development that wasn't yet on the map. He checked the date of the map: 2010, five years old. Yes, that must be it. Surely, the motel clerk would know where it was.

He quickly showered, shaved, and got dressed before making his way to the lobby of the motel. The girl from last night wasn't there, replaced instead by a large, burly man sitting at the front desk.

"May I help you?" he asked as Chambray approached, looking up from a copy of a newspaper called the *Hancock County Journal-Pilot*.

"I'm trying to find an address on Bridge Road. Problem is, Bridge Road doesn't seem to exist, at least on the map I got from the lobby last night. My GPS can't seem to find it, either."

The man stared at him for a second before speaking. "I've lived here all my life, mister, and I've never heard of any 'Bridge Road.' Are you sure you got the name right?"

"I know I got the name right," snapped Chambray. "Are you sure it isn't new or something?"

The man scratched his head and shrugged. "Could be," he said, "but if it is, I've never heard of it. You might check with the Chamber of Commerce. They'd know, for sure."

"And where is the chamber of commerce?"

The man rattled off directions and, thankfully, an address, which Chambray inputted into his phone. The Chamber of Commerce was just about five minutes from the hotel. That was pretty much the only good thing about living in a town the size of Carthage. You could get anywhere you needed to go inside of five minutes.

Thunder rumbled somewhere off in the distance, and the sky above seemed a little darker than it had mere moments before. All he needed was to get caught in a thunderstorm. Chambray hopped in his rental—a brand new silver Buick LaCrosse—and headed down U.S. highway 136 toward downtown Carthage. He followed the GPS, made his way around the town square, and pulled into a parking spot in front of the tiny Carthage Chamber of Commerce building.

"Can I help you?" asked an older man in a shirt and tie as Chambray pushed through the door into the tiny building. The badge on his shirt identified him as Leroy Perkins.

"I'm looking for an address, and it isn't on your map. It's 1 Bridge Road. Do you know where that's located?"

"Are you sure you got the address right? Doesn't ring a bell."

Chambray drove back toward the way he had come, fuming. It was becoming more and more obvious that the troll had indeed given him a fake address, and he should have investigated that possibility before flying halfway around the country to this dismal little town. Still, he wasn't ready to give up quite yet.

He hung a right on county road 1850 and it took him between the public swimming pool and the Jaycee Park, just as Leroy Perkins at the Chamber of Commerce had said it would.

He followed the curvy old road through the huge trees surrounding it, and before long the lake appeared on his left. The old man said that the only bridge in Carthage was just past the dam and, sure enough, he reached it in no time. He doubted that the troll was there, but he had to be sure.

Chambray parked his car on the bridge, got out, and looked around. There were no houses here, of course. Not that he really expected there to be. In fact, the closest thing to a house was the concrete building that stood across the road from the dam about a fourth of a mile back. He was about to get back in the vehicle and drive back to the concrete building when he heard a noise, like metal rubbing against metal.

"Hello, is anyone there?" He called out. It occurred to him that this whole thing might've been a setup to lure him here. He was probably being paranoid, but that didn't stop him from retrieving the tire iron from the trunk of the car.

"Hello?" he repeated, louder this time. "Is anyone there?"

Nothing.

The bridge, Perkins had told him, used to be a one-lane, rickety wooden affair, but had been replaced years ago by the metal and concrete monstrosity upon which he now stood.

Thunder sounded a little closer this time, and it began to drizzle. The sound he'd heard a few minutes ago must have also been thunder. He needed to get out of the rain and just call this whole thing an expensive lesson to listen to his wife.

Chambray jumped as a loud metal clang sounded from beneath his feet. What the hell? He clenched the tire iron in his fist and walked down the bridge to the grass, ignoring the rain, and then down into the dirt embankment. It was dark under the bridge, and he wished he'd brought a flashlight. Instead, he turned on the flashlight app on his iPhone. It would have to do.

A flash of lightning startled him, and then the heavens opened up and he was suddenly drenched. Rain poured down, turning the little dirt path he stood upon into mud in a matter of seconds. Hugging himself against the downpour, he made a mad dash and darted beneath the bridge.

Turning the cellphone-cum-flashlight all around him, he was surprised by what he didn't see. The cement surrounding him was completely free of graffiti, and in fact was devoid of beer bottles, used condoms, half-eaten food, or any of the usual items that sometimes collected beneath bridges.

Something caught his eye and he turned the light toward a large metal door set in the concrete. He moved forward, one hand clenching the tire iron and the other holding the iPhone out in front of him. There was a brass plaque beside the door, upon which was etched "1 Bridge Road." His heart began to beat faster. He reached out and clutched the door knob, twisted it, and pulled. The door opened easily, and light shone forth from whatever was inside.

Some part of Chambray told him to get out of there, to run up the muddy embankment, get in the rental, and head straight to the Quincy

248 | J o e D e R o u e n

airport. He pushed the fear down, clicked off the flashlight, and went through the door.

He found himself in a small hallway, lit by a simple lamp set into the wall. The hallway opened up into a large room, but that room was dark, and he couldn't make out what might lie beyond.

"Hello?" he called, his voice echoing in the hallway. "Is anyone here?"

No answer.

He walked over black and white tile, streaking it with mud. Slipping the iPhone into his pocket, he reached around the corner, feeling for a light switch. His phone beeped and he jumped, skittering back toward the metal door.

He took a deep breath and pulled out his iPhone. A secured network had been found. Did he want to connect to "1BridgeRoad," asked his phone? What the fuck? He ignored it, shoving the phone back in his pocket, and again crept toward the darkened room before him.

Chambray's fingers finally found a switch, and he flicked it on. Light filled the massive room in front of him and he found himself inside a huge library. The walls were covered in bookshelves that were overflowing with books. A large oak desk filled the center of the room, upon which sat a small laptop computer.

An overstuffed gray chair sat in front of the desk, empty. An open door opposite from where he stood led off to some other darkened room, while another door to his left looked like it opened up into a dining room.

He blinked, for a moment not trusting his eyes. The room was still there, an underground house beneath a bridge in a small Midwestern town in the middle of nowhere. Forgetting for a moment his goal, he padded over to the bookshelves and began to look through the books.

There was a first edition copy of Ray Bradbury's *Something Wicked This Way Comes* in pristine condition, along with works by Kage Baker, J.G. Ballard, Greg Bear, and more. He realized that the books were in alphabetical order, and, with a sense of excitement, moved down to the C's.

And there he was. The shelves contained all five of his books, including *Death by Tractor*, the second book in his *Farmhouse Murders* trilogy. They were surrounded by books by C.J. Cherryh, Lincoln Child, Anton Chekov, and more.

Next were the D's, which included Dahl, de Lint, DeRouen, Dann, and even Charles Darwin. Like the others, these books appeared to be all first editions and in perfect condition. He was almost ready to move to the E's when he heard a noise.

"Don't turn around," said a deep voice from behind him. "Just leave, and we'll forget this ever happened. You're not supposed to be here."

Chambray's hand clutched the tire iron so hard that his knuckles turned white. "Then why did you send me your address?"

"So you could send me the book, of course."

"It's not even finished yet. I just wanted your address, you stupid fuck."

He heard a sigh. "Yeah, I figured. But I wanted to give you the benefit of the doubt. I didn't expect you to show up here, though. I thought you'd probably send that detective of yours."

Chambray started to turn around, but stopped when the troll cleared his throat. How did he know about Rich Wayne? "Listen, you pretentious prick, I—"

"I said, you need to leave," the troll interrupted. "If you turn around...well, I'll have to follow the rules, and it won't be very pretty."

Follow the rules? What rules? "Just tell me something before I go. Why? Why go after my books? It's obvious you've never even read them."

"Oh, quite to the contrary. I've read them, all right," said the troll. "You've actually become one of my favorite authors over the years. The ending to *Death by Silo* was genius, one of the best I've ever read.

Death by Tractor was really good, too. Are you sure you haven't finished the third book?"

Chambray ignored the question. "But if you like my books, why did you leave me such awful reviews?"

He could almost feel the troll shrug. "It's my job. It's what I do. Every writer has a troll, even someone like, say, J.K. Rowling. Actually, she has two. Stephen King has three."

"Your *job*?" yelled Chambray, feeling his anger surge. "Your job is to ruin my career?"

"Is your career ruined?" countered the troll. "Didn't you just sign a new contract, the best you've ever been offered?"

How the hell did the troll know that? For that matter, how did he know about Rich Wayne? Chambray swung around almost in spite of himself, and immediately dropped the tire iron. Time seemed to slow as he heard it clang against the tile at his feet. He stared straight into a bare, muscular chest. The chest was a pale green and covered in wiry black hair.

He followed the chest up to the neck and finally to the face of a man wearing glasses who stood at least eight feet tall, had pointed ears, and whose teeth looked as sharp as razors. He wore a golden earring in one ear, and a silver ring in his nose. He was naked save for a furry loincloth, and he held a massive wooden club covered in sharp, metal spikes in one hand.

His breathe caught in his throat. His troll really was a troll. A real, honest-to-God troll. He backed away into the bookshelf, knocking a handful of books to the ground.

The troll sighed, exposing his teeth. "I asked you not to turn around, Mr. Chambray. I asked you to leave, but you just couldn't let it go, could you?"

"I'll leave," Chambray managed to squeak out, edging toward the still-open door that led to the outside.

"It's too late for that now, Mr. Chambray. Far too late." The troll moved in front of the door, his massive legs carrying him there in just two steps. He pushed the door closed and then locked it.

"No, no, it isn't," said Chambray, stumbling away from the troll.

The troll was upon him in second, clasping Chambray's right arm in his massive hand and wrenching it from its socket. The pain was excruciating, almost unbearable, and he watched in shock as the troll tossed aside his now useless limb. Blood poured out of his shoulder, where his arm used to be.

"Please, don't," he whispered, falling to his knees, clutching uselessly at his shoulder.

"It's too late," repeated the troll, raising the club above his head. "The worst thing is, I'll never find out the ending to the *Farmhouse Murders* trilogy."

"It was Jacob all along," Chambray screamed, holding his lone arm over his head. "Remember, they suspected him in the first book, but he had an alibi. But here's the thing. His brother was lying. Jacob killed them all."

The troll cocked his head. "Actually, that makes perfect sense," he said, as he swung the club down to meet Chambray's head. Everything exploded, and that was all Jonathan J. Chambray knew.

＊ ＊ ＊

The troll pushed the mop through the last of the blood, then wrung it out over a huge metal bucket. What a waste. Chambray could have been one of the great ones. Now, he was just dead, and the troll was out of a job.

No matter, though. He'd be assigned to a new writer soon enough, hopefully one with a little thicker skin. A writer who would actually listen to his wife. After all, most writers knew not to engage trolls.

He picked up the metal bucket and took it into the kitchen to join the rest of Chambray. Mixed with some flour and a little seasoning, the blood would make a good gravy. He may have lost his job, but at least he'd eat well tonight. He guessed it wasn't such a waste, after all.

Dark

Charlie woke in the darkness, a scream on her lips. She had no idea where she was or how she'd gotten there; she only knew she had to get out. She willed her hands to reach out into the blackness that surrounded her, but they ignored her, remaining motionless. She couldn't even feel them, and couldn't feel her legs, either.

What had happened? The last thing she remembered was her and Sara on their sailboat, named "the white owl," laughing and drinking margaritas, watching the waves lap at the shore some fifty yards away as they enjoyed the warm summer breeze. They were in love, and were celebrating Charlie finally having the courage to leave her husband and accept herself and her feelings for this beautiful, intelligent woman whom she'd known for only six months.

They'd made love for the first time on that rented sailboat. It had been tentative at first, clumsy even, but then their passion had taken over, and it felt like nothing Charlie had ever experienced before. She'd come, really come, for the first time in her life. Sara held her afterwards, kissing her, telling her how beautiful she was and how much she loved her.

What happened after that? She struggled to remember, fighting down the panic that slowly spread throughout her body. Why couldn't she move? Had the boat capsized? No, the boat was fine. A flash of memory. They'd been sailing just outside of Oak Bluffs, heading back to the docks, when, on a whim, they'd decided to set shore on the beach. They jumped hand in hand from the boat, giggling, marveling that they seemed to have the whole beach to themselves. The sun was just beginning to set and looked breathtakingly beautiful over the blue Massachusetts water.

Why was she so cold? She struggled again to move, but it was as if her body was no longer hers. She felt like shivering, would have welcomed the chatter of her teeth, but she remained motionless despite herself. What was happening to her?

The beach. They'd been on the beach. And then what? She concentrated on remembering the feel of the sand crunching beneath her toes, the taste of Sara's lips, the smell of…the smell of what? And then she remembered.

"It's getting a little cold," Charlie said, enjoying the musky smell of Sara's patchouli perfume as she snuggled closer to her.

They decided to build a fire. Charlie gathered various dry and brittle branches from the trees on the other side of the beach, while Sara ran back to the boat to look for a lighter. Soon they had a small blaze going, and Charlie began to sweat. She looked into Sara's eyes, smiled, and pulled her tank top up and over her head.

Had they made love again then, in the sand, as the sun went down? Charlie had wanted to, but didn't think they had. No, they'd decided to go skinny dipping first. They'd strewn their clothes around the fire before running, giggling and splashing, into the cold water that lapped at their sailboat.

The water felt wonderful on her bare skin, caressing her back and shoulders. She was in Sara's arms again, laughing and kissing, wanting nothing more than to spend the rest of her life with this gorgeous woman.

She pounded at the gates of her memory, but nothing else would come. She had a thought, but pushed it down. She could feel her heart beating in her chest, couldn't she? She was sure that she could, and wasn't there light there, just a hint of it, in the darkness?

Something had grabbed her foot, pulling her under the water. She screamed, her mouth filling with liquid, choking her, making her cough and spit. What was it? Some ancient darkness, wanting to drag her deep beneath the surface? No, it was just a submerged branch that had managed to wrap itself around her ankle. Sara pulled her and the branch came loose from whatever anchored it, floating to the surface.

They'd made their way back to the beach, shivering, laughing, and warming their naked bodies beside the fire. And then he was there, gun in hand. Her husband held the pistol in trembling fingers, tears on his cheeks. If he couldn't have her, nobody would. She heard the crack of the pistol and, after that, nothing. She hadn't drowned, she'd been murdered.

Now she knew why she couldn't move her arms or feel the beat of her own heart. She was dead. But at least Sara was alive. At least there was that, and hopefully Michael was rotting in a prison somewhere. She embraced the darkness and fell into a deep, dreamless slumber, never to awaken again.

The nurse stood over Charlene Montgomery, reading her chart. She'd been in a coma for almost three years. Apparently, her husband had caught her having an affair with another woman. He'd murdered the woman and then shot himself. By the time the paramedics arrived, Charlene was catatonic and her husband and Sara Stone were both dead. Such a tragedy.

The nurse noticed Charlene was shivering and added an extra blanket to her bed before leaving the room.

Charlie woke in the darkness, a scream on her lips. She had no idea where she was or how she'd gotten there, only knew that she had to get out. Why couldn't she move her hands?

Good Fortune

Grimsley Harkness sat alone at his dining room table with a fifty-two-year-old bottle of Glenfiddich scotch, carefully cutting open packets of fortune cookies and pulling out the little fortunes that lay hidden inside. Sometimes a cookie would break as he tried to wheedle out the pieces of paper, but that was okay. These he would throw into the wastebasket that he placed beside the table for just this occasion. He had a near-infinite supply of fortune cookies, so a few broken ones here and there wouldn't change a thing.

Harkness wasn't a brilliant man, but he was a cunning one. It was that instinct, his ability to identify opportunities and seize them by the throat, which led to White Owl Fortune Cookies becoming the largest fortune cookie factory in the country. However, as cunning as he was, he was just as cheap.

Every Halloween, he gave out fortune cookies. One to each child, and one only. The children never appreciated his generosity, and most November the Firsts he awoke to find the huge maple tree outside his house covered in toilet paper, or nasty messages scrawled in shoe polish on his car windows.

This Halloween would be different, very different, indeed, and if the entire neighborhood were to get together and burn down his house, well, more power to them.

Harkness now had exactly 200 fortuneless fortune cookies piled on the table before him, and so it was time to begin phase two. He opened up a ream of copy paper he'd purchased from Wal-Mart on clearance, and began cutting the pages into tiny strips the size of the now-discarded fortunes.

He was nothing if not methodical. He waited until he had cut all 200 identical strips from the sheets of paper before, in a spidery hand, he began writing on them. He wrote a fortune, set it aside, and took another drink of the scotch his board members had given him for Christmas last year.

To think last night he sat at this very same table, tears coursing down his face, his .357 Magnum shoved in his mouth, finger tightening on the trigger. It was then that he'd had this idea, his one last chance to get back at all those little shits who came begging for treats each and every year, and then, unsatisfied with their bounty, vandalized his house. Oh, he'd still kill himself, there was no doubt about that, but at least this way he'd go out with a different kind of bang.

Harkness looked down at his first attempt:

You will break your arm.

Not bad, he thought, *but surely I can be a little more inventive than that.* He wrote out each fortune with care, cackling gleefully at his wit as he read some of the best ones back to himself.

You were adopted.

Your parents hate you.

Daddy's sleeping with the babysitter.

You will never be loved.

A monster lives under your bed.

You'll poke your eye out.

Step on a crack, you'll break your mother's back.

If you touch yourself, you'll go blind.

Your dog will be run over.

You'll choke on candy.

Your father will lose his job.

These will be the last words you'll ever read.

Two hours later, his hand cramping, he had finally finished writing all 200 fortunes. He sat back for a moment, proudly taking in his handiwork. He still had to slide the fortunes into the cookies, of course, but he'd always felt a man should pause now and then to examine all he had accomplished.

It was then the phone rang. Harkness looked at the caller ID. It was that bitch from the board again, Betty Newsom. He decided to ignore the call, just as he'd ignored all the others for the past two days. He regretted ever taking the damned company public. What had seemed like a good idea at the time was now coming back to haunt him.

Three days ago, the comptroller of his company had embezzled ninety percent of the company's assets and fled the country. When word got out, the stock prices had plummeted, essentially making the company worthless. White Owl Fortune Cookies, Inc., the once-tiny business he'd inherited from his father, had, for all intents and purposes, ceased to exist.

Yet, he couldn't think about that now. He took a deep breath, followed by another shot of his single malt scotch, and got back to work. Thirty minutes later, it was done. All of the cookies had their new fortunes tucked safely inside. Now it was just a matter of waiting for the first of what would hopefully be many young visitors to darken his doorstep.

Harkness carefully placed each cookie back into its plastic wrapper, sealing the plastic with a bit of hot glue. He waited a moment and then tested one. You could hardly tell it had been opened at all, and he doubted the children would look twice before ripping off the plastic and cracking open the cookie to get at the fortune inside.

He looked at the bottle of scotch, noting he'd managed to down half the bottle. But what did that matter? He had no one to share it with. He and Marjorie had never had children, and she'd died nearly ten years ago.

"To Marjorie," he whispered, holding the bottle aloft in a toast before taking another long drink.

Harkness stood anxiously by the front door, watching through the small window set into the frame as the sun slowly set over his little neighborhood. The first trick-or-treaters should be showing up soon. He had long since drained the bottle of Glenfiddich, but was still feeling a warm, pleasant buzz, which only heightened his glee at the prospect of the little bastards reading their fortunes.

There! Hand on the door handle, he stared through the window as a black couple approached with a little boy dressed as a pirate. The boy looked to be six or seven. Harkness grabbed the plastic laundry basket he'd used to gather up all the cookies and flung open the door.

"Happy Halloween!" he yelled, a little too enthusiastically.

The child jumped back against his mother, who tousled his hair. That's what was wrong with kids today, he thought, always being coddled. In his day, parents didn't go trick or treating with their children.

"Twick-or-tweet," the child said with a lisp, holding out a plastic bucked that was shaped like a pumpkin.

Harkness withdrew one of the fortune cookies from his basket and dropped it into the kid's bucket. He watched as it landed on a Hershey bar and slid behind a miniature bag of Skittles.

It went like that for the next two hours until, one by one, he had given out all of the cookies. Harkness breathed a sigh of relief as he flicked off the porch light, the universal sign for "We're all out of candy."

He was almost sad it was over, and that he hadn't made more. He wished he could stick around to see the reaction of his neighbors once their little snots read the fortunes, but he had a date with his handgun. He imagined it would be quite the scandal. *Man Hands out Doctored Fortune Cookies, Commits Suicide*, would read the local newspaper. He chuckled at the thought.

He walked back to the dining table, where his .357 still sat, beside the empty bottle of scotch. Opening the chamber, he once again checked the bullets. They were still there, of course. Where would they have gone? Shaking his head, he took one last look around his house before shoving the muzzle of the gun into his mouth.

The doorbell rang, startling him, and he nearly pulled the trigger. His heart pounding, he slipped the gun from his mouth. The room around him grew dark for a moment as he stood up, and he briefly wondered if he might be dead, after all. But no: that accursed doorbell rang again, followed by pounding on the door.

"I'm all out of cookies!" he yelled, stumbling toward the front of the house.

Peering through the window, he saw it was a skinny, red-headed boy who was maybe fourteen or fifteen years old. He thought the boy might live in the two-story ranch house opposite his, but wasn't sure.

"Open up, old man!" yelled the boy, pounding his fists on the door once again.

Harkness opened the door just a crack. Before he could say anything, however, the teenager pushed hard against the door. The frame caught Harkness in the nose, immediately bloodying it.

"I'll call the police, that's what I'll do!" Harkness threatened, wishing he hadn't left his gun on the dining table.

"You hurt my little brother!" shouted the boy. "You broke his arm. Why did you do that? *How* did you do that?"

Harkness stared at the boy. "What do you mean?"

"As soon as he got home, he opened that stupid fortune cookie you gave him. And then he tripped against the fireplace and broke his arm. I looked at the fortune after my mom took him to the hospital. It said, 'You will break your arm.' How did you know?"

Harkness almost smiled, but stopped himself. "I don't know what you're talking about, young man."

It was just a coincidence. It had to be, didn't it? The kid read the fortune, got scared, tripped, and broke his arm. A self-fulfilling prophecy! It made perfect sense.

"You gave him the cookie."

"I seriously doubt the factory they came from would have included a fortune like the one you described, boy."

"My name isn't 'boy,' old man. It's Jeffrey. Jeffrey Newton. We've lived across the street from you for five years."

"And my name isn't 'old man,'" he countered. "It's Mr. Harkness, and I'll thank you to leave my home right now before I call the police."

"I'll go," Jeffrey said, "but I'm keeping an eye on you, Mr. Harkness. There better not be any other *accidents* in my neighborhood."

With that, the boy turned and stalked out the door, slamming it behind him. He was gone just as quickly as he'd shown up.

The audacity! To come into his home, accuse him of such crimes, and slam the door on his way out. What was the world coming to? And then Harkness had to suppress a giggle at the thought of Jeffrey's little brother breaking his arm. What delicious irony. His fortune really had foretold the future, in its own way.

The doorbell rang just as he was about to walk back to the dining room table and the handgun that awaited him. Opening the door, he half expected to see the boy again. Instead, a tall brunette woman stood on his doorstep. She didn't look happy.

"My name is Lizzie Drummond. Did you give this to my little boy?" she asked, holding out a small piece of paper.

He took the piece of paper from her hand. It was one of his fortunes, the one that read, "Daddy's sleeping with the babysitter."

"Madame, I assure you, I did not."

"How did you know?" she said, not acknowledging his response. "When Joshua showed it to my husband, he turned white as a sheet. I'd suspected, but the look on his face when he read that fortune pretty much confirmed it."

Harkness didn't know what to say, or how to respond. He simply stood there, staring at her. What in the world was going on?

"Anyway, while I do appreciate finally knowing the truth," she continued, not even giving him time to respond, "I don't appreciate you going through my son to do it. I want you to stay away from me and Josh, and if you don't, well, what I'll do to you will make what I'm about to do to my husband look tame by comparison."

With that, the woman turned around and walked across the street.

Once could be a coincidence, but twice? He walked with purpose to the dining room table, ignoring the gun, and carefully slipped the fortune out of one of the cookies. Cutting off a slip of paper, he wrote the first thing he could think: "You will get flowers delivered to your door in the next thirty seconds." He slipped it inside the empty cookie and waited.

This was insane. He knew it wouldn't work, but quickly broke the cookie in half, removed the fortune, and read it out loud. He looked at his watch, counting down the seconds. 25. 26. 27. 28. 29. 30.

The doorbell rang, and he nearly leapt out of his chair. His heart beating wildly in his chest, he hurried to the door and flung it open. It was a florist, and he had a bouquet of black lilies in his arms.

"Hello, sir. I have a delivery for Mr. Grimsley Harkness," the young man said, holding out the flowers. "I'm sorry it's so late. Normally we don't make deliveries at this hour, but my truck broke down."

Harkness stared at the flowers. The fortune had worked, but who would send him black lilies? He grabbed the bouquet, not bothering to tip the delivery man, and took it back to his dining table. There was no card attached, but he didn't care. It didn't matter who sent the flowers, because his fortunes were coming true.

He cut another fortune-sized piece of paper from the sheet, and carefully wrote, "You will reach in your pocket and find a legally-valid cashier's check made out in your name for $100,000,000. You will also live forever, being healthy and disease-free, and you will meet the most beautiful woman in the world, who will fall head-over-heels in love with you." His hands were cramping by the time he was finished, having managed to fit the entire fortune on that tiny strip of paper. He read it over again, confirming that he had covered all the bases and left no margin for error.

Harkness removed the fortune from one of the leftover cookies and inserted the one he had just written in its place, and then sealed it back into its plastic. He was about to crack it open when someone began banging on his front door. Another angry parent? He was determined to ignore it when he heard Jeffrey's voice calling out.

"Open up, Mr. Harkness! I know you're in there. We need to talk."

He sighed, sitting the cookie beside the handgun. He was curious to know what the boy wanted, and besides, what could happen? The world was his for the taking. He pushed himself up from the table and walked back to the door.

"It's happening all over the neighborhood," said Jeffrey, pushing inside the moment that Harkness opened the door. "Jordan Kessler somehow managed to poke her eye out with a Pixie stick, Jake Monahan's dog got run over, and Chase Weaver choked and almost died on a Tootsie Roll, just like their fortunes said would happen."

Harkness wanted to jump with glee, but instead he said, "That's preposterous, boy! It's all just coincidence. Now get out of here before I call the police."

Jeffrey folded his arms and stared straight into the older man's eyes. "Go right ahead. I'd love to hear what they'd think about all of this." He opened his palm, revealing a handful of fortunes he'd evidently collected from the neighborhood children.

The old man held the boy's gaze for nearly half a minute before looking away. He finally asked, "What do you want?"

"What do you mean?" asked Jeffrey.

"What do you want to not tell anyone about this? Everyone wants something. What do *you* want?"

Now that he wasn't planning to kill himself, he couldn't very well have people finding out what he'd done. He had an idea on how to fix this, if he could just get the kid to go for the bait.

"I want my brother's arm to not be broken. I want Jordan not to be half-blind, and I want Chase's dog to be alive again. How's that?"

"I will do all of that," Harkness lied, "but what do you want for yourself?"

"I want you to promise never to do this, ever again."

"Tell you what, why don't I surprise you? Follow me."

Harkness walked to the dining table, gesturing for the boy to take a seat. Jeffrey stared for a moment at the gun, finally pulling out a chair and sitting down opposite Harkness.

Grimsley Harkness grabbed another fortune cookie, removed the plastic, and maneuvered the old fortune out from inside. He tossed it aside without looking at it, and then cut on a strip of paper and began to write. When he was done, he sealed the cookie back in its plastic wrapper and sat it in front of Jeffrey.

"That's it?" Jeffrey asked, picking up the fortune cookie.

"That's it," Harkness replied, his heart racing. "Open it, and you'll get everything you wanted, and more."

"So everyone will be fixed?"

The phone rang just then, almost making Harkness jump. Why couldn't people leave him alone? "Hold that thought. I want to see you open it, see how happy you are."

He stood from the table, crossed the room, and stared at the Caller ID. It was Betty Newsom again. He turned off the ringer, deciding to ignore the old bat. After he opened his fortune, he'd never have to deal with her or any of the other board members ever again.

Harkness walked back to the dining table and sat down opposite the boy. "Well, what are you waiting for? Open the damned thing."

Jeffrey ripped off the plastic, cracked opened the cookie, and read the fortune. "Wow, Mr. Harkness. Thank you."

Harkness stared, dumbfounded. "For what?"

"For the money, for living forever, and for the beautiful woman, though I'm probably a little too young for that one. Though there's nothing here about my brother's arm or any of the other kids. What's up with that, Mr. Harkness?"

Harkness grabbed the fortune cookie sitting beside his .357 and stared at it. That was *his* fortune! Had the boy switched them? Without even thinking, he ripped the cookie out of the plastic wrapper and cracked it open, reading the fortune inside.

You are dead.

Jeffrey Newton carefully replaced the real fortunes in the cookies with ones he had written, one each for his brother, Jordan, Chase, and Jake, and then sealed them back in the plastic with the hot glue gun he'd found on the table. Maybe it would work and maybe it wouldn't, but if it didn't, he'd do what he could for all of them once he cashed that $100,000,000 check he'd found in his pocket.

He methodically packed up the rest of the cookies from the table, along with the scissors, ballpoint pen, ream of paper, and of course the glue gun, and put them all in a plastic Wal-Mart bag he'd found in Mr. Harkness' kitchen. If anyone else had been hurt by the old man's fortunes, he'd do his best to set things right, either through the fortune cookies or old-fashioned cash.

Jeffrey took one last look at poor, old Mr. Harkness, lying dead on the floor with one gnarled hand still clutching his chest. He almost felt sorry for the man, but then remembered that fortune had been meant for him. Shrugging, he walked out the front door, closing it behind him. Tomorrow, after he opened up a bank account, he thought he'd buy himself a new bicycle. After all, if he was going to live forever, he might as well start enjoying it.

Poetry

I wrote a lot of poetry when I was a teenager and into my early twenties. A lot of angst-filled, depressing poetry. Most of it wasn't very good. Here are a few gems among the rubbish.

Twirl

I held her as we danced,
Twirling 'pon the precipice,
Moving together to the music,
Apart to our own rhythm.

A blade lashed out,
Blood dripping to the ground,
I pushed her away from me,
She called my name as she fell.

Imagine my surprise:
The knife was in my hand,
The blood,
hers.

A Flower Falls 'Way

A flower grown, blossoming bright,
Reaching the sun on midsummer's night,
Taken root in the soul's soiled earth,
Shining today, to celebrate birth,

Delicate flower petals so strong,
Dancing to the wind's summer song,
Rooted in rock its soul flies free,
'Twas always as it were meant to be

Love burns bright green its stem,
Worn so proudly a pink jeweled diadem,
Compassion's water flowing to feed,
Grown from the joy of a simple seed…

And lo—the image of flower falls 'way,
Touched but once by the warm summer day,
Heather, a flower, though yes may it be,
A flower's beauty compares nothing to thee

Would My Wish Work Again?

The poet was walking through the forest one night,
Lost in his thoughts, he clutched himself tight,
Trailing further down the path, away from the light,
He felt so empty that he cried.

A movement in the distance caught the poet's eye,
A falling star, breaking through from the sky,
He made a silent wish, truth from a lie,
As the forest grew ablaze with light.

Blinded by the glow, he fell to his knees,
Lost in the forest, amidst all the trees,
In a moment the light cleared, and again he could see,
In the clearing, there stood an angel.

"Oh angel," said the poet, confused and afraid,
"Did you come to me, by the wish that I made?"
And then he wondered what price he had paid,
To look into her eyes so bright.

"You wished for me, and I did appear.
Don't be so frightened, there's nothing to fear.
We can talk and I'll hold you, but don't get too near."
The angel looked unsure of her words.

The poet arose from the ground just then,

Went to her, held her, and called her a friend,
They laughed and they talked, and held each other again,
And then it was her time to go.

"Oh, my sweet poet, how I wish you would see,
I know what you sought, and I know it's not me,
I must fly to the heavens, soaring and free."
Her hand touched his face in farewell.

He knew she was right, the situation was wrong,
To ever be more than a secret sung song,
Ah, but for her, his heart did it long,
But he bade her farewell just the same.

The poet walked away through the forest that night,
Lost in his thoughts of holding her tight,
Trailing back down the path, away from the light,
He felt so empty that he cried.

And he wondered, would my wish work again?

The Moment Now

She smiles and takes his hand
Dancing in the wind his breath taken
She runs from him wanting him to come
Taunting whispering sweet caresses

Promises of today, the moment now
Tomorrow a distant gleam in her eye
He catches her they tumble
Lying in the grass he notices she's gone

He cries hammering his fists
Against her memory he rages
Anger gives ways 'gainst sweet sorrow
He finds her in his heart

A Promise Kept

His heart broken, the adept stumbled,
Nearly fell, as the seagull flew away,
He called out after her, searching,
Crying, as his spells failed him.

He paused in his angst, remembering of
Sweeter times, pressed against his soul;

Gliding the winds, her wings beat fast,
She came to him, as he brewed his spells,
They shared joy, she taught him to fly,
He taught her a little magic.

They shared wonders anew, as well as
Ancient riddles and wanderings,
Companions in friendship,
Sharing magical bonds.

One day, incantations went awry,
Cast 'pon them both, revealing,
Their innermost secrets to each other,
He saw what he knew, and she saw love.

In a fleeting moment, they shared the sight,
What they dared not voice; spoken,

What they dared not feel; embraced,
In that moment, she flew away.

Why 'o why must it be this way, he raged,
Anger's lightning blazing thunderstrokes;

Night and day he toiled, new enchantments,
Crystal balls gazed, for a lone seagull,
He sought out great wizards and magicians,
And not one could help him on his quest.

Creating potions, scrying mirrors,
Gazing to the stars, looking for answers,
He cursed her, then himself, the world,
His spells, for failing him.

For days and nights, he did not rest,
His seagull gone, perhaps lost forever,
Why had his spells been so careless,
Why did he scare her so?

He wept, anger turning to sadness,
Might-have-beens to never-coulds.
He missed the beat of her wings,
and the beat of her heart.

The Adept folded into himself,
Sleep calling to his weary mind;

Images swam 'round him, calling his name,
As the mist encircled his psyche,
Pulling at him with questions,
And he knew why she'd left.

Fear beneath her wings, revealed,
Desire's blood, and gentle whispers,
Of love, and hope, and a yearning,
For what she thought could never be.

She was afraid, not of her secrets,
But of his, now that she knew them,
She yearned stronger, and feared,
Never knowing his kiss.

The answer came to him in a dream,
A woman taken form from his seagull,
Kissing sweet promises, whispering,
I'll come back, as she drifted away.

In that instant, he let her go,
Smiling, remembering, hoping;

The next morning the sun spoke to him,
Calling him to the window, promising warmth,
The shutters fell open, the wind blew in,
And she flew in after, a promise kept.

Rain

Water's touch brings me to life,
Rain dancing on my skin,
Lightning marks my way,
Brightness against the darkened sky,
Thunder calling me back again.

Troubles fall 'way, sadness forgotten,
Tears melting from the rain's wet kiss,
With a start, I'm alive again,
Power so long lost is mine again,
In a crashing rainstorm, joyful bliss.

Strength has returned, tempered with knowledge,
Power and responsibility intertwined,
I've longed for it, lusted after it,
It's back now. Mine!
Smiling, I let it go, mortal again.

But a little wiser...
And not so weak.

Merryland Revisited

Zara Boone awoke with a pounding headache. She tried to open her eyes, failed miserably, then fell back into a fitful sleep.

Sometime later she awoke again, her head still pounding, but this time she forced herself to open her eyes. She was lying on the grass in the middle of a clearing, a forest on one side and a crystal blue lake on the other. A pleasant breeze caressed her cheek, and she could smell summer flowers in the air.

She blinked, took in the scene again, and rolled over on one elbow. And then she remembered her grandmother, Seattle Slim, and everything else. Her heart began to race. Why wasn't she dead? She forced herself into a sitting position and instantly regretted it. Her head felt like it might explode.

"You'll feel better soon," said a familiar British voice. "At least you're finally awake."

Zara turned her gaze to the little purple dragon hovering just a few feet away. She could smell cherry tobacco intermingling with the summer flowers as he puffed away on his trademark pipe.

"Professor Plum?" she asked, squeezing her eyes closed.

When she opened them again the little dragon was gone, replaced by a tall, gaunt man wearing gray slacks and a blue Polo shirt. He, too, was smoking a pipe, but that's where the similarities ended.

"I take it by your expression that you're finally seeing me as I really am," he said, sharing the same British accent that Professor Plum had spoken with just a moment ago. "That's good, and about time."

"Grandpa Michael," she said, using the name she'd called him when she was just a little girl, "why aren't I dead? Merryland…just existed in my grandmother's head, right?"

"That's what I always believed," said Michael Brennan, shrugging. He waved his arms, indicating the forest, the lake, and everything around it. "Apparently, I was wrong. Very wrong. Now, come on. It's time to get you up and moving."

Brennan held out a hand to Zara and she took it, pulling herself to her feet. She threw her arms around the man who had once been her grandfather, hugging him tight.

They stood that way for a while, and it was finally Zara who separated. "She has my body, right?"

Brennan nodded. "As she's taken so many more during her long, twisted lifetime."

"So why do I feel…real? Why can I touch you?"

"I wish I knew."

"Professor Plum wasn't always you, was it?"

"No, Zara. Professor Plum came from your imagination, a few months after I…after I died."

"You mean after you were murdered," Zara said flatly, and Brennan nodded.

"Murdered, then. You were always one to cut to the heart of the matter, Zara, even as a little girl. Yes, I was murdered, and it was after that you invented Professor Plum. And you did seem to base him on your memory of me, pipe and all. Eventually, Lucy incorporated him into her stories, though he was your creation, not hers."

"But how did you take on his form?"

"For years I just wandered that house, hiding from your grandmother and her friends. But I got stronger, and, finally, I was able to manifest myself as your Professor Plum, to wrest control of your creation from Lucy. I just wish it'd been in time to save you."

"You did your best, Michael," said a woman's voice from behind them. "That's all we can ask."

Zara spun on her heels, coming face-to-face with a woman about her age. She sported long, blonde hair and was wearing a blue peasant blouse and a white skirt that ended just past her knees. She looked familiar, somehow, and then she realized: it was her Grandmother, but much younger.

"You bitch!" she yelled, leaping for the woman's throat.

She felt strong hands holding her back, but struggled against them. Zara didn't know why her grandmother had come back, but she was going to make her pay for what she had done.

"Easy, girl," said Brennan, holding her tight. "It's not what you think."

"I'm not her," the other woman said quickly. "I'm the real Lucy Gold. She stole my body, too."

Zara stared at the woman, and felt Brennan release his grip from around her shoulders.

"She's telling the truth," said Brennan.

"So, you're my real grandmother," Zara said, relaxing a little. "When did she take your body?"

"I was twenty eight, and it was right before Sara's fifth birthday. My precious little Sara. At least she escaped this nightmare."

Lucy didn't know that Sara was dead. Zara glanced at Brennan, who shook his head almost imperceptibly. She nodded. There was no reason to cause the woman any more pain.

Zara cleared her throat. "So, are they real? Seattle Slim, Scottie, and the rest of them?"

"If they are, they disappear when Lucy," Brennan said, then paused, looking at the real Lucy, "or whatever her real name is, isn't here."

"So it's just us three?" asked Zara.

"Not exactly," said the real Lucy Gold. "When *she's* here, we can't do anything. We can watch but we can't interact. But as soon as she's gone—"

"'We?'" interrupted Zara. "There's more of you?"

"Oh, indeed there are," Lucy said. "We just didn't want to overwhelm you by forcing you to meet us all at once. Girls?"

One by one, women in all sorts of clothing, hairstyles, shapes, and sizes appeared all around Lucy. First, a plump woman sporting long, brown hair and dressed in Victorian-style clothing seemed to step out of thin air, and then a skinny redhead with her hair in a bun wearing a white prairie dress materialized beside her.

Next, a World War II-era WAC appeared in front of Zara, joined seconds later by a 1920's era flapper dressed all in black with a matching feather boa. Another redhead materialized next to the WAC, this one wearing a long green and brown dress and primitive-looking brown sandals on her feet.

The women continued to appear, thousands of them, stretching across the meadow and going on for as far as the eye could see. One about a dozen yards away was dressed in animal skins and held a club-like branch in her hand. She had no shoes, and her hair was long and tangled. Hundreds if not thousands of women who on the surface had nothing in common other than looking very, very pissed. Zara shook her head. How long had this been going on?

"Now you understand," said Lucy, reaching out to take Zara's hand. "This goes back many generations, for thousands of years. We're all here, and we're all powerless when *she* comes to exchange bodies. And she'll just keep doing it. There's nothing we can do."

"Well, that's not exactly true," said Michael Brennan, putting an arm on Zara's shoulder.

"Explain," said Lucy, eyes on the old man.

"Well, from what you told me, you've tried to escape, and you can't, and when she's here, you can't interact or even materialize. Correct?"

Lucy looked annoyed. "Tell me something I don't know."

"You're looking at it. Me. I got here, I came from the 'real world,' and I took possession of Zara's Professor Plum, however briefly. And if I could get here, if I could interact..."

"Then there's a way back," Zara said, finishing for him. "Someway, somehow, there's a way back. And if there's a way back, if Michael can get *here*, then we can get *there*."

"But the portal is closed," countered Lucy. "You can't get back. You tried, while Zara was unconscious. It didn't work."

"But can't you feel it?" Brennan asked, and then immediately shook his head. "No, of course you can't. Why would you?"

"What are you talking about?"

"Your body is gone, dead and buried, like everyone else here, including me—everyone, that is, except for Zara. That connection, however tenuous, still exists. And if that connection exists, we can manipulate it, we can draw upon it, we can use it. There has to be a way back, if not for all of you, then at least for Zara."

"Don't you think we've tried that?" Lucy sounded annoyed. "All our bodies were still alive at some point."

"Oh, I'm sure you have, but that was all before I got here. If I got here without her bringing me here, I think I can get back. And if I can get back, I think I can bring Zara with me. We have to follow her connection. There's a way, we just have to find it."

Lucy stood still for a moment, and then exchanged glances with her ancestors stretching back thousands of years. And then as one, they all nodded.

"If there's a way," said the woman in the prairie dress, speaking in a heavy southern drawl, "we'll get you back."

The WAC stepped forward. "All we ask is that once you get your body back, you send that bitch back here to us, preferably stripped of her powers."

"Wouldn't that be poetic justice?" said Lucy, smiling for the first time since Zara had met her.

She could feel the connection that Michael had referenced, that was true, but stronger than the connection to her own body was the connection she felt to Tildie and to Matt. If Michael could somehow get her back, she felt certain she could use those connections to her benefit.

So maybe there would be a little poetic justice, after all.

About the Author

 Joe was born in Carthage, Illinois, and currently lives in Rogers, Arkansas with his wife Andee, their teenage son Fletcher, and their cats Milo, Lucky, and Archer. Joe is a freelance writer, web designer, and substitute teacher, and also serves on the Arkansas Arts Academy school board. In addition to writing, he enjoys purchasing (and occasionally watching) copious amounts of Blu-Ray discs, listening to music, playing video games, and collecting Mego action figures from the 1970s. Connect with Joe at JoeDeRouen.com.